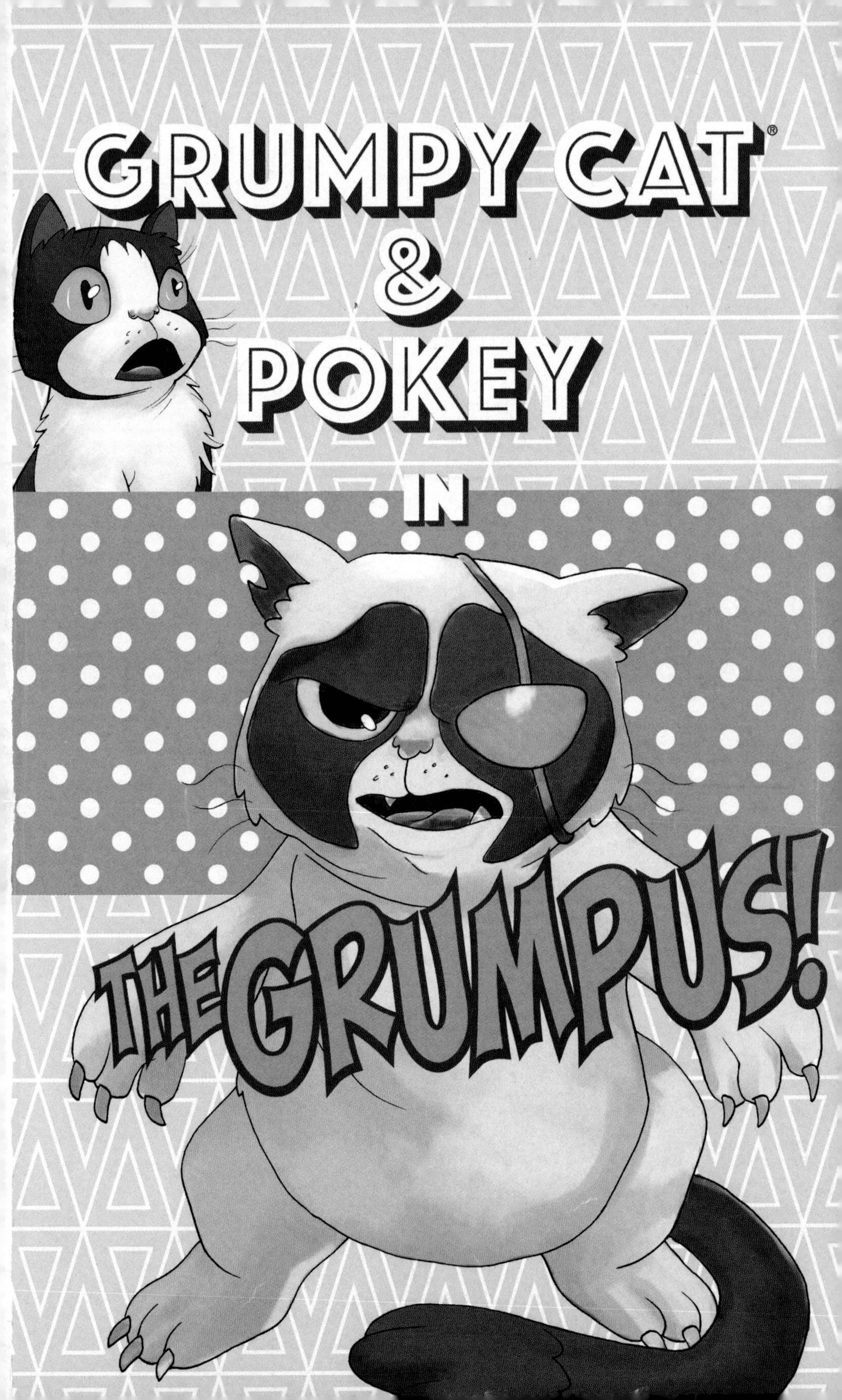
GRUMPY CAT®
&
POKEY
IN
THE GRUMPUS!

## HIDE AND EEK!

Written by: **Ben McCool**
Art & Colors by: **Steve Uy**
Letters by: **Bill Tortolini**

## SOMETHING GRUMPY THIS WAY COMES

Written by: **Royal McGraw**
Art & Colors by: **Michelle Nguyen**
Letters by: **Bill Tortolini**

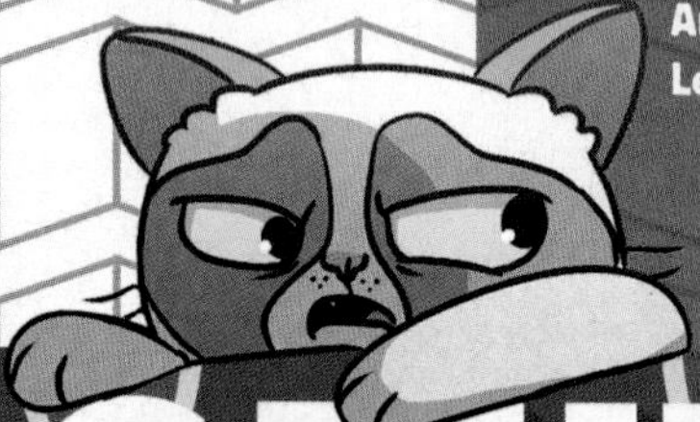

# GRUMPY CAT® & POKEY

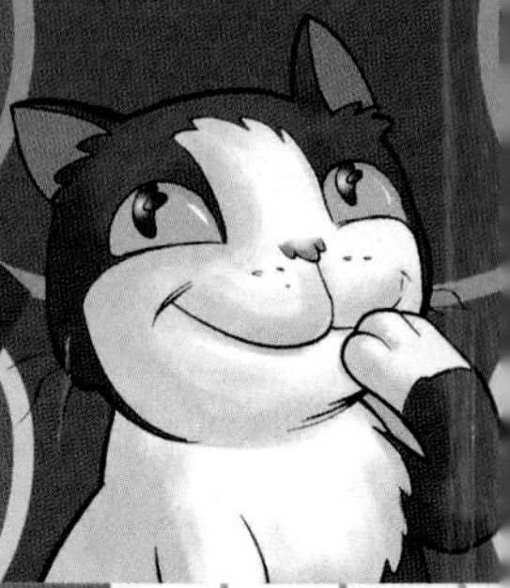

## GRUMPUS

Written by: **Ben Fisher**
Art by: **Ken Haeser & Buzz Hasson**
Colors by: **Mohan**
Letters by: **Bill Tortolini**

## SURFING CAT

Written by: **Ben McCool**
Art & Colors by: **Steve Uy**
Letters by: **Bill Tortolini**

## GRUMP-E

Written by: **Ben Fisher**
Art by: **Ken Haeser**
Colors by: **Mohan**
Letters by: **Bill Tortolini**

## CAT-ASTROPHE
Written by: **Derek Fridolfs**
Art by: **Derek Fridolfs**
Colors by: **Mohan**
Letters by: **Bill Tortolini**

## THE GENIE'S LAMP
Written by: **Ben Fisher**
Art by: **Ken Haeser**
Colors by: **Mohan**
Letters by: **Bill Tortolini**

## IN THE GRUMPUS!

## EVERY WITCH WAY
Written by: **Derek Fridolfs**
Art & Colors by: **Steve Uy**
Letters by: **Bill Tortolini**

## CAT CALLING
Written by: **Ilias Kyriazis**
Art & Colors by: **Ilias Kyriazis**
Letters by: **Bill Tortolini**

Edited by:
**Rich Young & Anthony Marques**

Collection Design by:
**Cathleen Heard**

# DYNAMITE.

[facebook] [instagram] [tumblr] [twitter] [YouTube]

Nick Barrucci, CEO / Publisher
Juan Collado, President / COO

Joe Rybandt, Executive Editor
Matt Idelson, Senior Editor
Anthony Marques, Associate Editor
Kevin Ketner, Editorial Assistant

Jason Ullmeyer, Art Director
Geoff Harkins, Senior Graphic Designer
Cathleen Heard, Graphic Designer
Alexis Persson, Production Artist

Chris Caniano, Digital Associate
Rachel Kilbury, Digital Assistant

Brandon Dante Primavera, V.P. of IT and Operations
Rich Young, Director of Business Development

Alan Payne, V.P. of Sales and Marketing
Keith Davidsen, Marketing Director
Pat O'Connell, Sales Manager

For more Grumpy & Pokey, visit DYNAMITE.COM and GRUMPYCATS.COM!

Online at www.DYNAMITE.com
On Facebook /Dynamitecomics
On Instagram /Dynamitecomics
On Tumblr dynamitecomics.tumblr.com
On Twitter @dynamitecomics
On YouTube /Dynamitecomics

Online at www.GRUMPYCATS.com
On Facebook /TheOfficialGrumpyCat
On Instagram @RealGrumpyCat
On Twitter @RealGrumpyCat

Hardcover:
ISBN-13: 978-1-52410-246-3

Paperback:
ISBN-13: 978-1-52410-247-0

First Printing
10 9 8 7 6 5 4 3 2 1

PEFC Certified
Printed on paper from
sustainably managed
forests and controlled
sources
PEFC/01-31-106
www.pefc.org

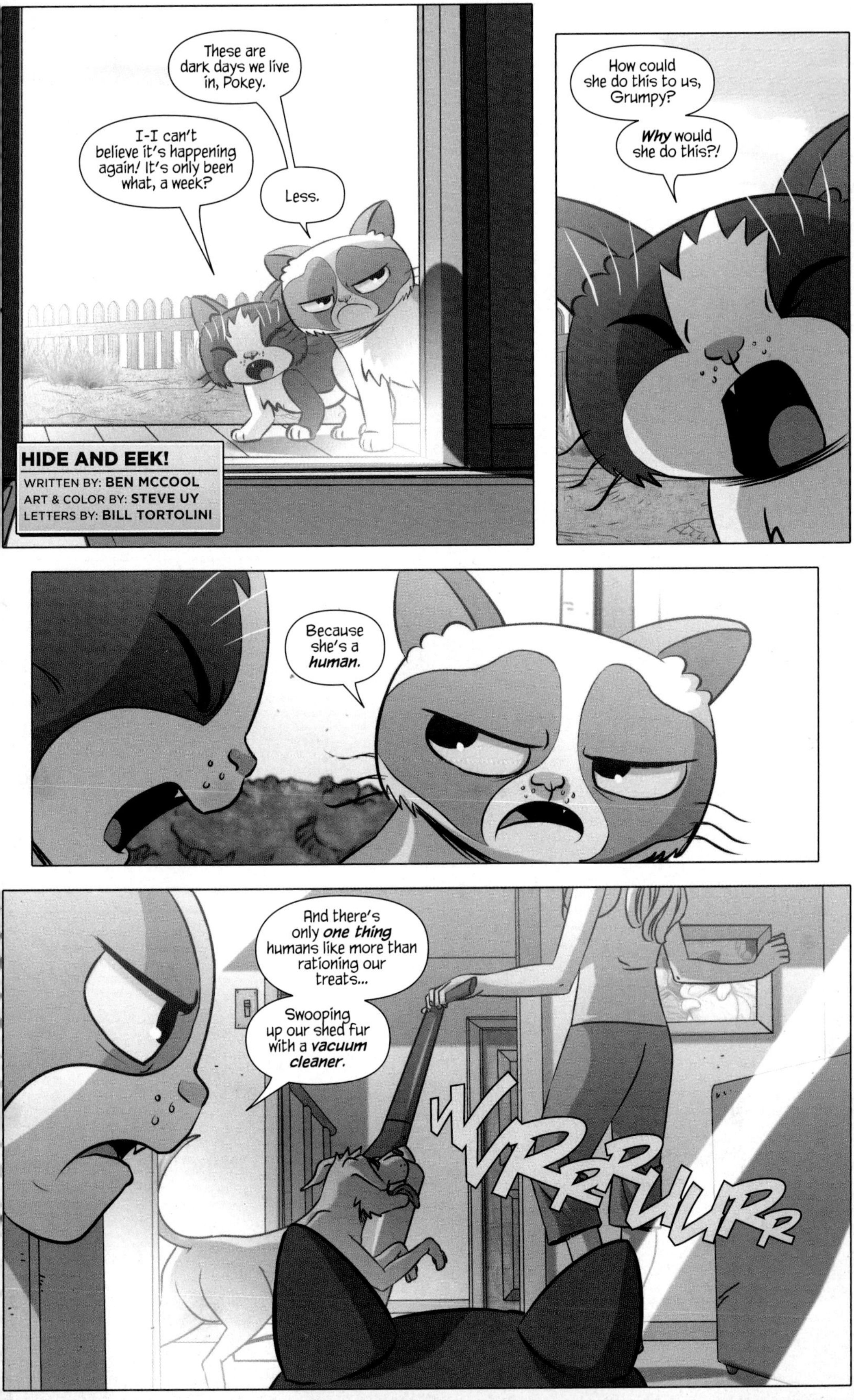
These are dark days we live in, Pokey.
I-I can't believe it's happening again! It's only been what, a week?
Less.
HIDE AND EEK!
WRITTEN BY: BEN MCCOOL
ART & COLOR BY: STEVE UY
LETTERS BY: BILL TORTOLINI
How could she do this to us, Grumpy?
Why would she do this?!
Because she's a human.
And there's only one thing humans like more than rationing our treats...
Swooping up our shed fur with a vacuum cleaner.
WRRRRUUURR

Look at the dog, prancing around to its torturous tune...

What is *wrong* with him?

I've got news for you -- the dog is a *dimwit.*

He makes even *you* seem smart.

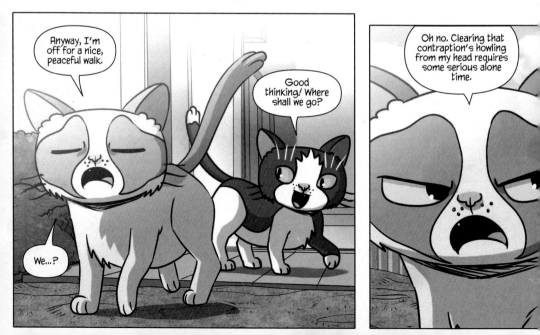

Anyway, I'm off for a nice, peaceful walk.

Good thinking! Where shall we go?

We...?

Oh no. Clearing that contraption's howling from my head requires some serious alone time.

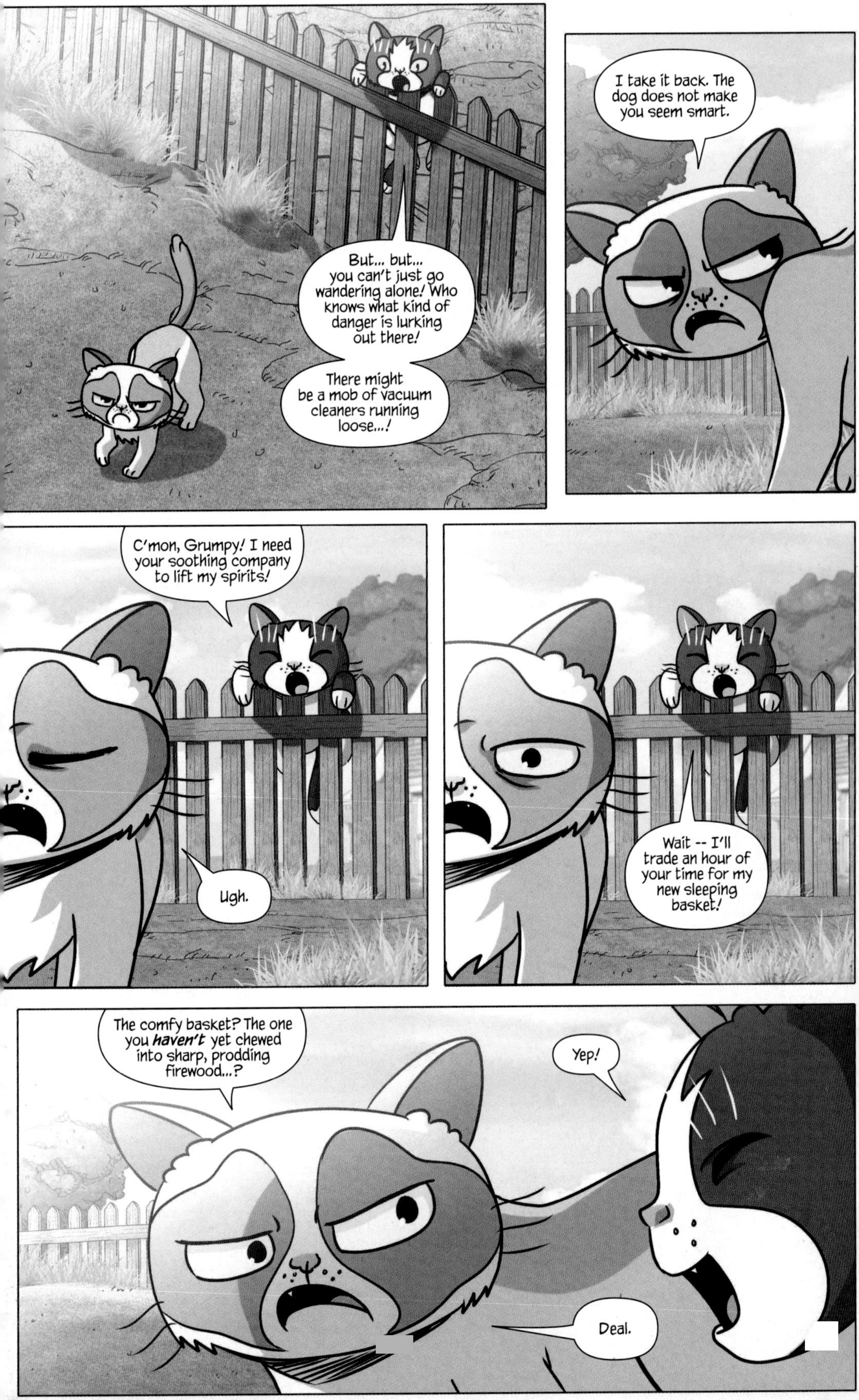
But... but... you can't just go wandering alone! Who knows what kind of danger is lurking out there!
There might be a mob of vacuum cleaners running loose...!
I take it back. The dog does not make you seem smart.
C'mon, Grumpy! I need your soothing company to lift my spirits!
Ugh.
Wait -- I'll trade an hour of your time for my new sleeping basket!
The comfy basket? The one you ***haven't*** yet chewed into sharp, prodding firewood...?
Yep!
Deal.

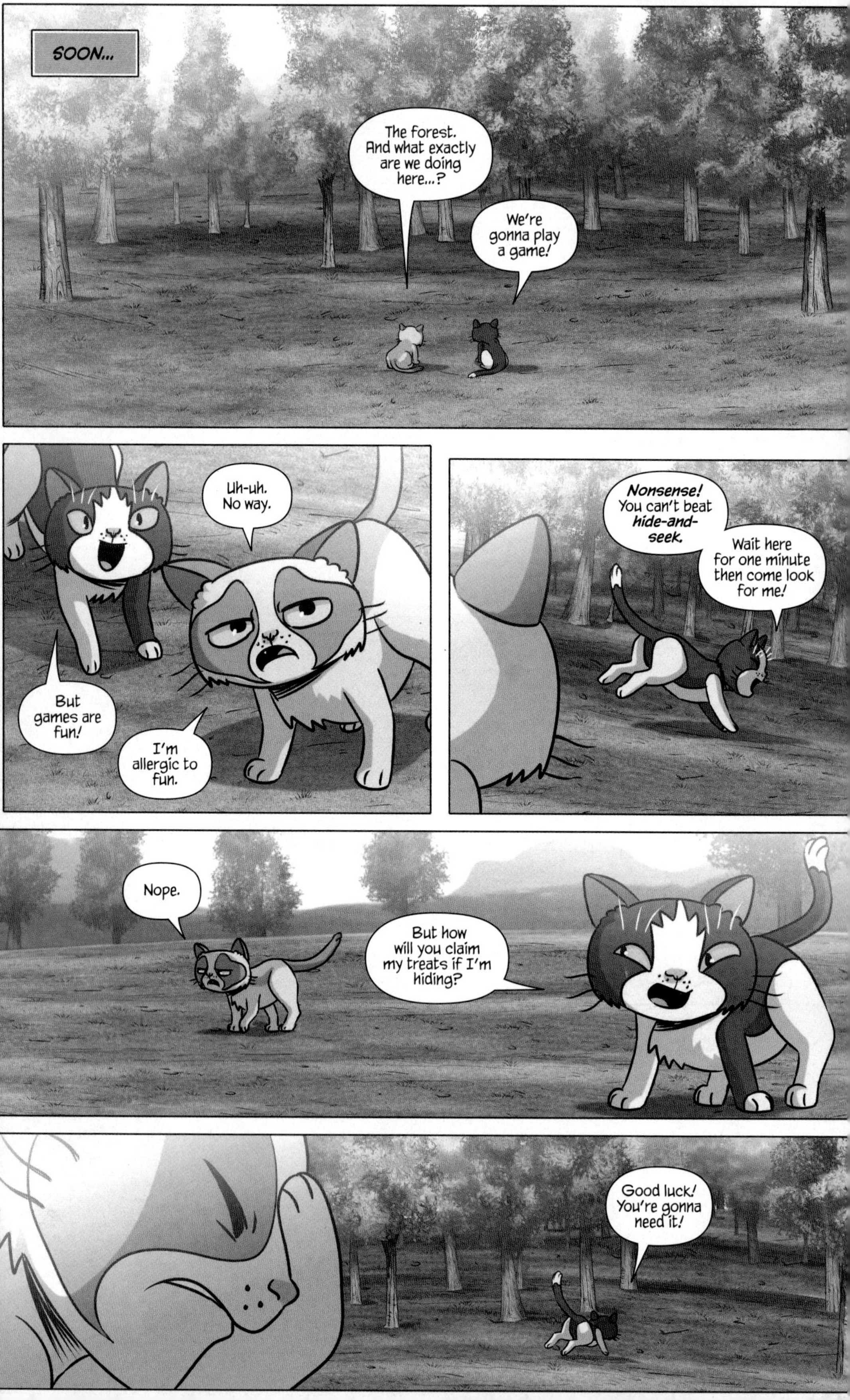
SOON...
The forest. And what exactly are we doing here...?
We're gonna play a game!
Uh-uh. No way.
But games are fun!
I'm allergic to fun.
Nonsense! You can't beat hide-and-seek.
Wait here for one minute then come look for me!
Nope.
But how will you claim my treats if I'm hiding?
Good luck! You're gonna need it!

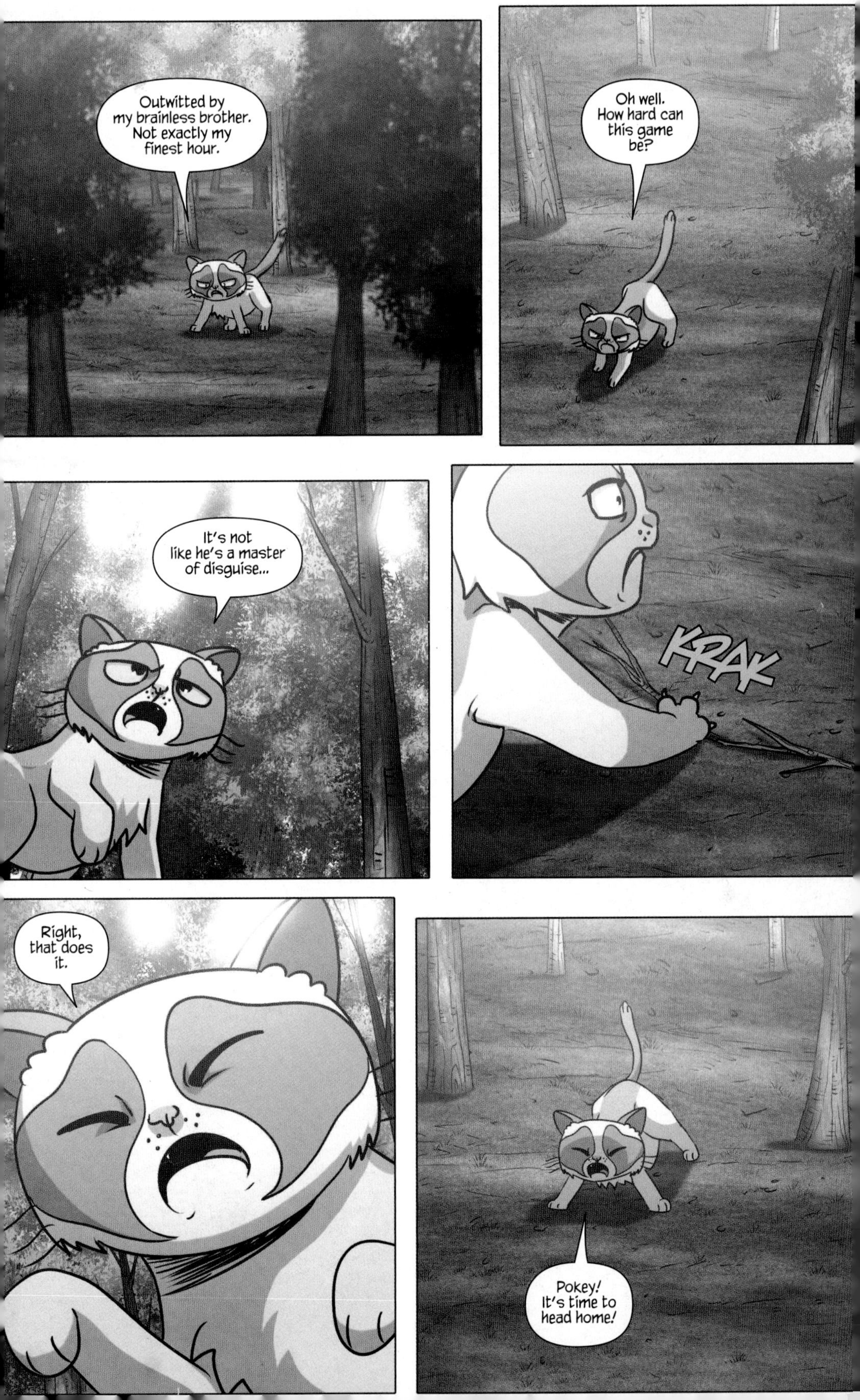
Outwitted by my brainless brother. Not exactly my finest hour.
Oh well. How hard can this game be?
It's not like he's a master of disguise...
KRAK
Right, that does it.
Pokey! It's time to head home!

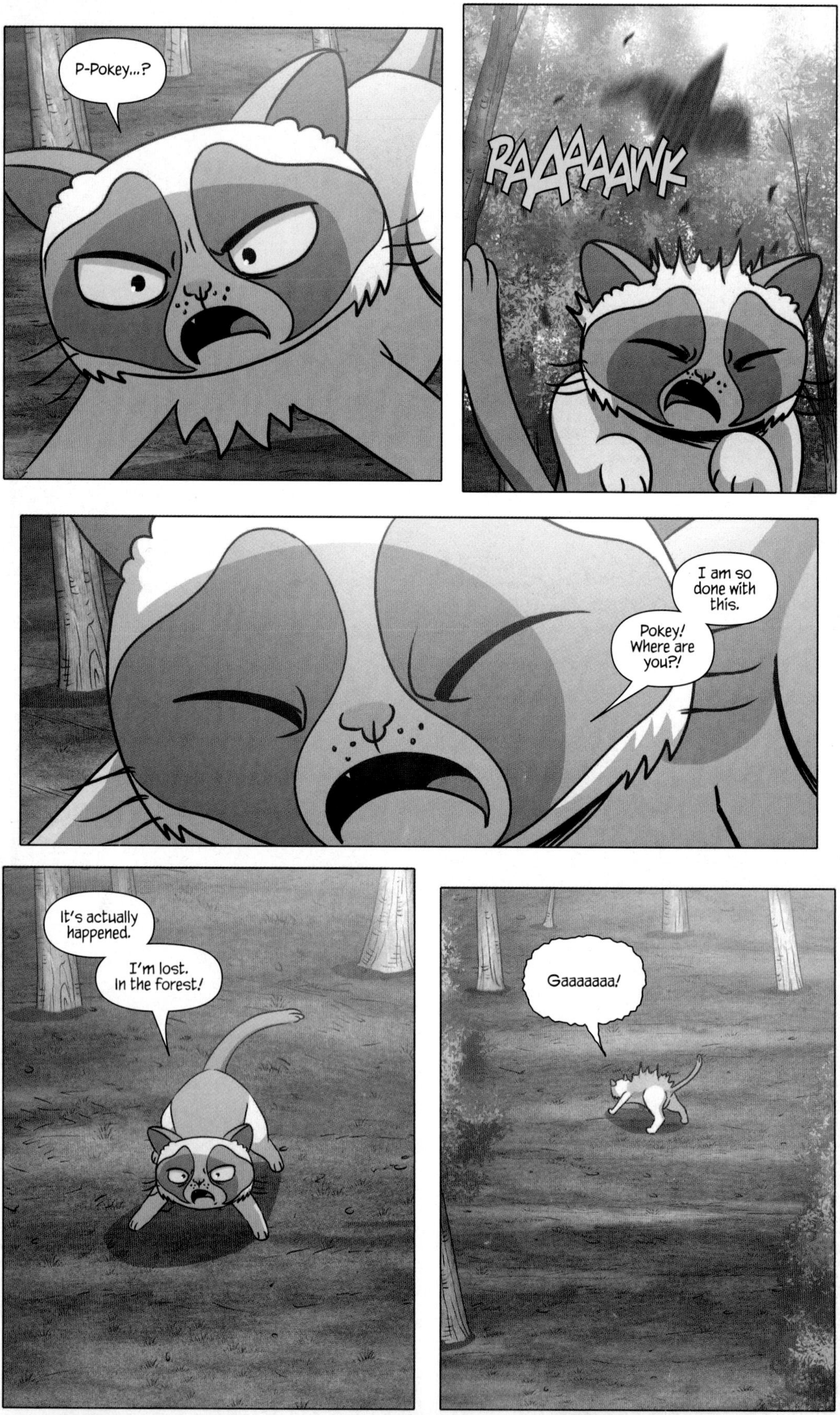

P-Pokey...?
RAAAAAWK
I am so done with this.
Pokey! Where are you?!
It's actually happened.
I'm lost. In the forest!
Gaaaaaaa!

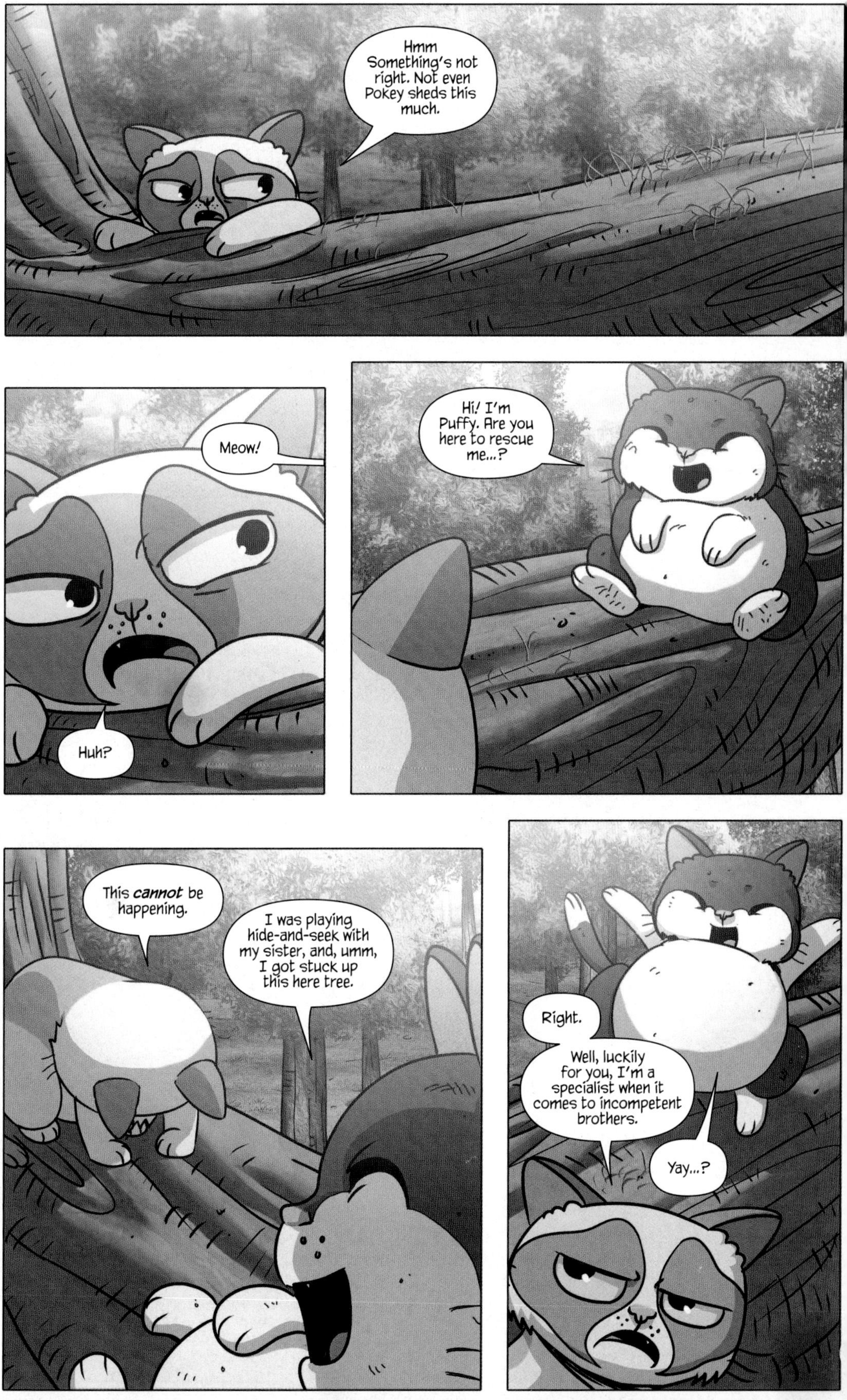
Hmm
Something's not right. Not even Pokey sheds this much.
Meow!
Huh?
Hi! I'm Puffy. Are you here to rescue me...?
This *cannot* be happening.
I was playing hide-and-seek with my sister, and, umm, I got stuck up this here tree.
Right.
Well, luckily for you, I'm a specialist when it comes to incompetent brothers.
Yay...?

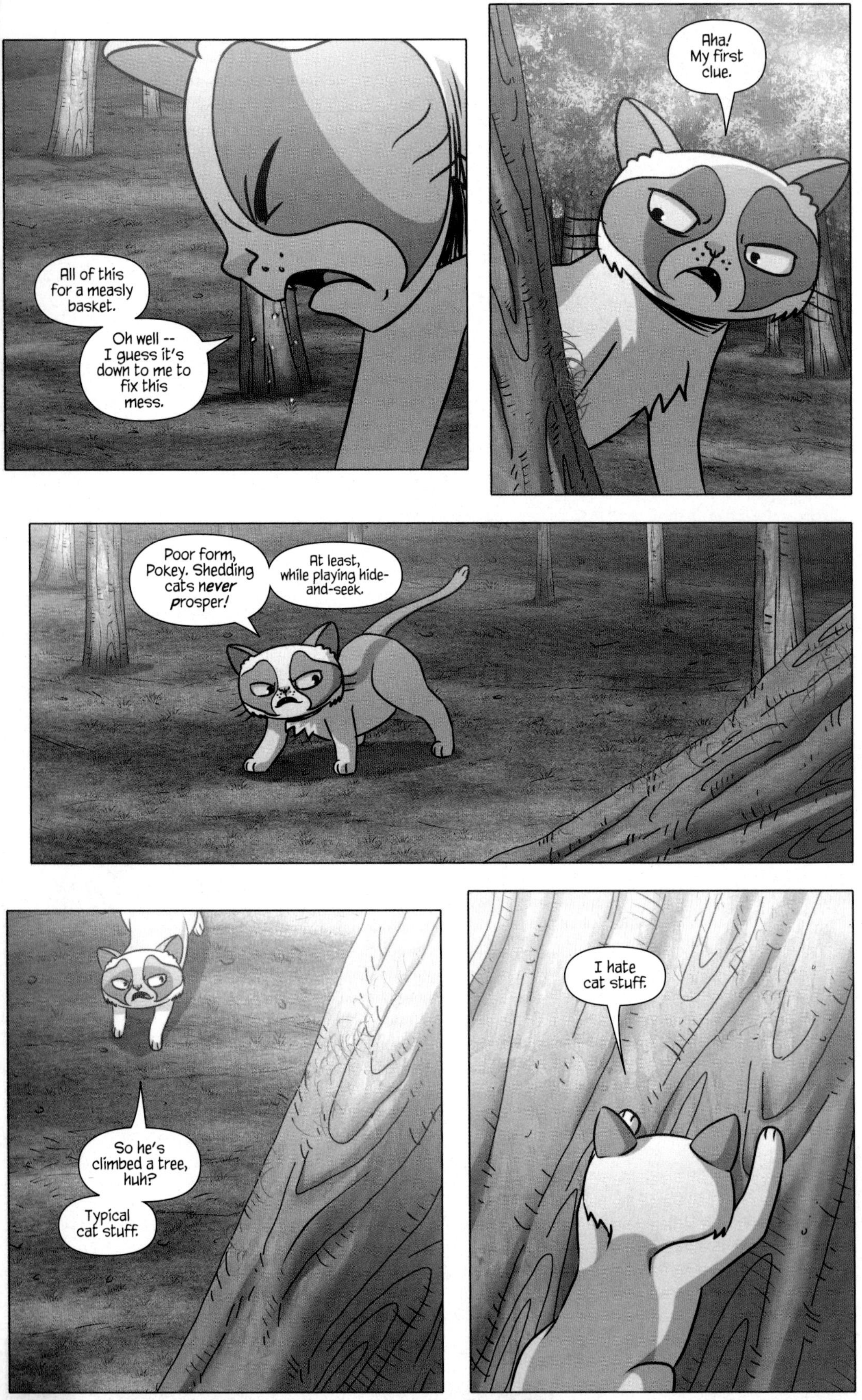
All of this for a measly basket.
Oh well -- I guess it's down to me to fix this mess.
Aha! My first clue.
Poor form, Pokey. Shedding cats *never* prosper!
At least, while playing hide-and-seek.
So he's climbed a tree, huh?
Typical cat stuff.
I hate cat stuff.

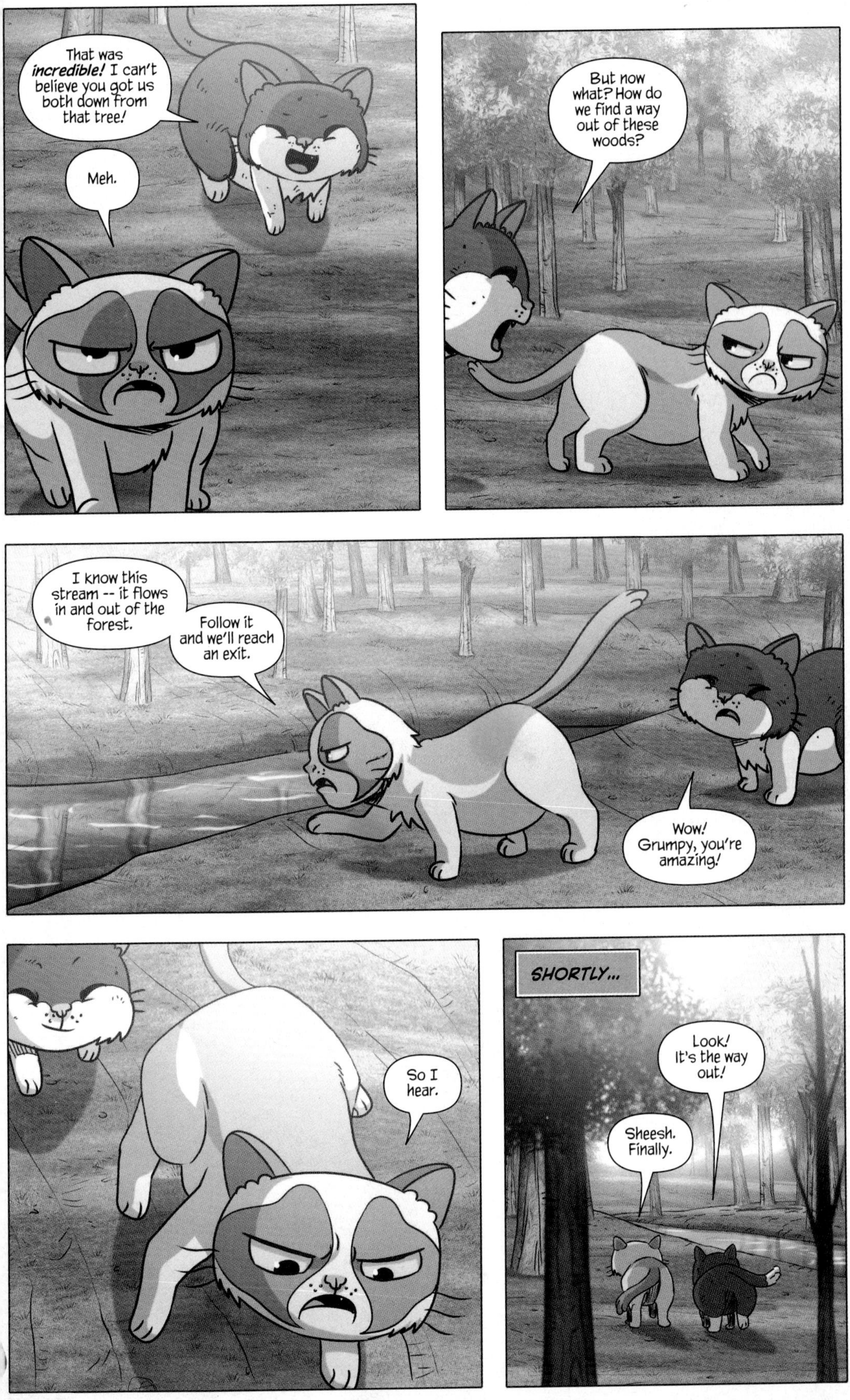
That was *incredible!* I can't believe you got us both down from that tree!
Meh.
But now what? How do we find a way out of these woods?
I know this stream -- it flows in and out of the forest.
Follow it and we'll reach an exit.
Wow! Grumpy, you're amazing!
So I hear.
SHORTLY...
Look! It's the way out!
Sheesh. Finally.

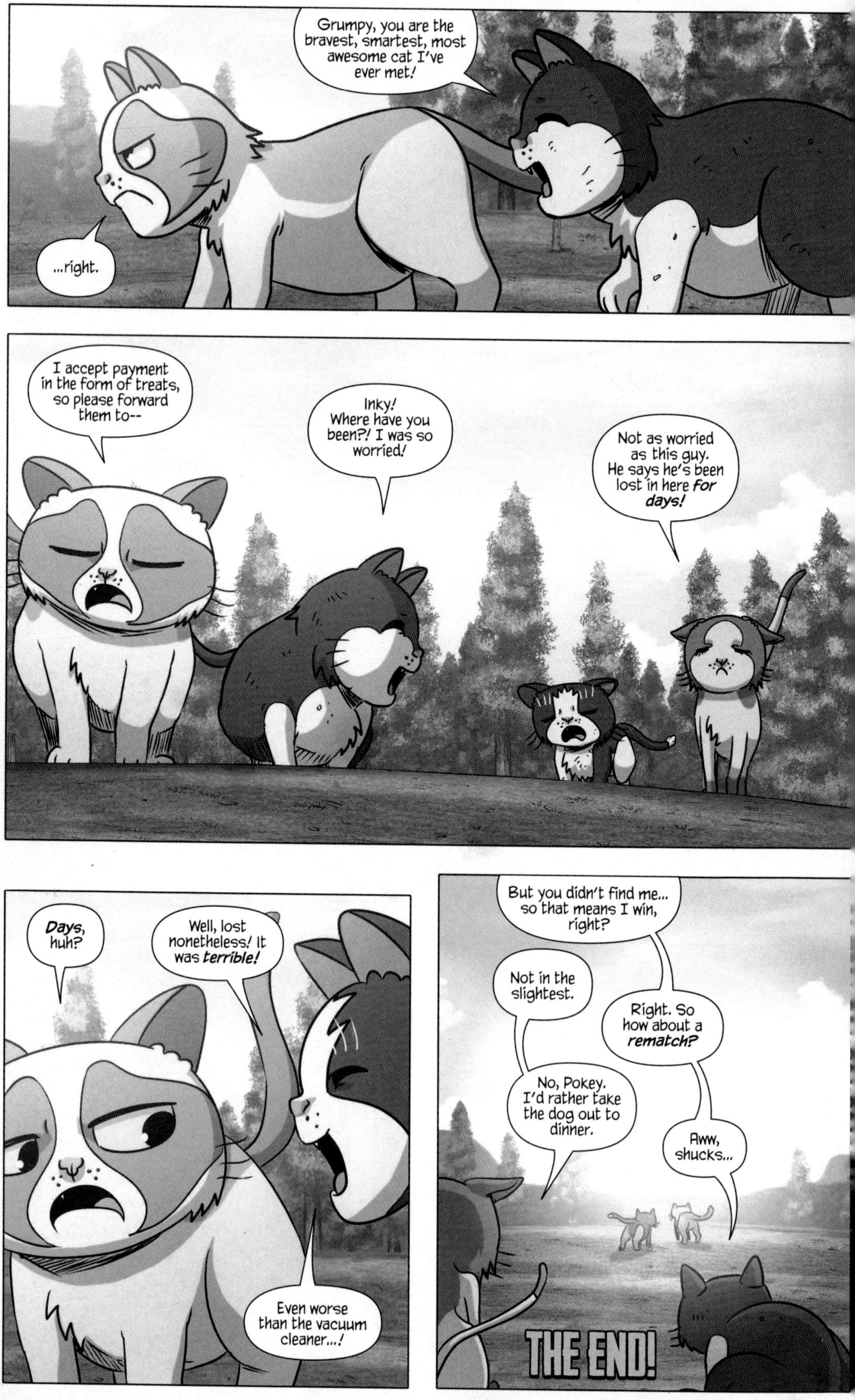

Grumpy, you are the bravest, smartest, most awesome cat I've ever met!
...right.
I accept payment in the form of treats, so please forward them to--
Inky! Where have you been?! I was so worried!
Not as worried as this guy. He says he's been lost in here *for days!*
*Days*, huh?
Well, lost nonetheless! It was *terrible!*
Even worse than the vacuum cleaner...!
But you didn't find me... so that means I win, right?
Not in the slightest.
Right. So how about a *rematch?*
No, Pokey. I'd rather take the dog out to dinner.
Aww, shucks...
THE END!

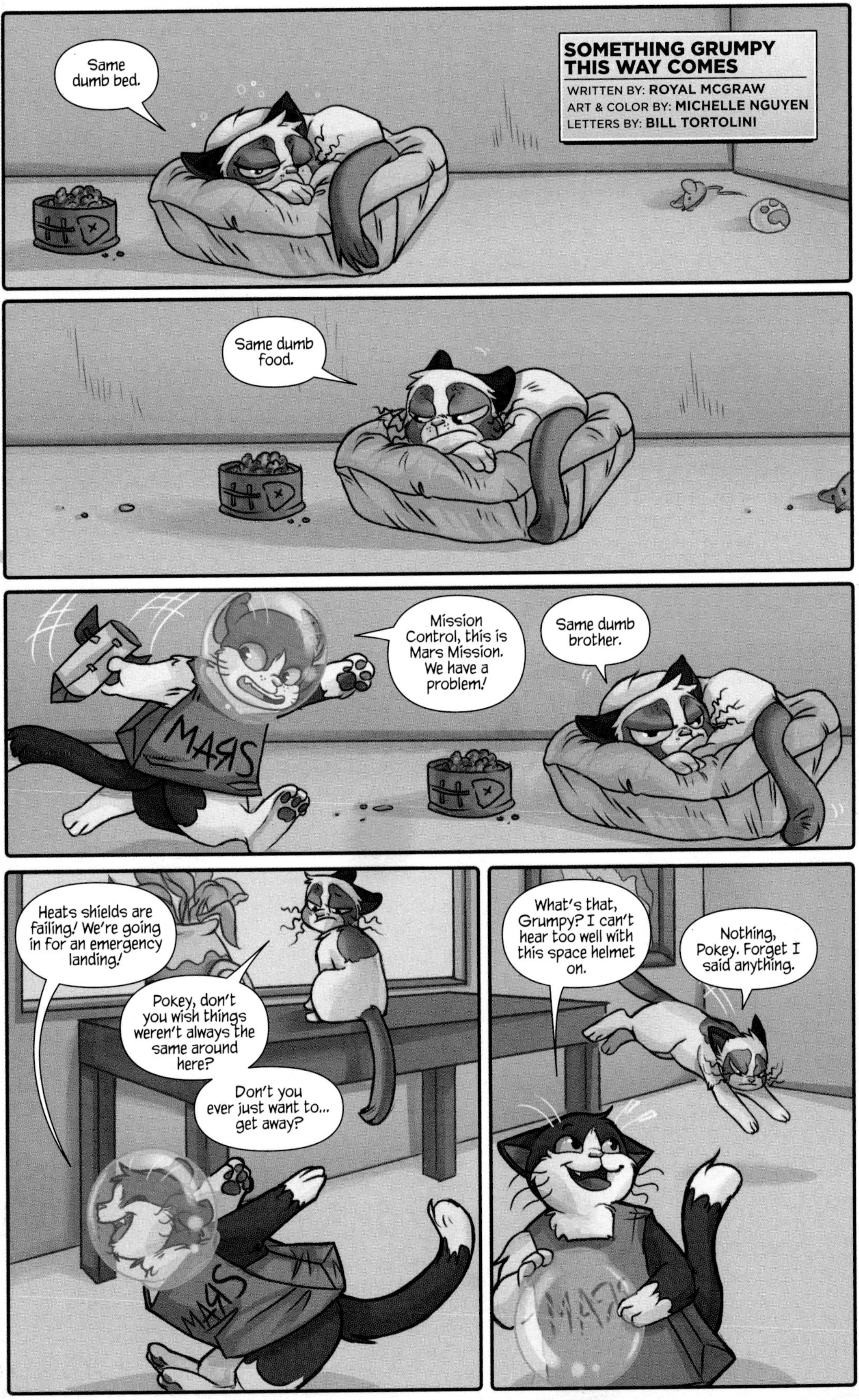
SOMETHING GRUMPY THIS WAY COMES
WRITTEN BY: ROYAL MCGRAW
ART & COLOR BY: MICHELLE NGUYEN
LETTERS BY: BILL TORTOLINI
Same dumb bed.
Same dumb food.
Mission Control, this is Mars Mission. We have a problem!
Same dumb brother.
MARS
Heats shields are failing! We're going in for an emergency landing!
Pokey, don't you wish things weren't always the same around here?
Don't you ever just want to... get away?
What's that, Grumpy? I can't hear too well with this space helmet on.
Nothing, Pokey. Forget I said anything.

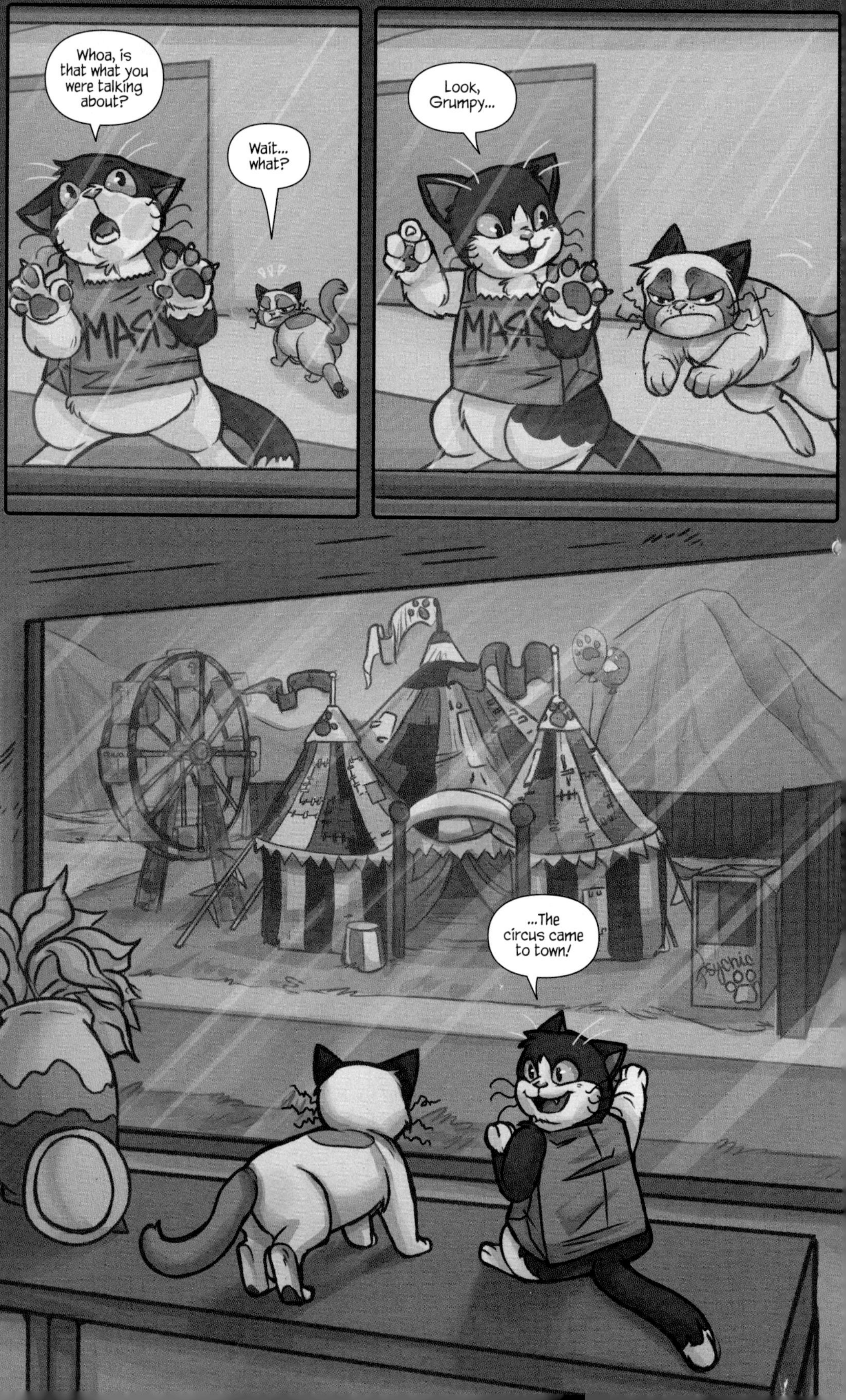
Whoa, is that what you were talking about?
Wait... what?
MARS
Look, Grumpy...
MARS
...The circus came to town!
Psychic

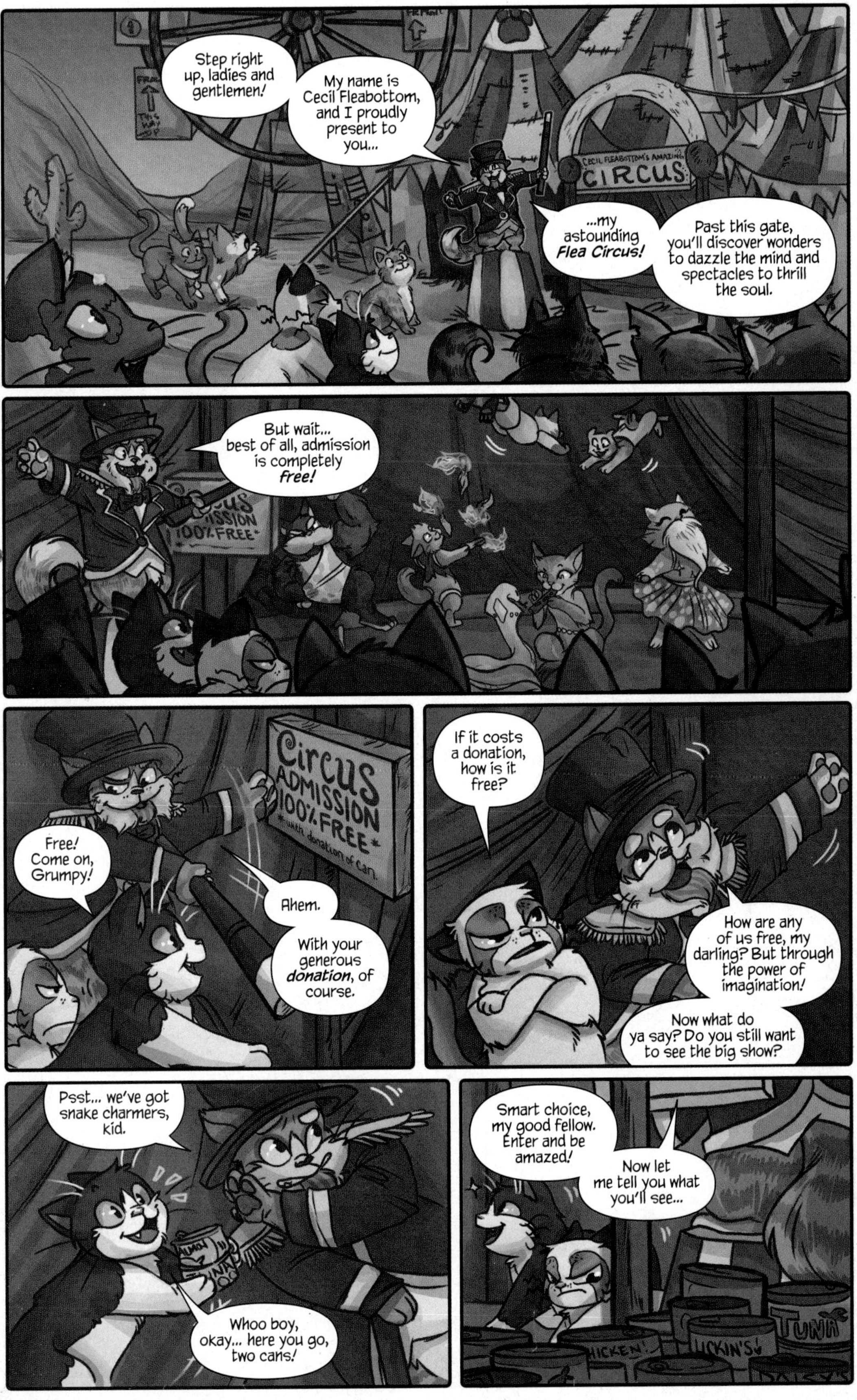
Step right up, ladies and gentlemen!
My name is Cecil Fleabottom, and I proudly present to you...
CIRCUS
...my astounding *Flea Circus!*
Past this gate, you'll discover wonders to dazzle the mind and spectacles to thrill the soul.
But wait... best of all, admission is completely ***free!***
100% FREE*
Circus ADMISSION 100% FREE* *with donation of can.
Free! Come on, Grumpy!
Ahem.
With your generous ***donation***, of course.
If it costs a donation, how is it free?
How are any of us free, my darling? But through the power of imagination!
Now what do ya say? Do you still want to see the big show?
Pssst... we've got snake charmers, kid.
Whoo boy, okay... here you go, two cans!
Smart choice, my good fellow. Enter and be amazed!
Now let me tell you what you'll see...
CHICKEN!
LICKIN'S
TUNA

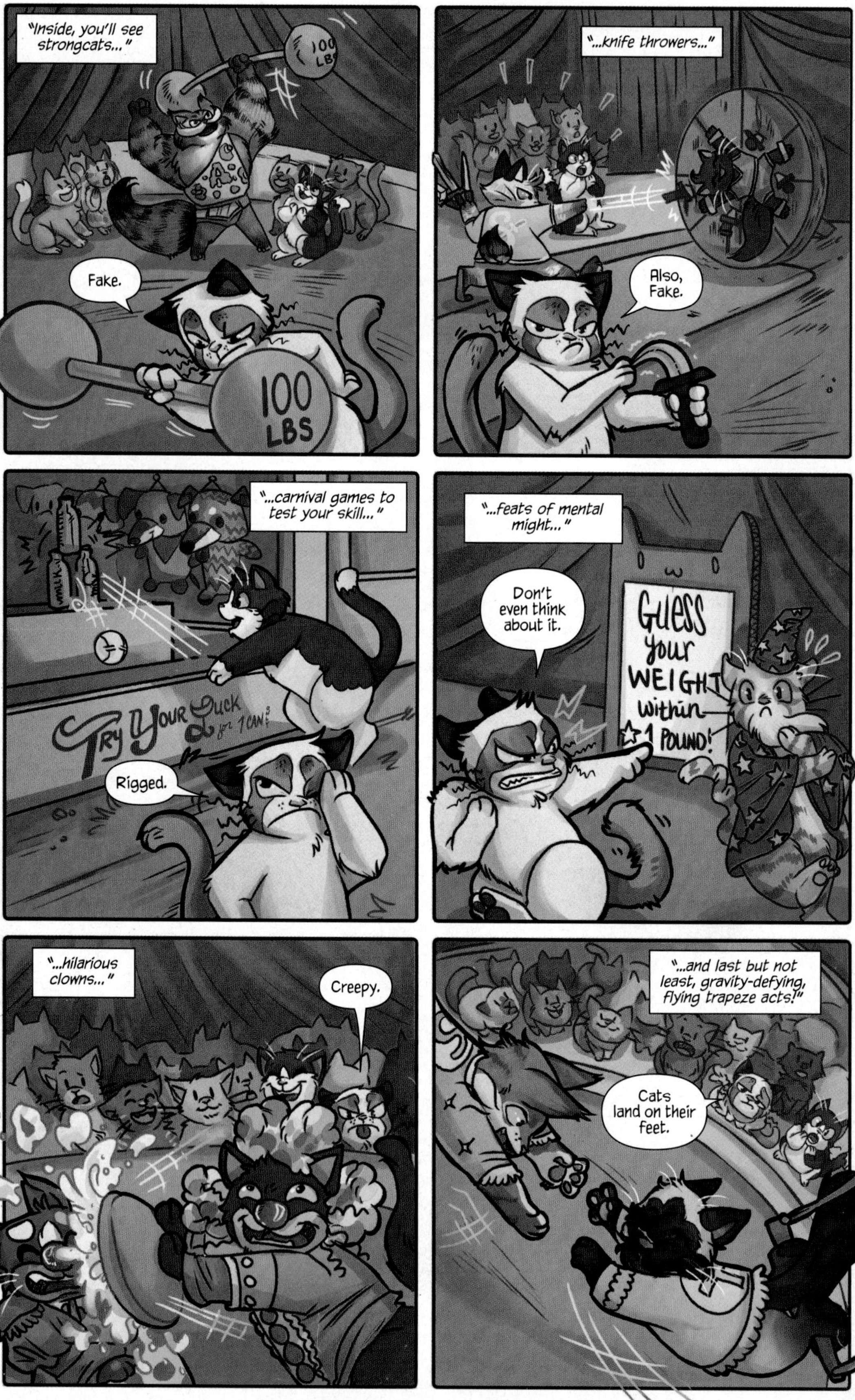
"Inside, you'll see strongcats..."
100 LBS
Fake.
100 LBS
"...knife throwers..."
Also, Fake.
"...carnival games to test your skill..."
Try Your Luck
Rigged.
"...feats of mental might..."
Don't even think about it.
Guess your WEIGHT within 1 POUND!
"...hilarious clowns..."
Creepy.
"...and last but not least, gravity-defying, flying trapeze acts!"
Cats land on their feet.

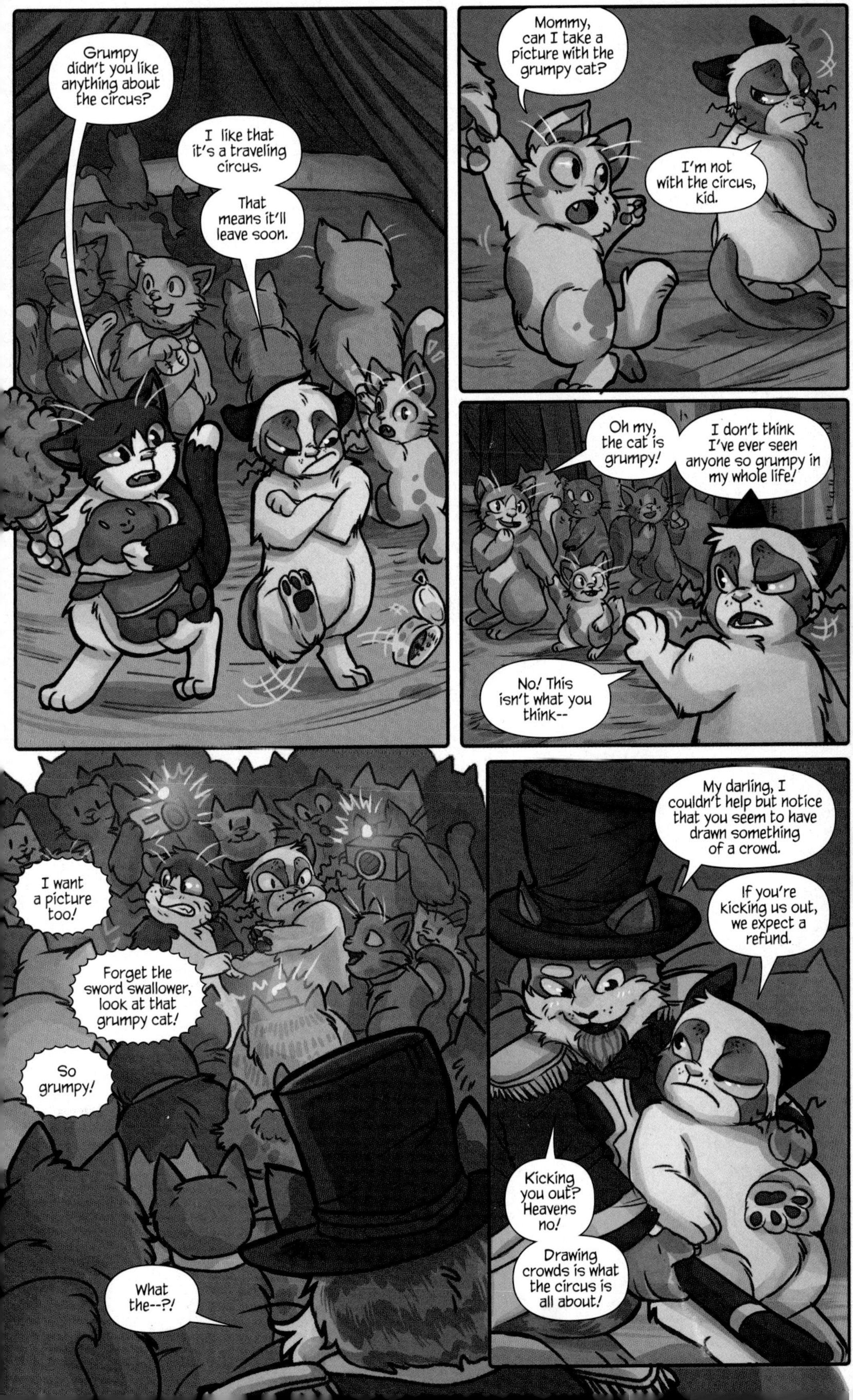
Grumpy didn't you like anything about the circus?
I like that it's a traveling circus.
That means it'll leave soon.
Mommy, can I take a picture with the grumpy cat?
I'm not with the circus, kid.
Oh my, the cat is grumpy!
I don't think I've ever seen anyone so grumpy in my whole life!
No! This isn't what you think--
I want a picture too!
Forget the sword swallower, look at that grumpy cat!
So grumpy!
What the--?!
My darling, I couldn't help but notice that you seem to have drawn something of a crowd.
If you're kicking us out, we expect a refund.
Kicking you out? Heavens no!
Drawing crowds is what the circus is all about!

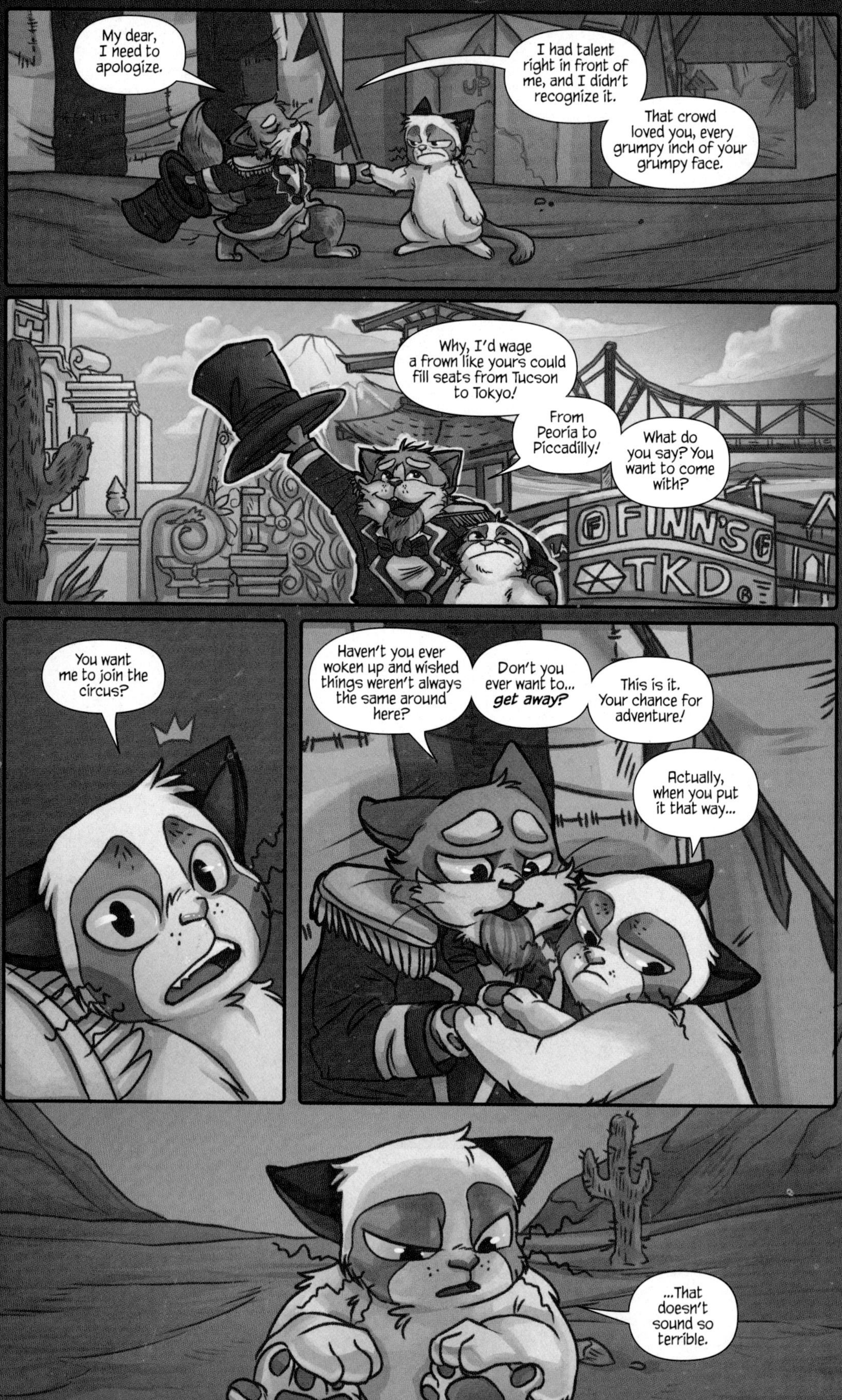
My dear, I need to apologize.
I had talent right in front of me, and I didn't recognize it.
That crowd loved you, every grumpy inch of your grumpy face.
Why, I'd wage a frown like yours could fill seats from Tucson to Tokyo!
From Peoria to Piccadilly!
What do you say? You want to come with?
FINN'S
TKD
You want me to join the circus?
Haven't you ever woken up and wished things weren't always the same around here?
Don't you ever want to... *get away?*
This is it. Your chance for adventure!
Actually, when you put it that way...
...That doesn't sound so terrible.

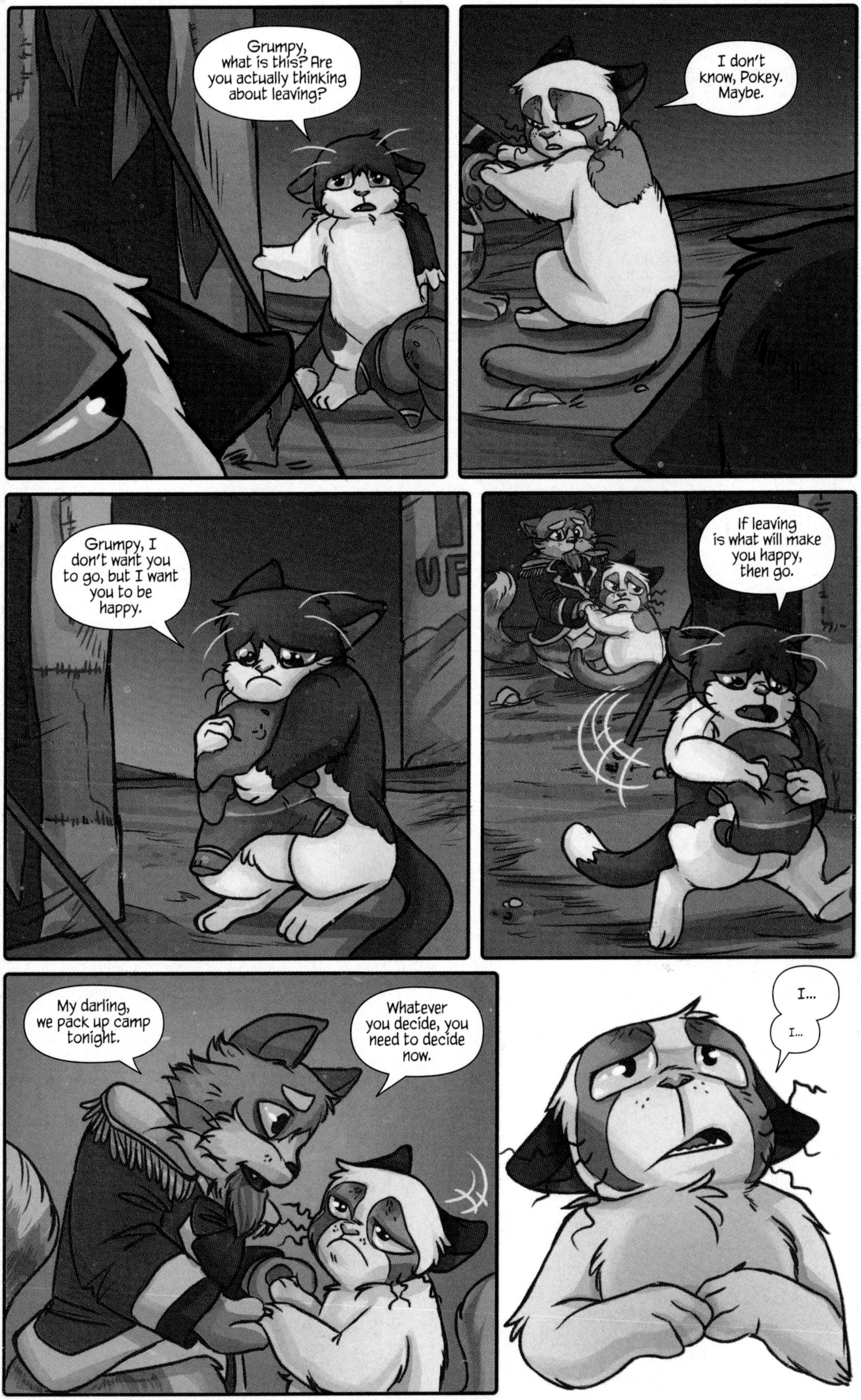
Grumpy, what is this? Are you actually thinking about leaving?
I don't know, Pokey. Maybe.
Grumpy, I don't want you to go, but I want you to be happy.
If leaving is what will make you happy, then go.
My darling, we pack up camp tonight.
Whatever you decide, you need to decide now.
I...
I...

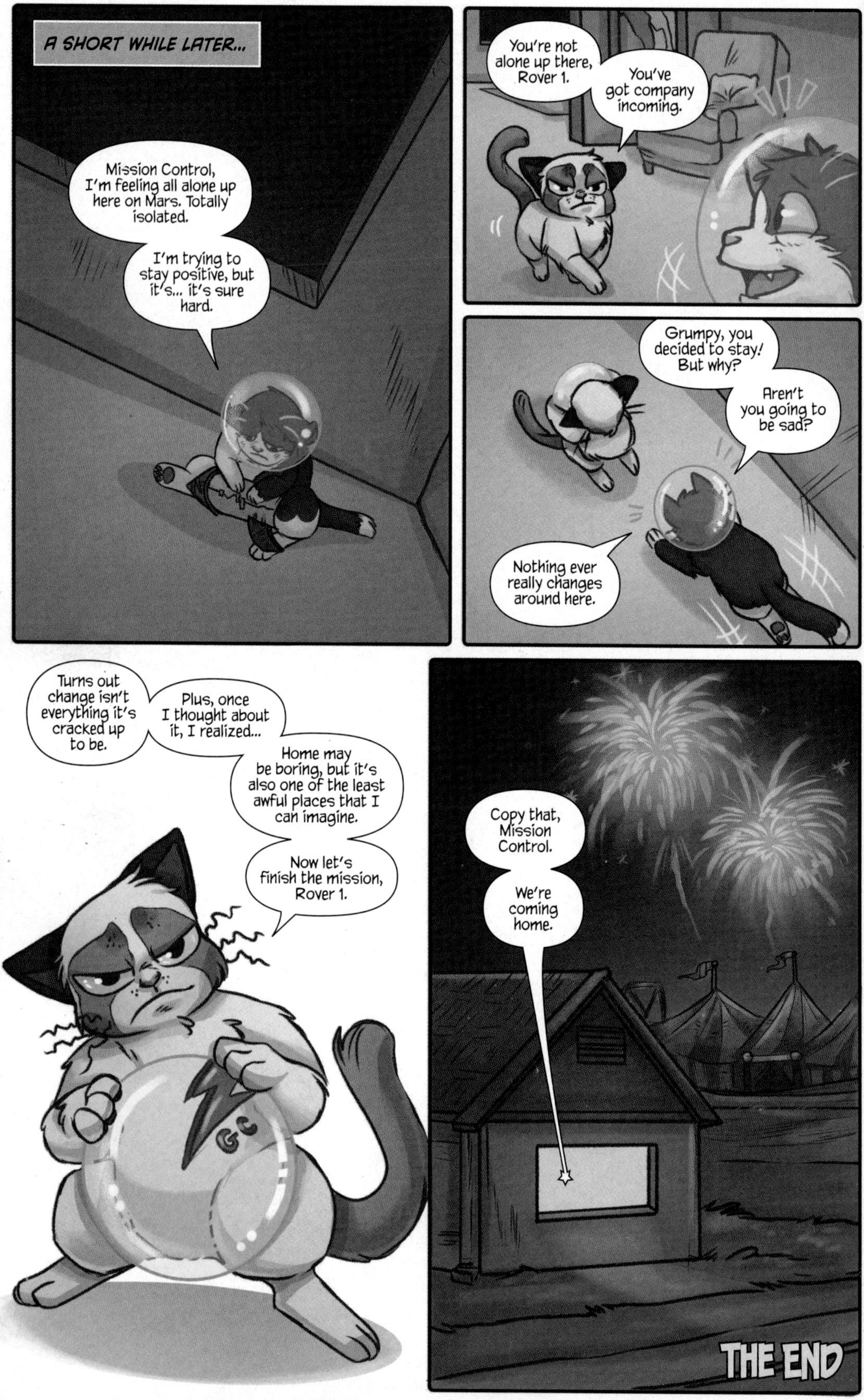
A SHORT WHILE LATER...
Mission Control, I'm feeling all alone up here on Mars. Totally isolated.
I'm trying to stay positive, but it's... it's sure hard.
You're not alone up there, Rover 1.
You've got company incoming.
Grumpy, you decided to stay! But why?
Aren't you going to be sad?
Nothing ever really changes around here.
Turns out change isn't everything it's cracked up to be.
Plus, once I thought about it, I realized...
Home may be boring, but it's also one of the least awful places that I can imagine.
Now let's finish the mission, Rover 1.
GC
Copy that, Mission Control.
We're coming home.
THE END

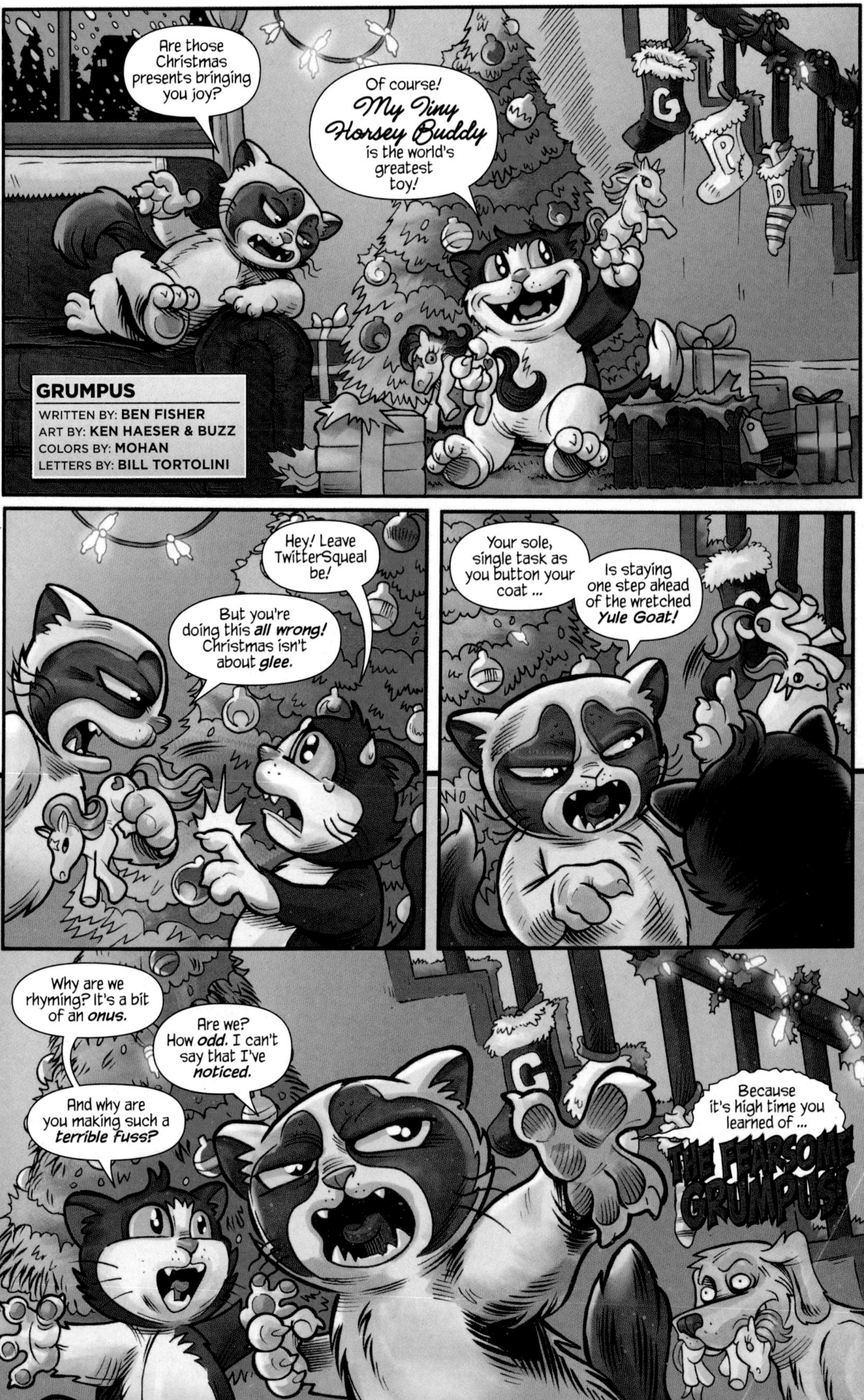
Are those Christmas presents bringing you joy?
Of course! My Tiny Horsey Buddy is the world's greatest toy!
GRUMPUS
WRITTEN BY: BEN FISHER
ART BY: KEN HAESER & BUZZ
COLORS BY: MOHAN
LETTERS BY: BILL TORTOLINI
Hey! Leave TwitterSqueal be!
But you're doing this all wrong! Christmas isn't about glee.
Your sole, single task as you button your coat ...
Is staying one step ahead of the wretched Yule Goat!
Why are we rhyming? It's a bit of an onus.
Are we? How odd. I can't say that I've noticed.
And why are you making such a terrible fuss?
Because it's high time you learned of ...
THE FEARSOME GRUMPUS!

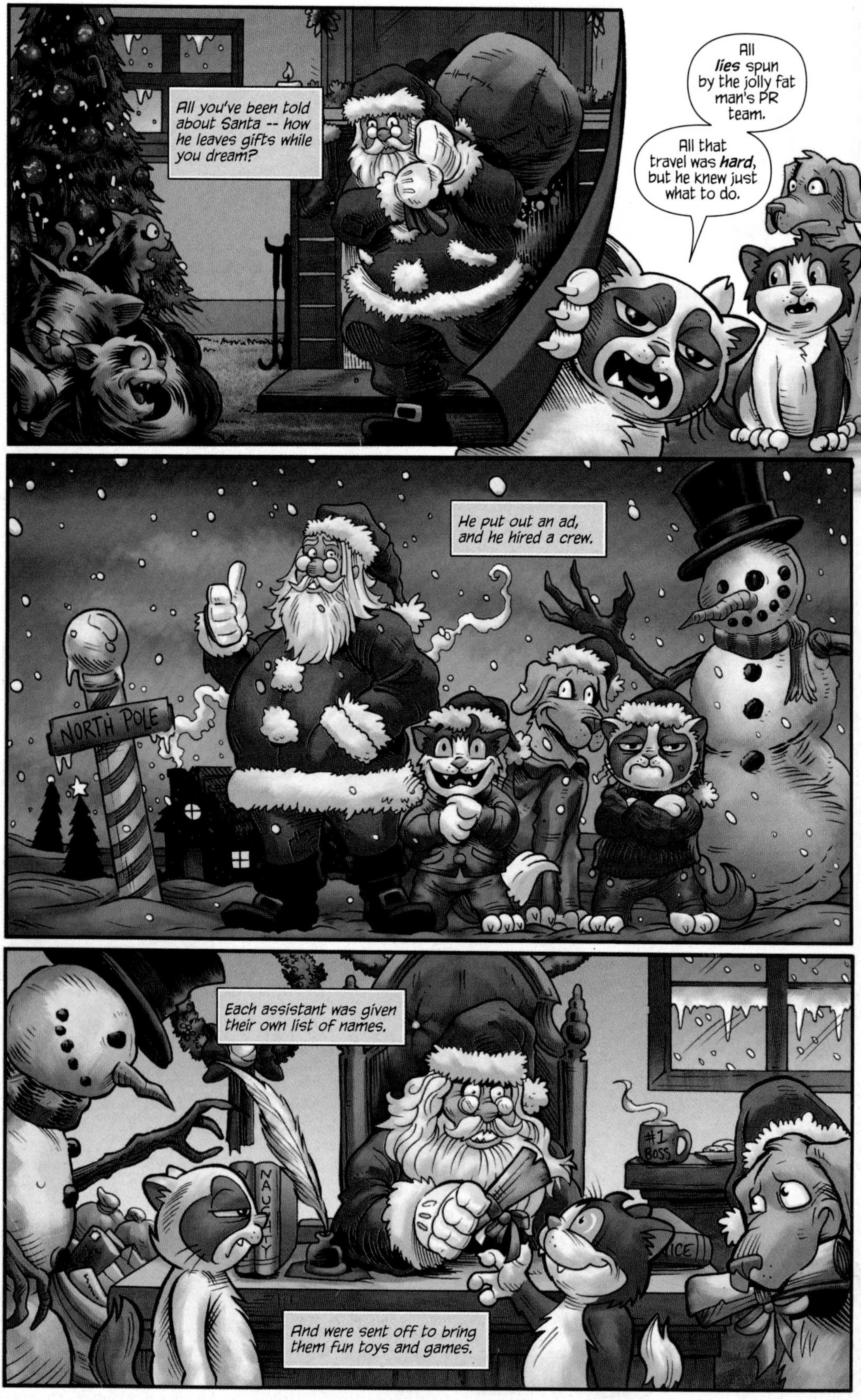
All you've been told about Santa -- how he leaves gifts while you dream?
All *lies* spun by the jolly fat man's PR team.
All that travel was *hard*, but he knew just what to do.
He put out an ad, and he hired a crew.
NORTH POLE
Each assistant was given their own list of names.
NAUGHTY
#1 BOSS
And were sent off to bring them fun toys and games.

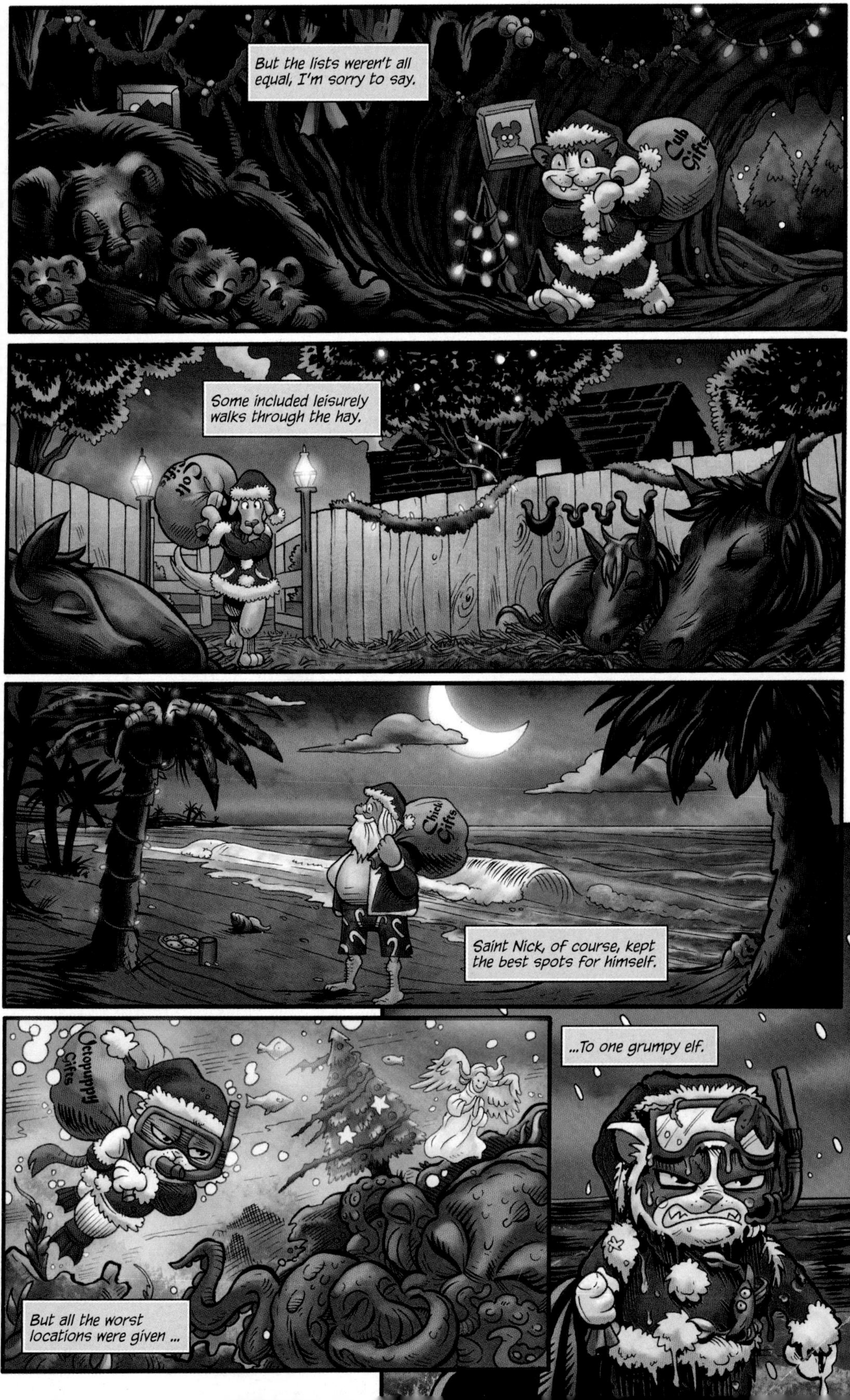

But the lists weren't all equal, I'm sorry to say.
Cub Gifts
Some included leisurely walks through the hay.
Colt Gifts
Chick Gifts
Saint Nick, of course, kept the best spots for himself.
Octopuppy Gifts
But all the worst locations were given ...
...To one grumpy elf.

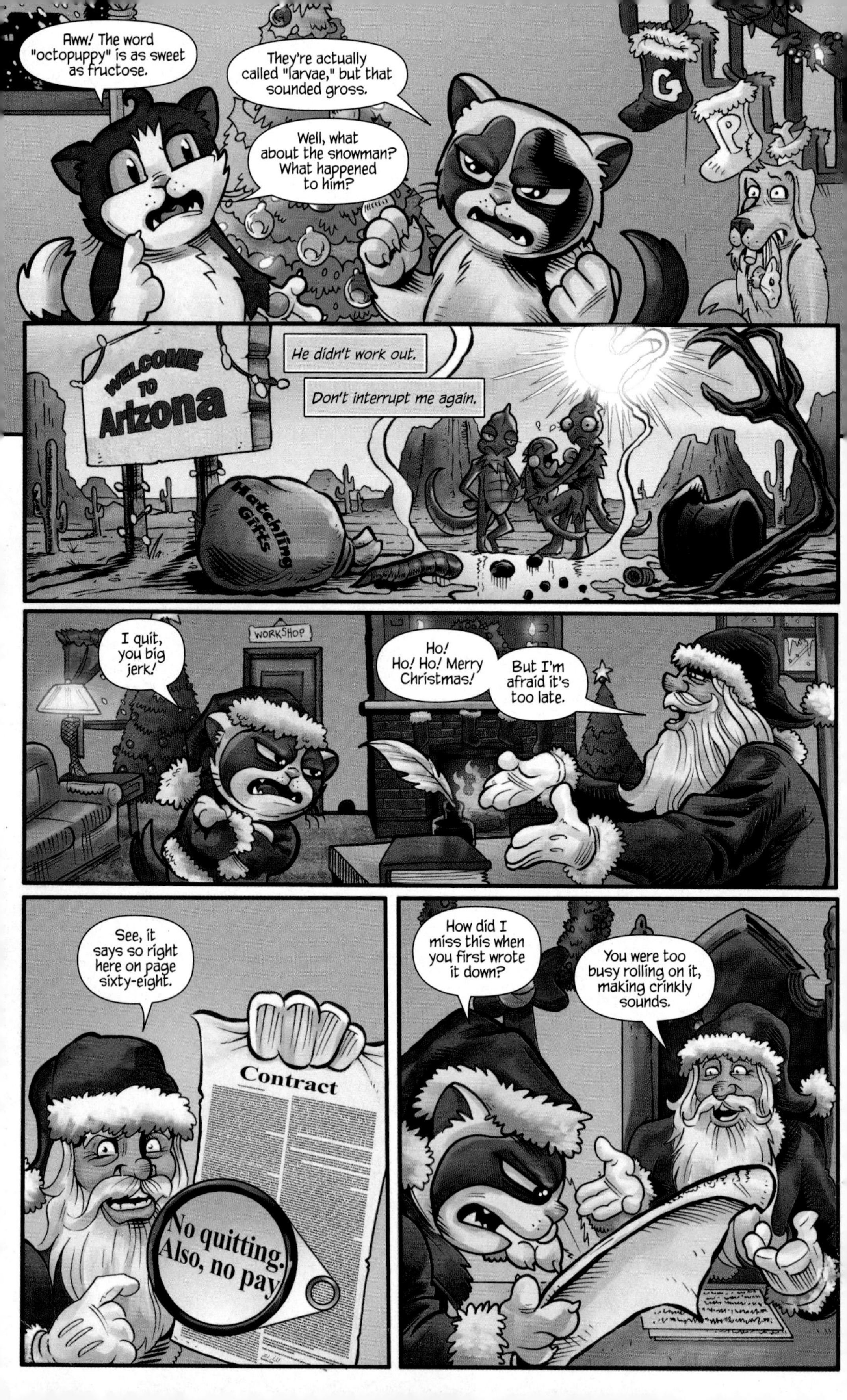

Aww! The word "octopuppy" is as sweet as fructose.
They're actually called "larvae," but that sounded gross.
Well, what about the snowman? What happened to him?
G
P
WELCOME TO Arizona
He didn't work out.
Don't interrupt me again.
Hatchling Gifts
WORKSHOP
I quit, you big jerk!
Ho! Ho! Ho! Merry Christmas!
But I'm afraid it's too late.
See, it says so right here on page sixty-eight.
Contract
No quitting. Also, no pay
How did I miss this when you first wrote it down?
You were too busy rolling on it, making crinkly sounds.

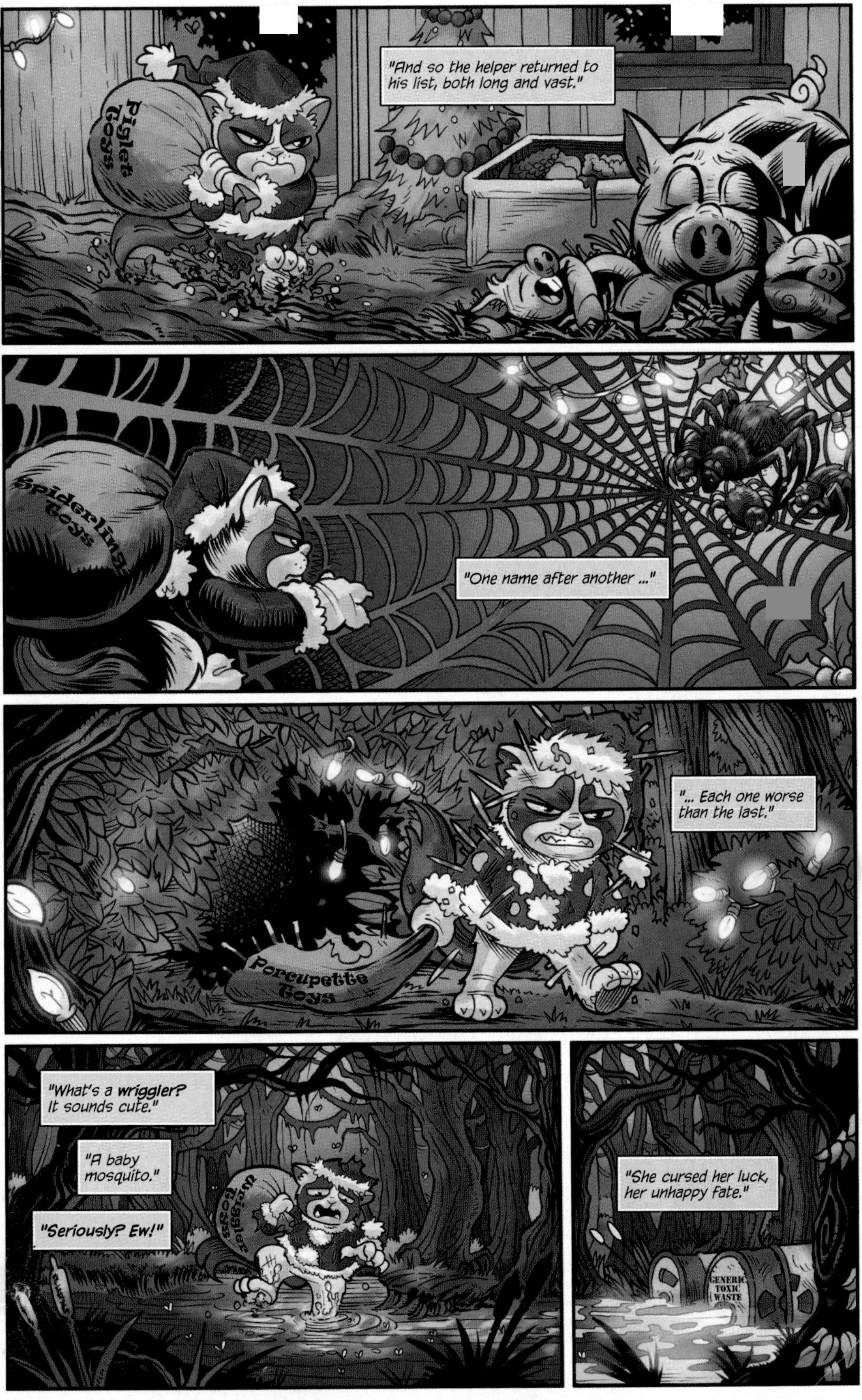
"And so the helper returned to his list, both long and vast."
Piglet Toys
Spiderling Toys
"One name after another ..."
"... Each one worse than the last."
Porcupette Toys
"What's a **wriggler?** It sounds cute."
"A baby mosquito."
**"Seriously? Ew!"**
Wriggler Toys
"She cursed her luck, her unhappy fate."
GENERIC TOXIC WASTE

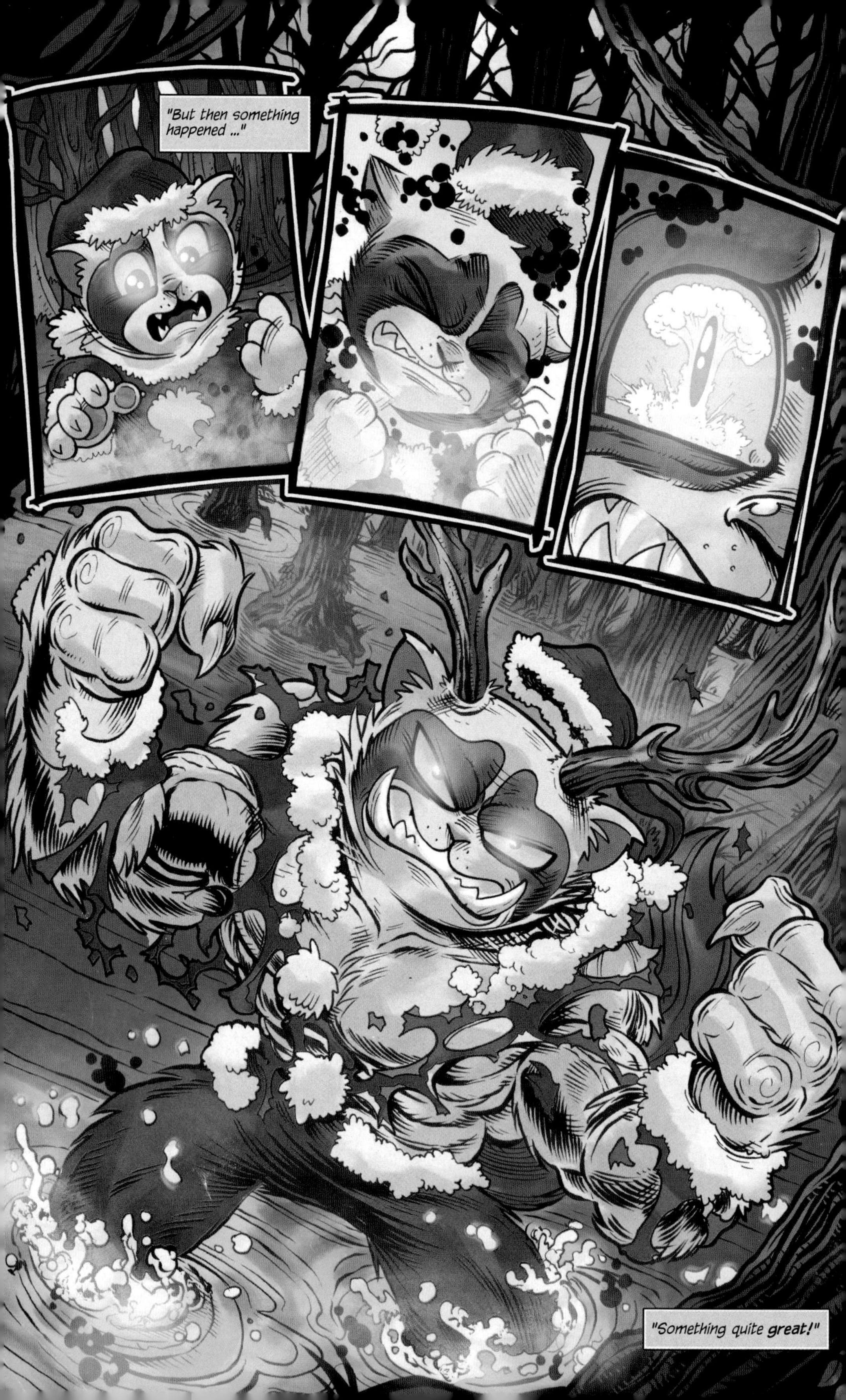
"But then something happened ..."
"Something quite great!"

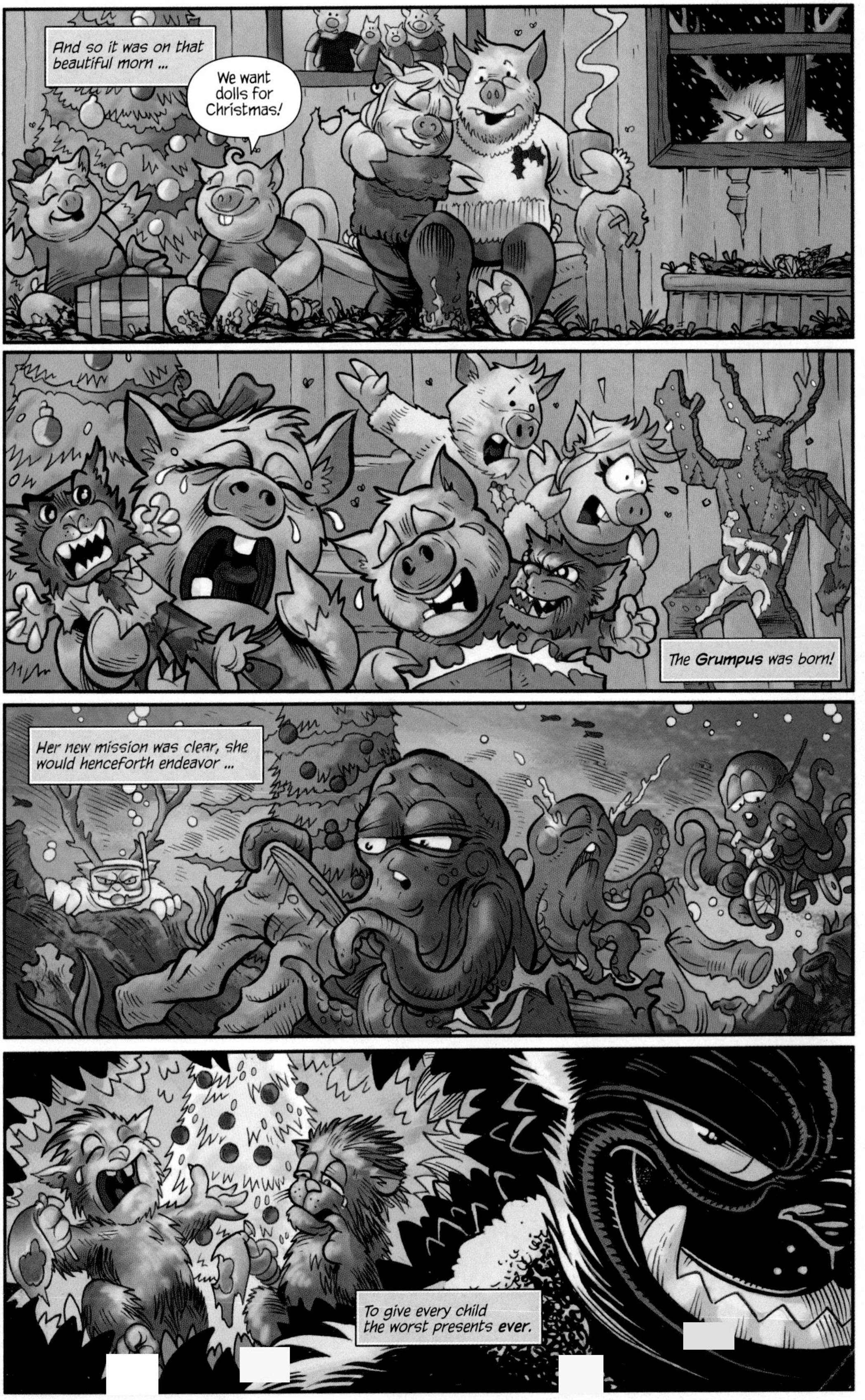
And so it was on that beautiful morn ...
We want dolls for Christmas!
The **Grumpus** was born!
Her new mission was clear, she would henceforth endeavor ...
To give every child the worst presents **ever**.

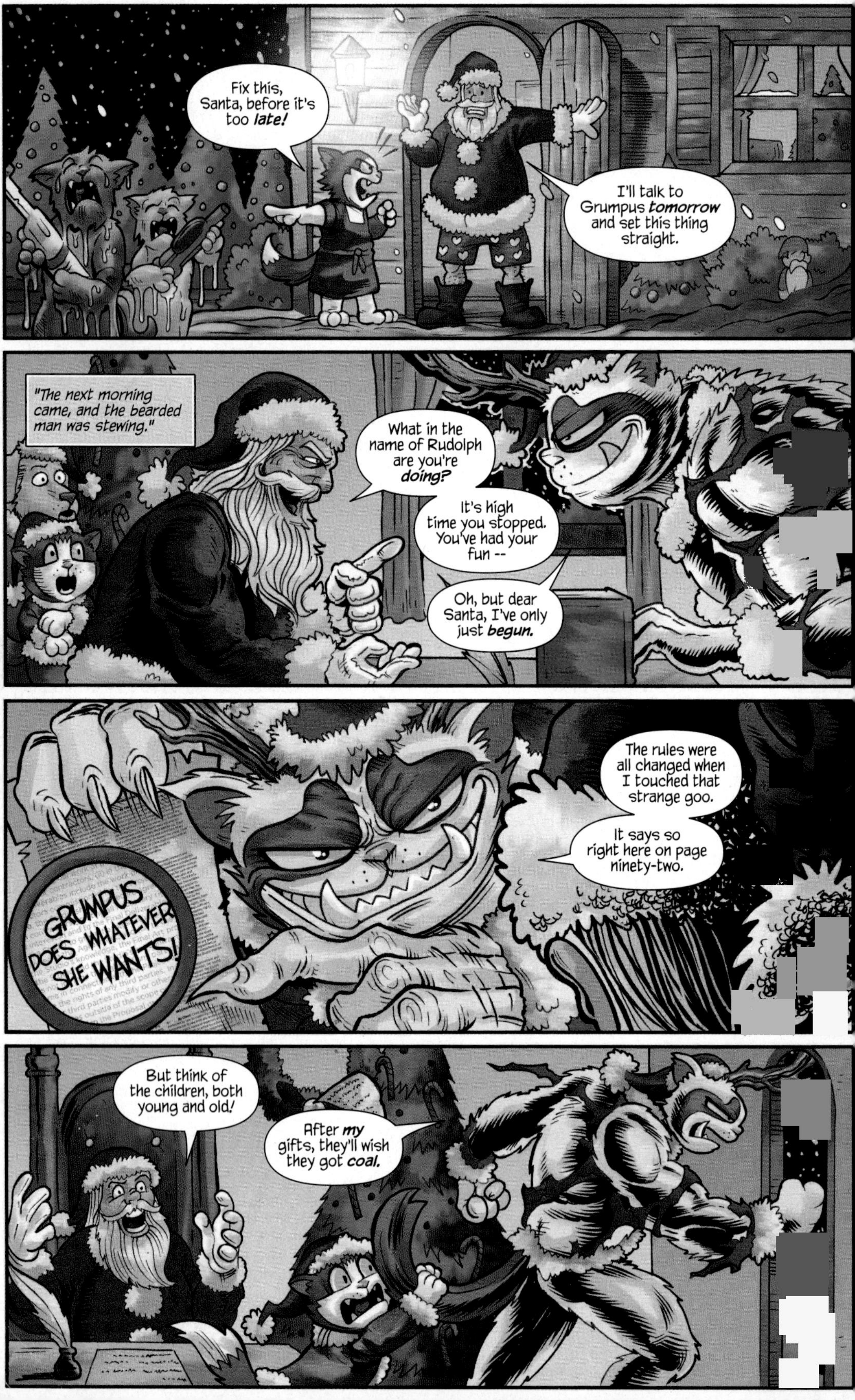
Fix this, Santa, before it's too late!
I'll talk to Grumpus tomorrow and set this thing straight.
"The next morning came, and the bearded man was stewing."
What in the name of Rudolph are you're doing?
It's high time you stopped. You've had your fun --
Oh, but dear Santa, I've only just begun.
GRUMPUS DOES WHATEVER SHE WANTS!
The rules were all changed when I touched that strange goo.
It says so right here on page ninety-two.
But think of the children, both young and old!
After my gifts, they'll wish they got coal.

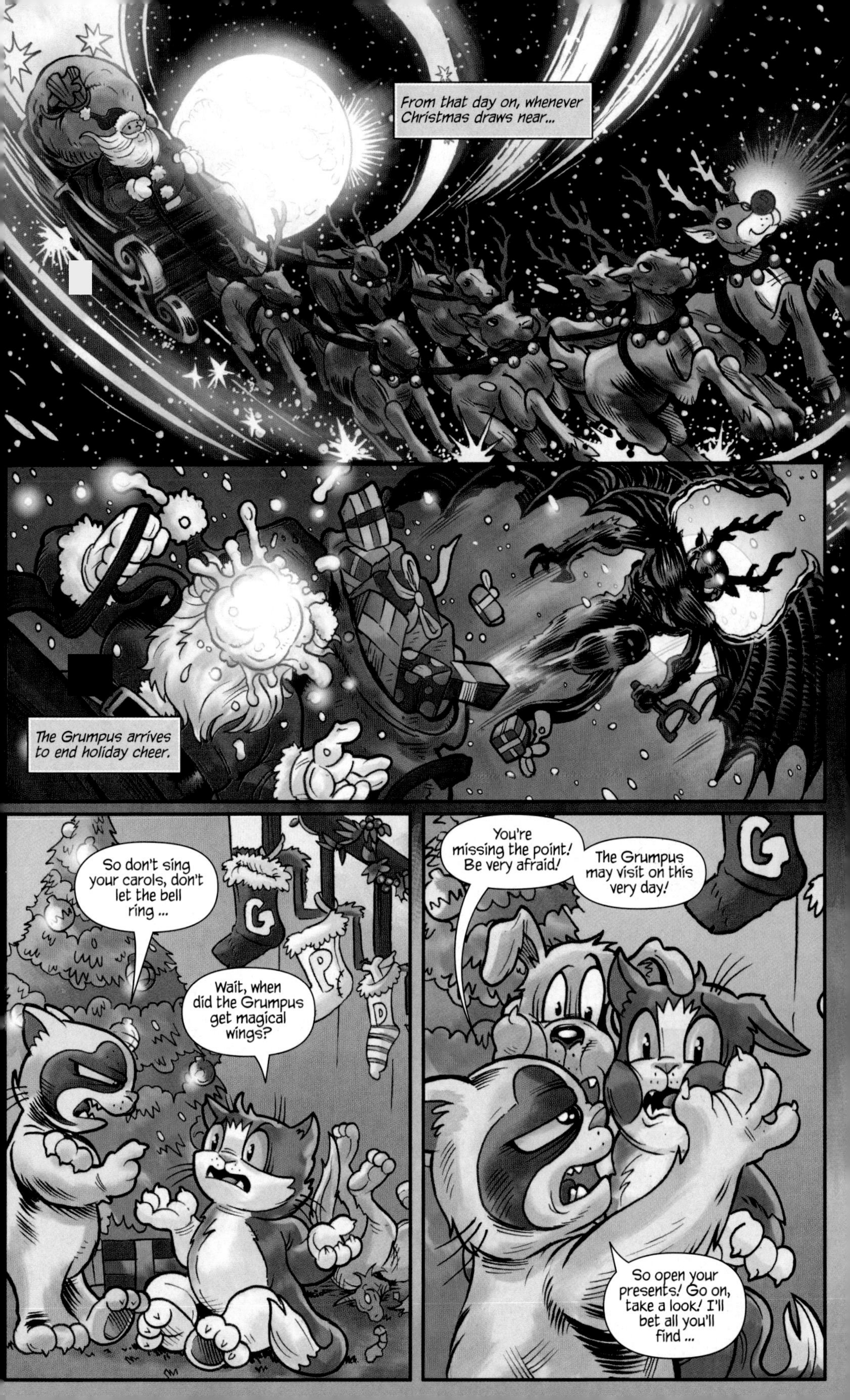
From that day on, whenever Christmas draws near...
The Grumpus arrives to end holiday cheer.
So don't sing your carols, don't let the bell ring ...
Wait, when did the Grumpus get magical wings?
You're missing the point! Be very afraid!
The Grumpus may visit on this very day!
So open your presents! Go on, take a look! I'll bet all you'll find ...

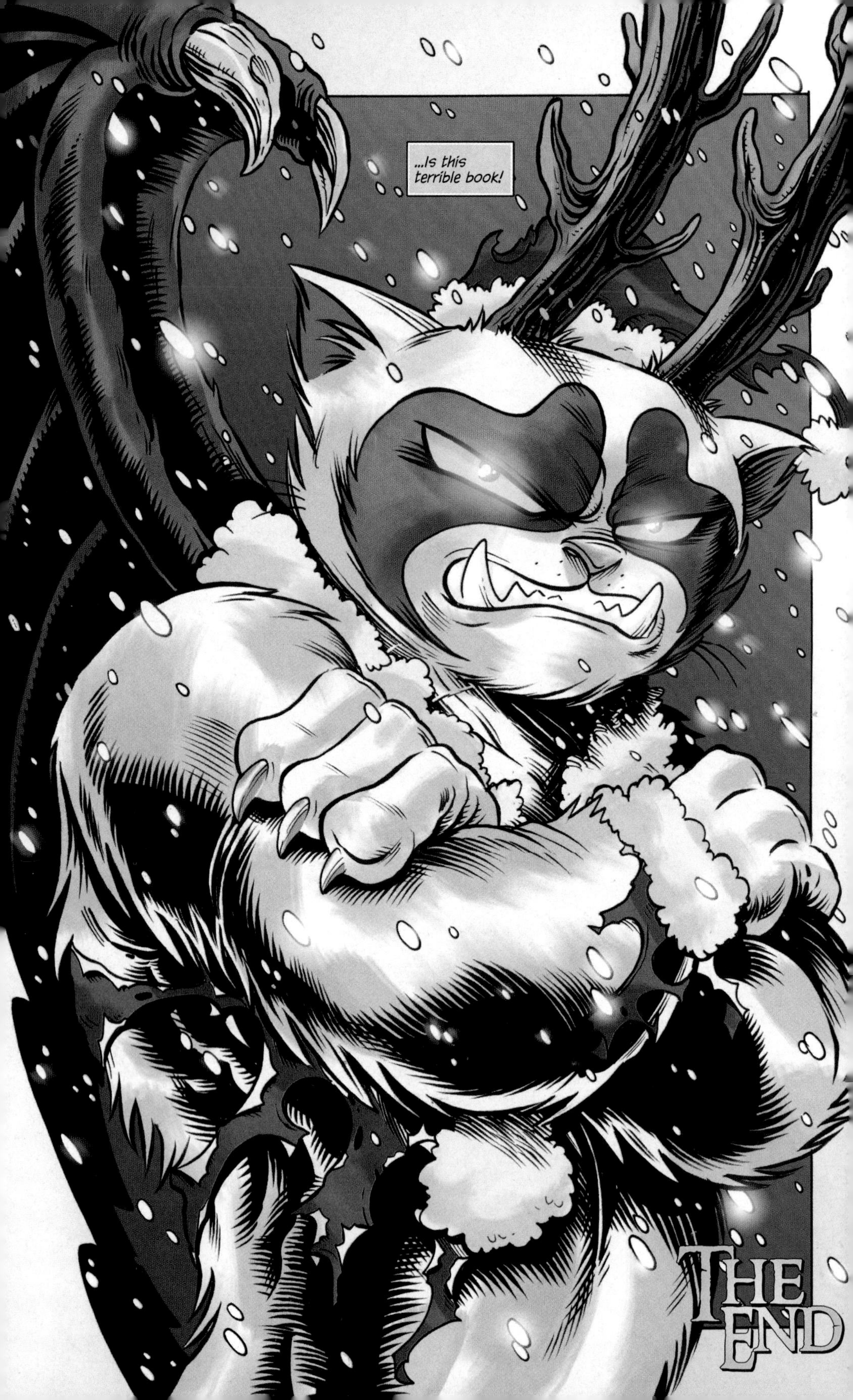
...Is this
terrible book!
THE
END

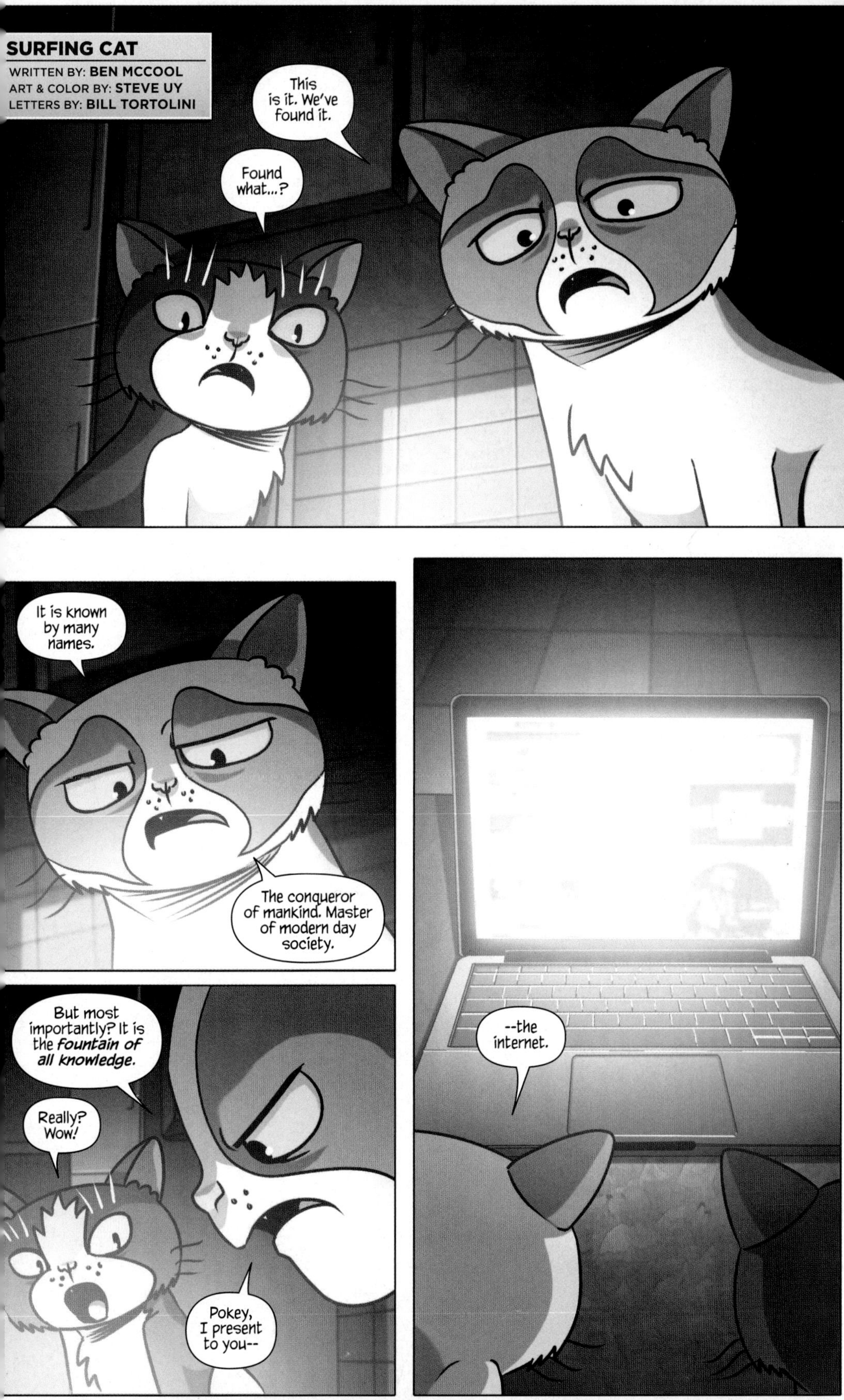
SURFING CAT
WRITTEN BY: BEN MCCOOL
ART & COLOR BY: STEVE UY
LETTERS BY: BILL TORTOLINI
This is it. We've found it.
Found what...?
It is known by many names.
The conqueror of mankind. Master of modern day society.
But most importantly? It is the *fountain of all knowledge.*
Really? Wow!
Pokey, I present to you--
--the internet.

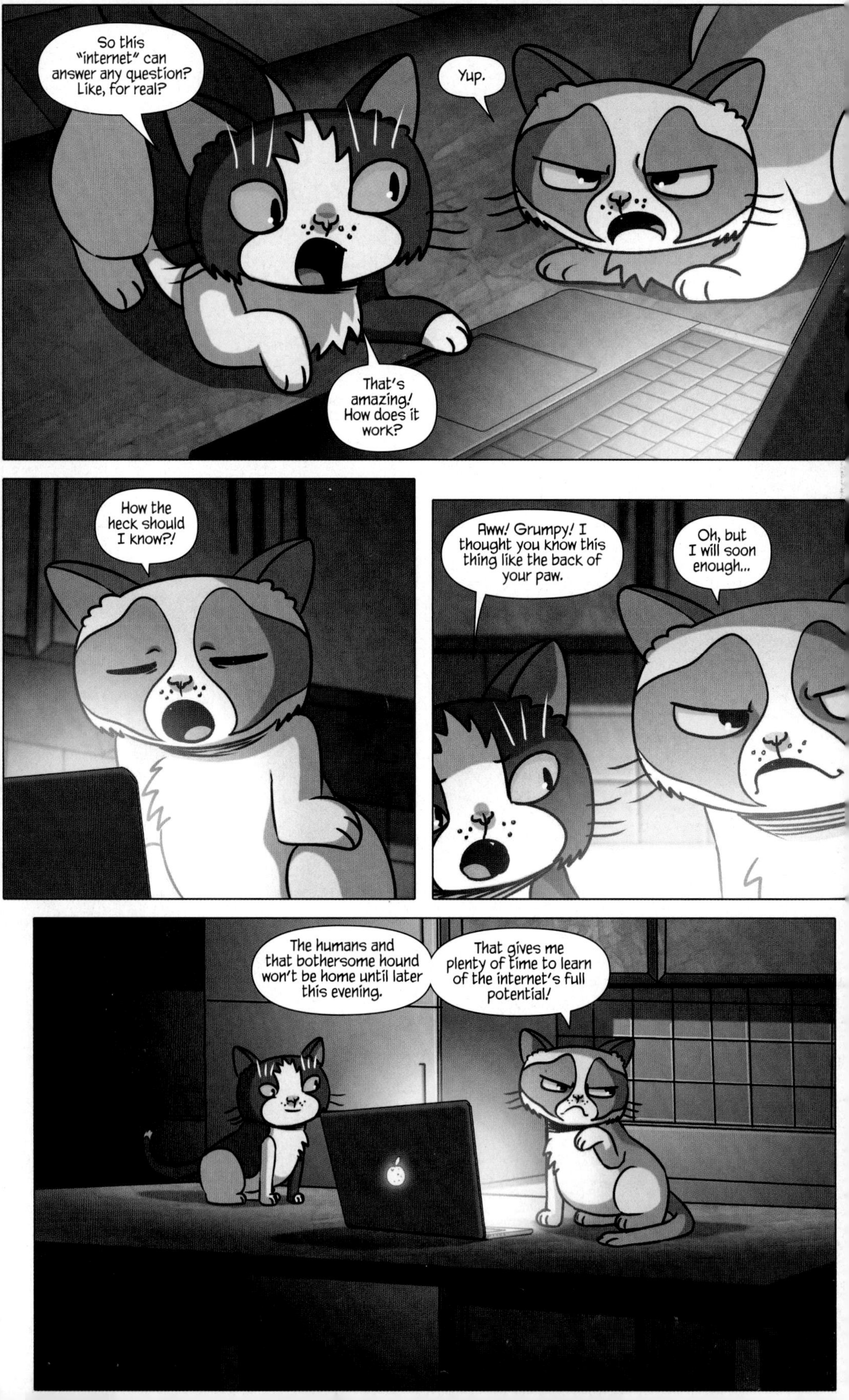
So this "internet" can answer any question? Like, for real?
Yup.
That's amazing! How does it work?
How the heck should I know?!
Aww! Grumpy! I thought you know this thing like the back of your paw.
Oh, but I will soon enough...
The humans and that bothersome hound won't be home until later this evening.
That gives me plenty of time to learn of the internet's full potential!

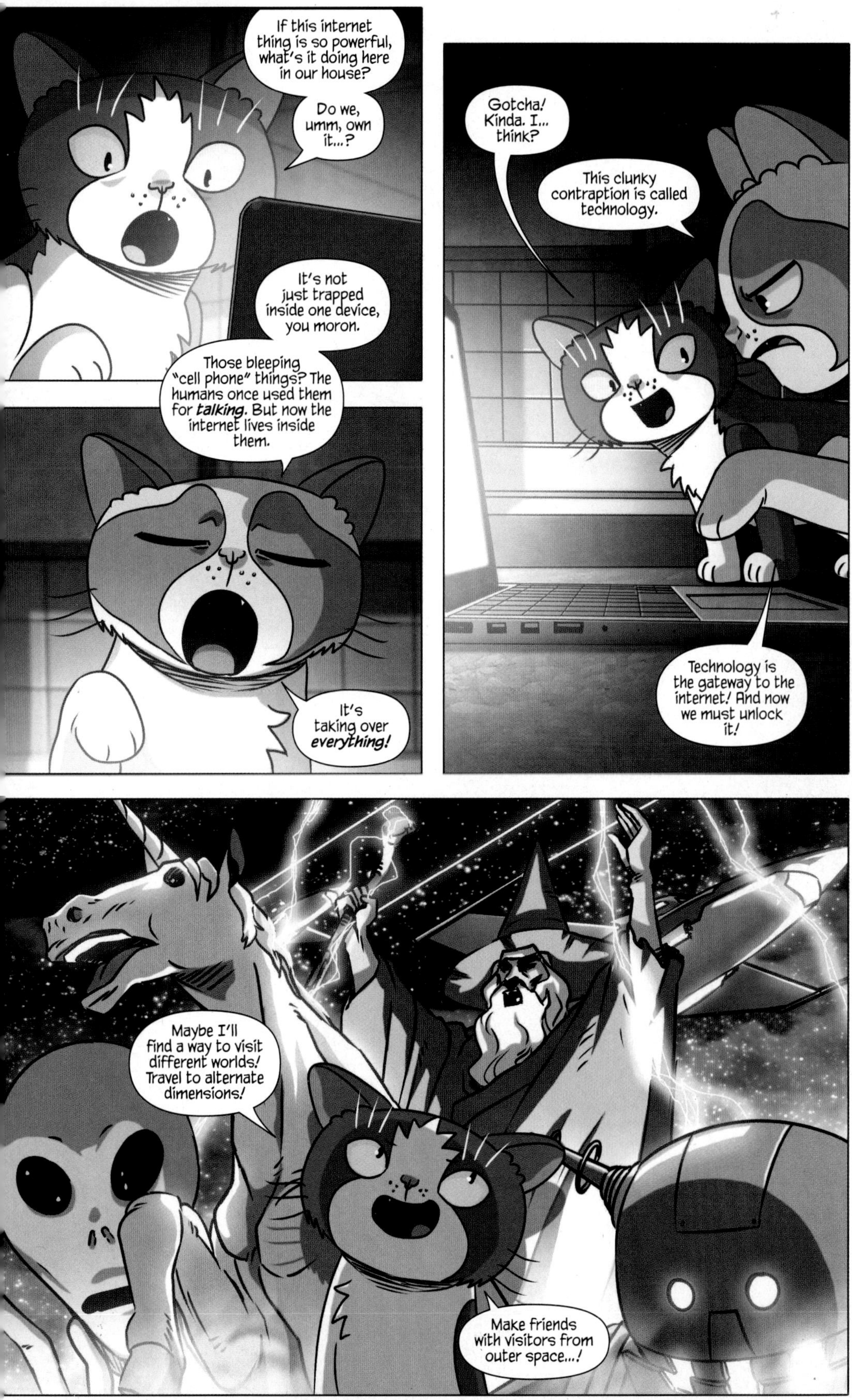

If this internet thing is so powerful, what's it doing here in our house?
Do we, umm, own it...?
It's not just trapped inside one device, you moron.
Those bleeping "cell phone" things? The humans once used them for *talking*. But now the internet lives inside them.
It's taking over *everything!*
Gotcha! Kinda. I... think?
This clunky contraption is called technology.
Technology is the gateway to the internet! And now we must unlock it!
Maybe I'll find a way to visit different worlds! Travel to alternate dimensions!
Make friends with visitors from outer space...!

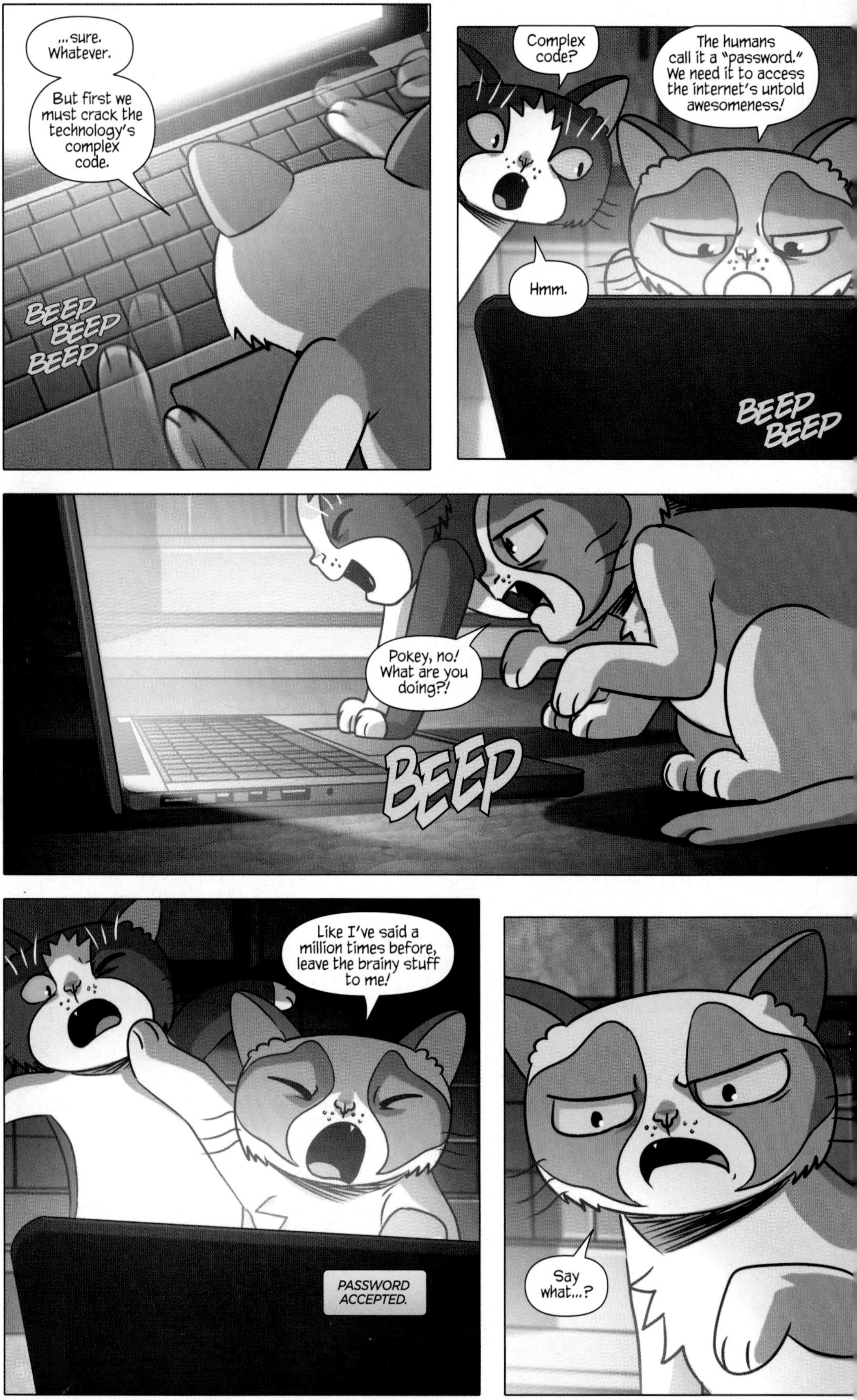
...sure. Whatever.
But first we must crack the technology's complex code.
BEEP BEEP BEEP
Complex code?
The humans call it a "password." We need it to access the internet's untold awesomeness!
Hmm.
BEEP BEEP
Pokey, no! What are you doing?!
BEEP
Like I've said a million times before, leave the brainy stuff to me!
PASSWORD ACCEPTED.
Say what...?

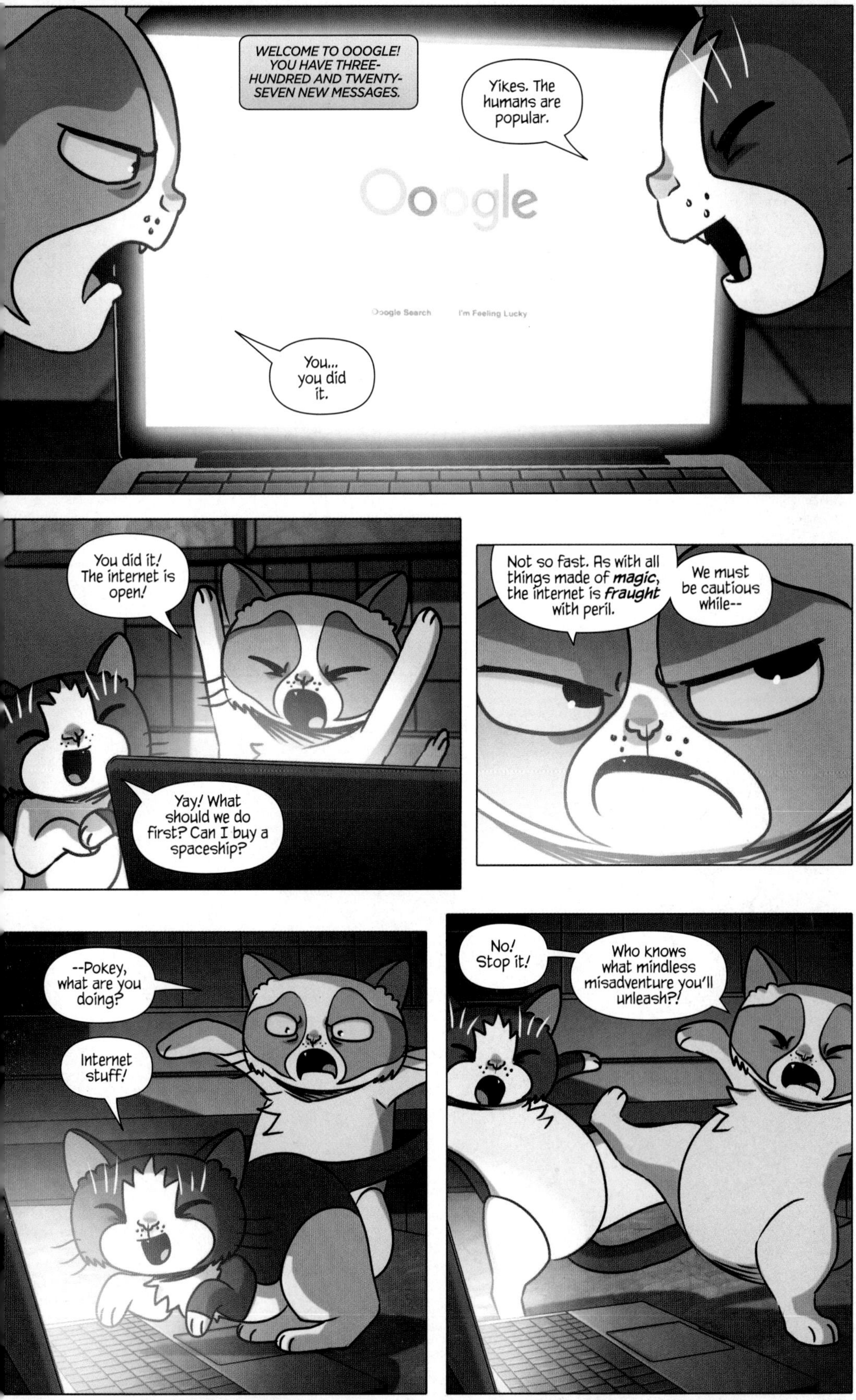
WELCOME TO OOOGLE! YOU HAVE THREE-HUNDRED AND TWENTY-SEVEN NEW MESSAGES.
Yikes. The humans are popular.
Ooogle
Ooogle Search
I'm Feeling Lucky
You... you did it.
You did it! The internet is open!
Yay! What should we do first? Can I buy a spaceship?
Not so fast. As with all things made of *magic*, the internet is *fraught* with peril.
We must be cautious while--
--Pokey, what are you doing?
Internet stuff!
No! Stop it!
Who knows what mindless misadventure you'll unleash?!

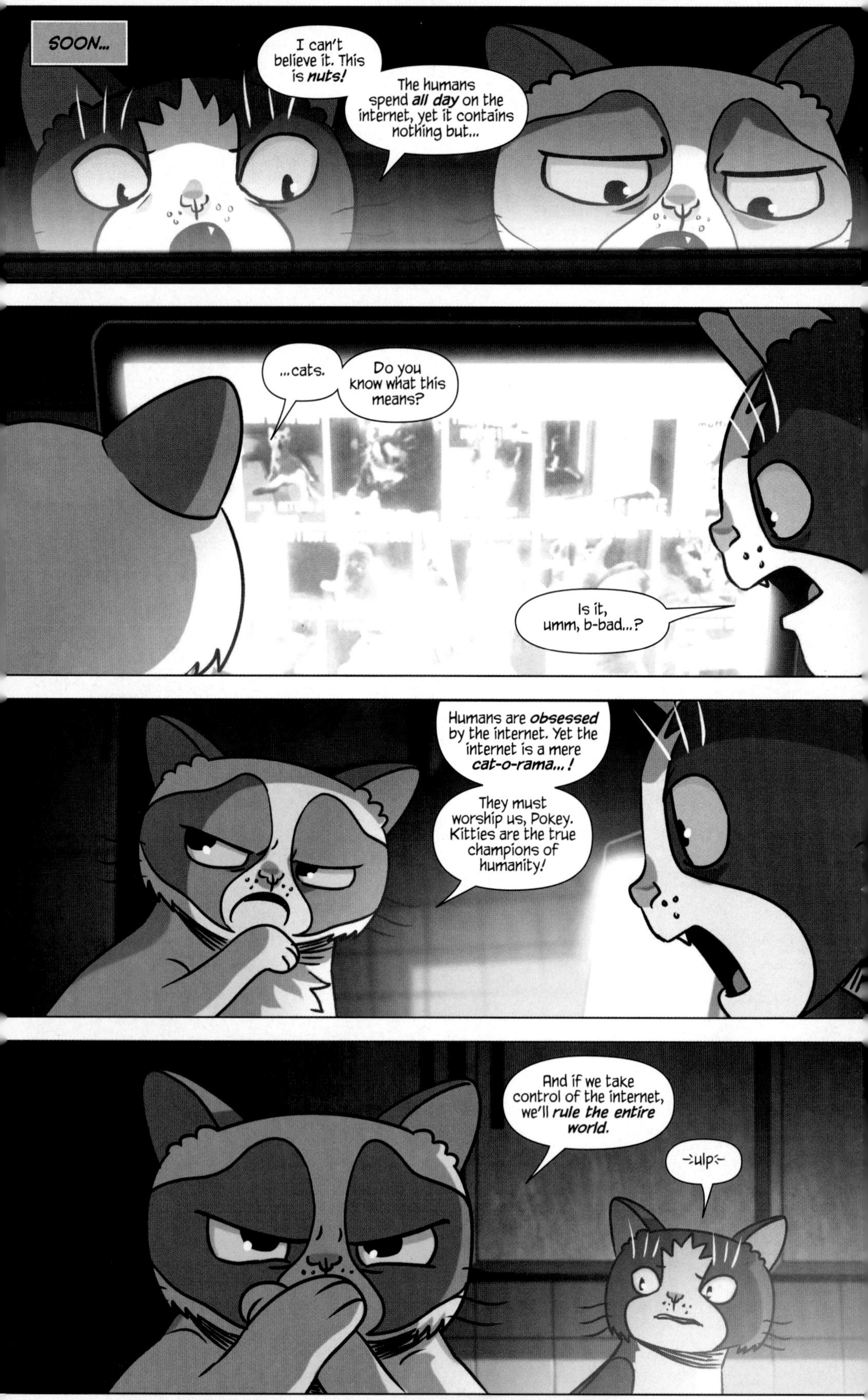
SOON...
I can't believe it. This is *nuts!*
The humans spend *all day* on the internet, yet it contains nothing but...
...cats.
Do you know what this means?
Is it, umm, b-bad...?
Humans are *obsessed* by the internet. Yet the internet is a mere *cat-o-rama...!*
They must worship us, Pokey. Kitties are the true champions of humanity!
And if we take control of the internet, we'll *rule the entire world.*
-ulp-

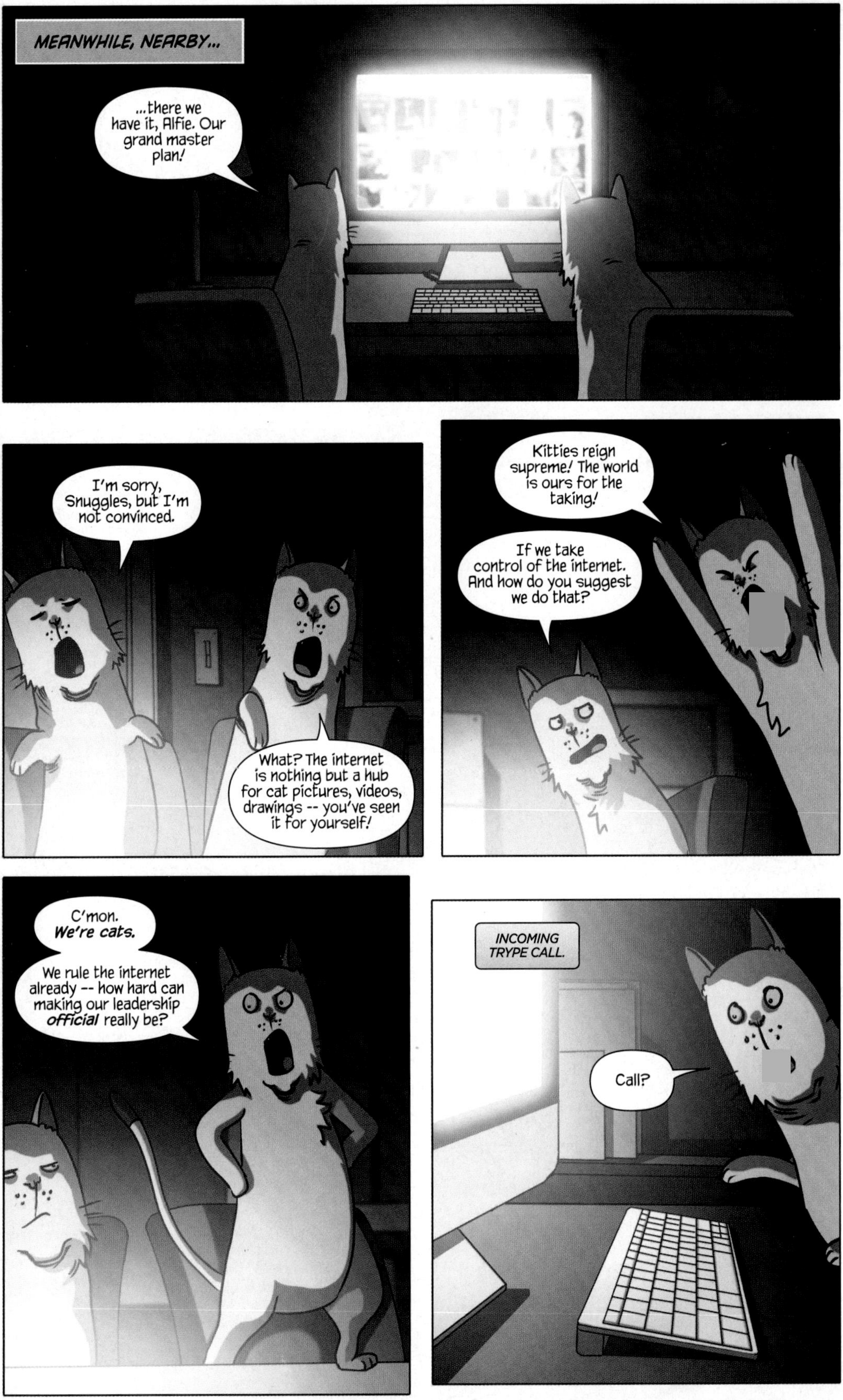
MEANWHILE, NEARBY...
...there we have it, Alfie. Our grand master plan!
I'm sorry, Snuggles, but I'm not convinced.
What? The internet is nothing but a hub for cat pictures, videos, drawings -- you've seen it for yourself!
Kitties reign supreme! The world is ours for the taking!
If we take control of the internet. And how do you suggest we do that?
C'mon. **We're cats.**
We rule the internet already -- how hard can making our leadership *official* really be?
INCOMING TRYPE CALL.
Call?

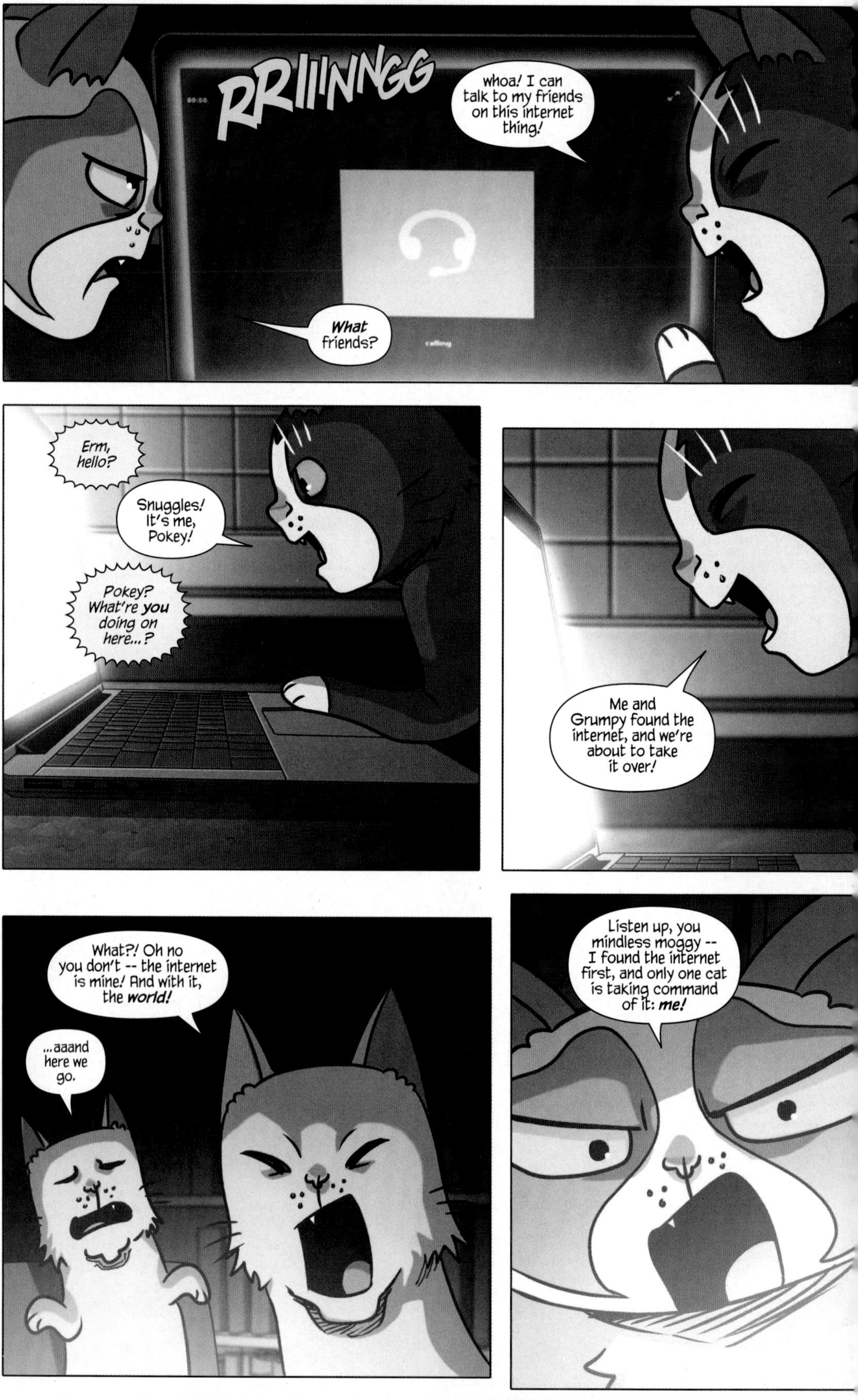
RRIIINNGG
whoa! I can talk to my friends on this internet thing!
What friends?
Erm, hello?
Snuggles! It's me, Pokey!
Pokey? What're you doing on here...?
Me and Grumpy found the internet, and we're about to take it over!
What?! Oh no you don't -- the internet is mine! And with it, the world!
...aaand here we go.
Listen up, you mindless moggy -- I found the internet first, and only one cat is taking command of it: me!

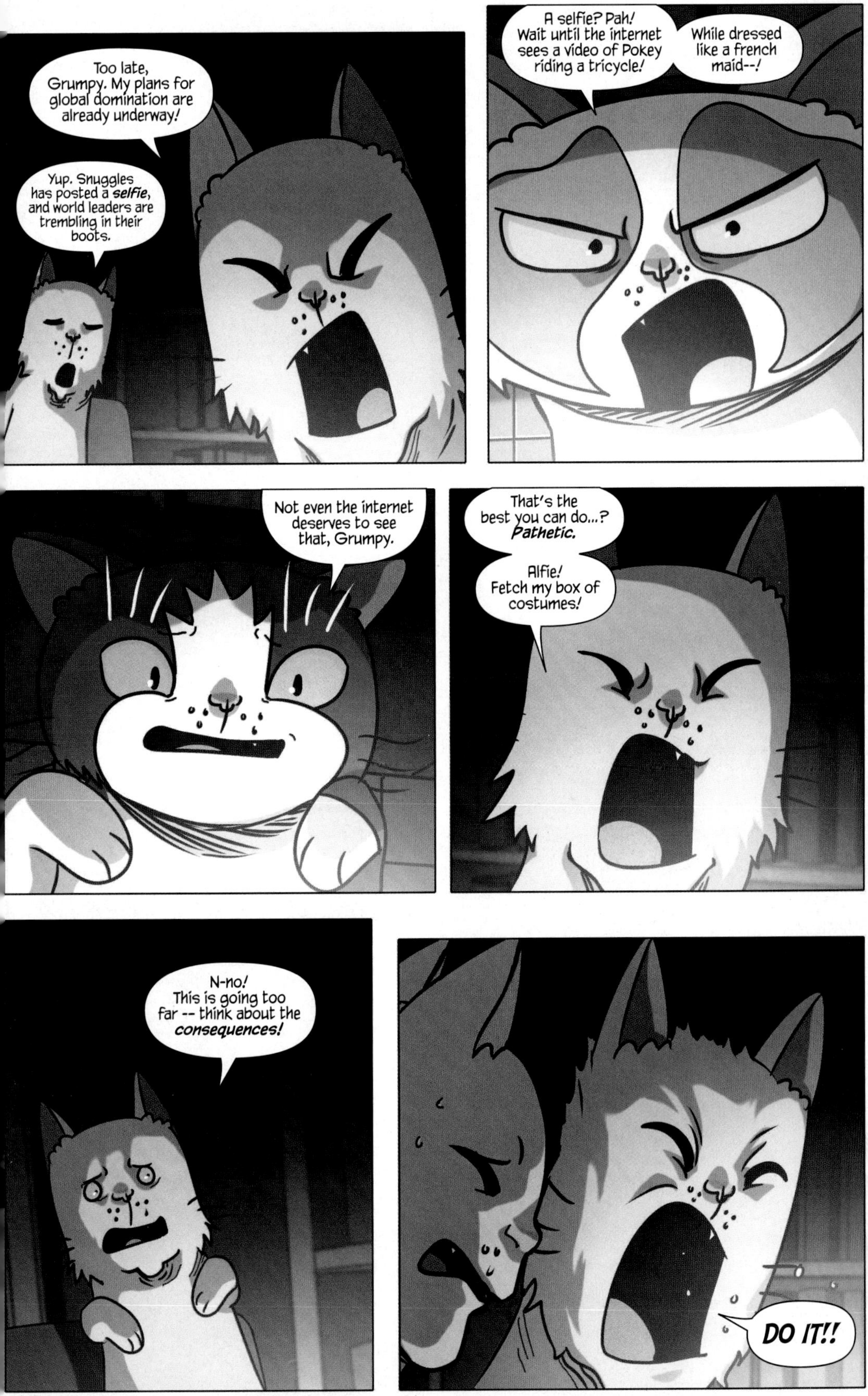
Too late, Grumpy. My plans for global domination are already underway!
Yup. Snuggles has posted a *selfie*, and world leaders are trembling in their boots.
A selfie? Pah! Wait until the internet sees a video of Pokey riding a tricycle!
While dressed like a french maid--!
Not even the internet deserves to see that, Grumpy.
That's the best you can do...? *Pathetic.*
Alfie! Fetch my box of costumes!
N-no! This is going too far -- think about the *consequences!*
DO IT!!

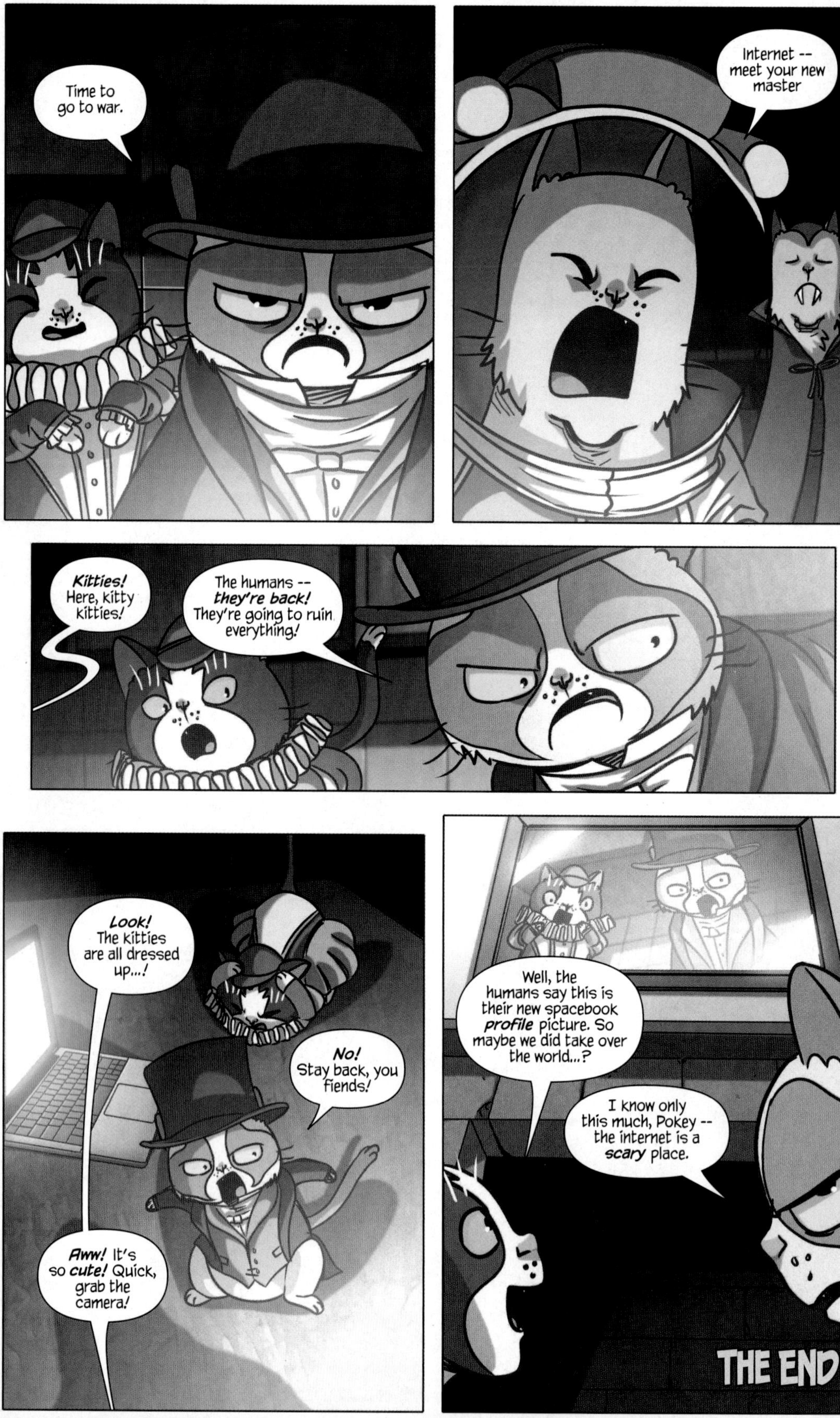
Time to go to war.
Internet -- meet your new master
Kitties! Here, kitty kitties!
The humans -- they're back! They're going to ruin everything!
Look! The kitties are all dressed up...!
No! Stay back, you fiends!
Aww! It's so cute! Quick, grab the camera!
Well, the humans say this is their new spacebook profile picture. So maybe we did take over the world...?
I know only this much, Pokey -- the internet is a scary place.
THE END

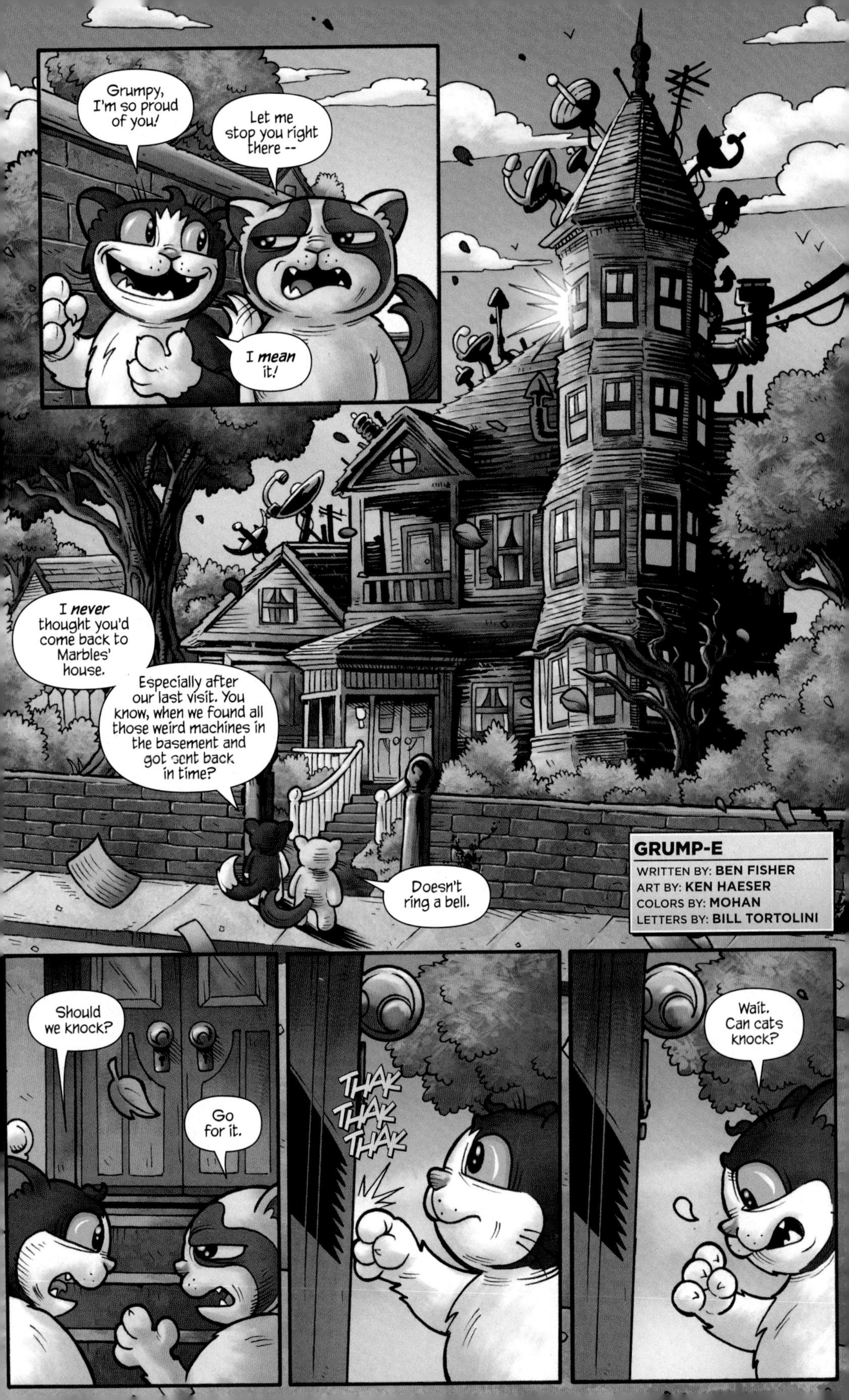
Grumpy, I'm so proud of you!
Let me stop you right there --
I mean it!
I never thought you'd come back to Marbles' house.
Especially after our last visit. You know, when we found all those weird machines in the basement and got sent back in time?
Doesn't ring a bell.
GRUMP-E
WRITTEN BY: BEN FISHER
ART BY: KEN HAESER
COLORS BY: MOHAN
LETTERS BY: BILL TORTOLINI
Should we knock?
Go for it.
THAK THAK THAK
Wait. Can cats knock?

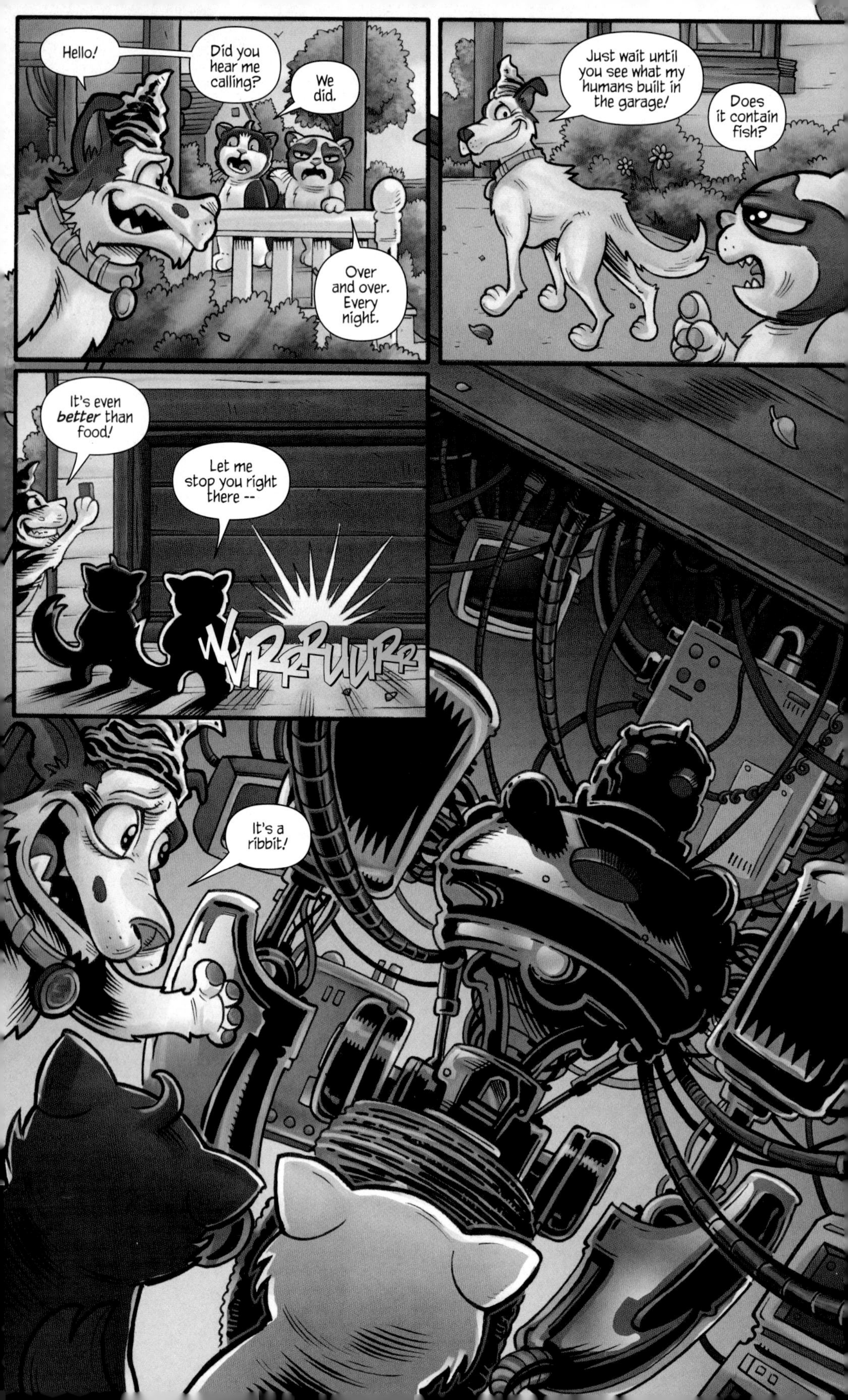
Hello!
Did you hear me calling?
We did.
Over and over. Every night.
Just wait until you see what my humans built in the garage!
Does it contain fish?
It's even **better** than food!
Let me stop you right there --
WVRRRUURR
It's a ribbit!

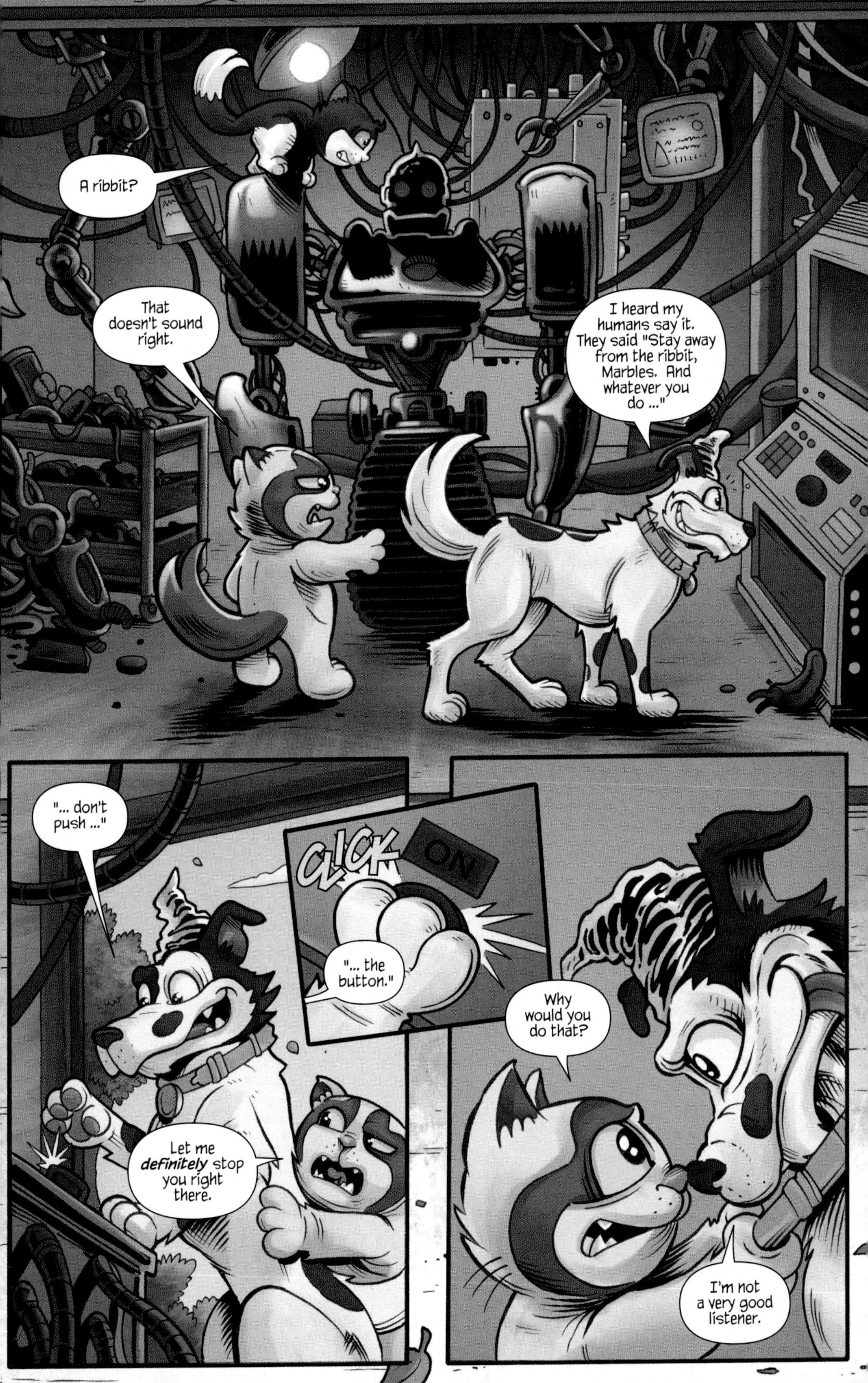
A ribbit?
That doesn't sound right.
I heard my humans say it. They said "Stay away from the ribbit, Marbles. And whatever you do ..."
"... don't push ..."
CLICK
ON
"... the button."
Let me *definitely* stop you right there.
Why would you do that?
I'm not a very good listener.

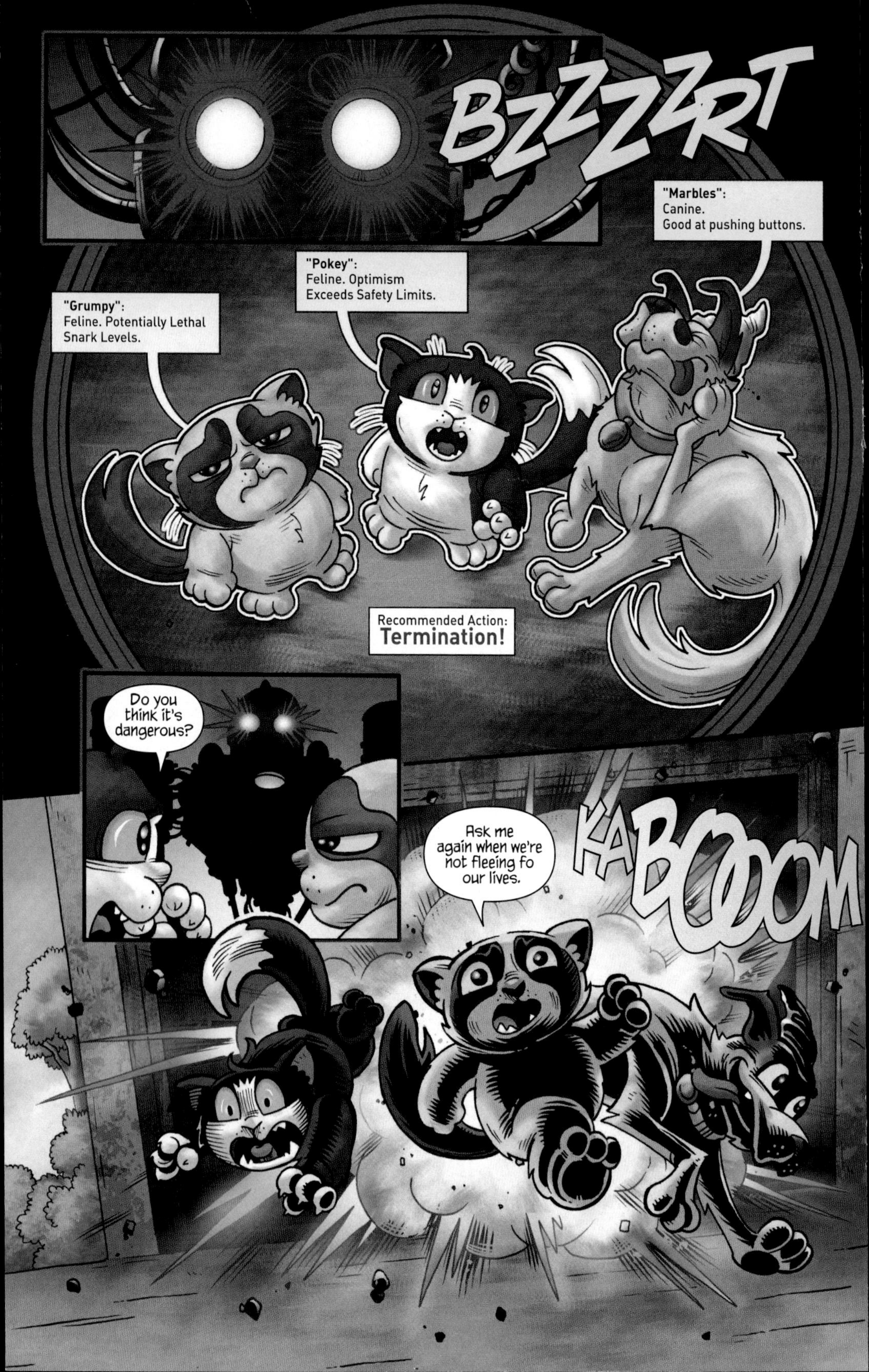
BZZZZRT
"Grumpy":
Feline. Potentially Lethal
Snark Levels.
"Pokey":
Feline. Optimism
Exceeds Safety Limits.
"Marbles":
Canine.
Good at pushing buttons.
Recommended Action:
Termination!
Do you think it's dangerous?
Ask me again when we're not fleeing fo our lives.
KABOOOM

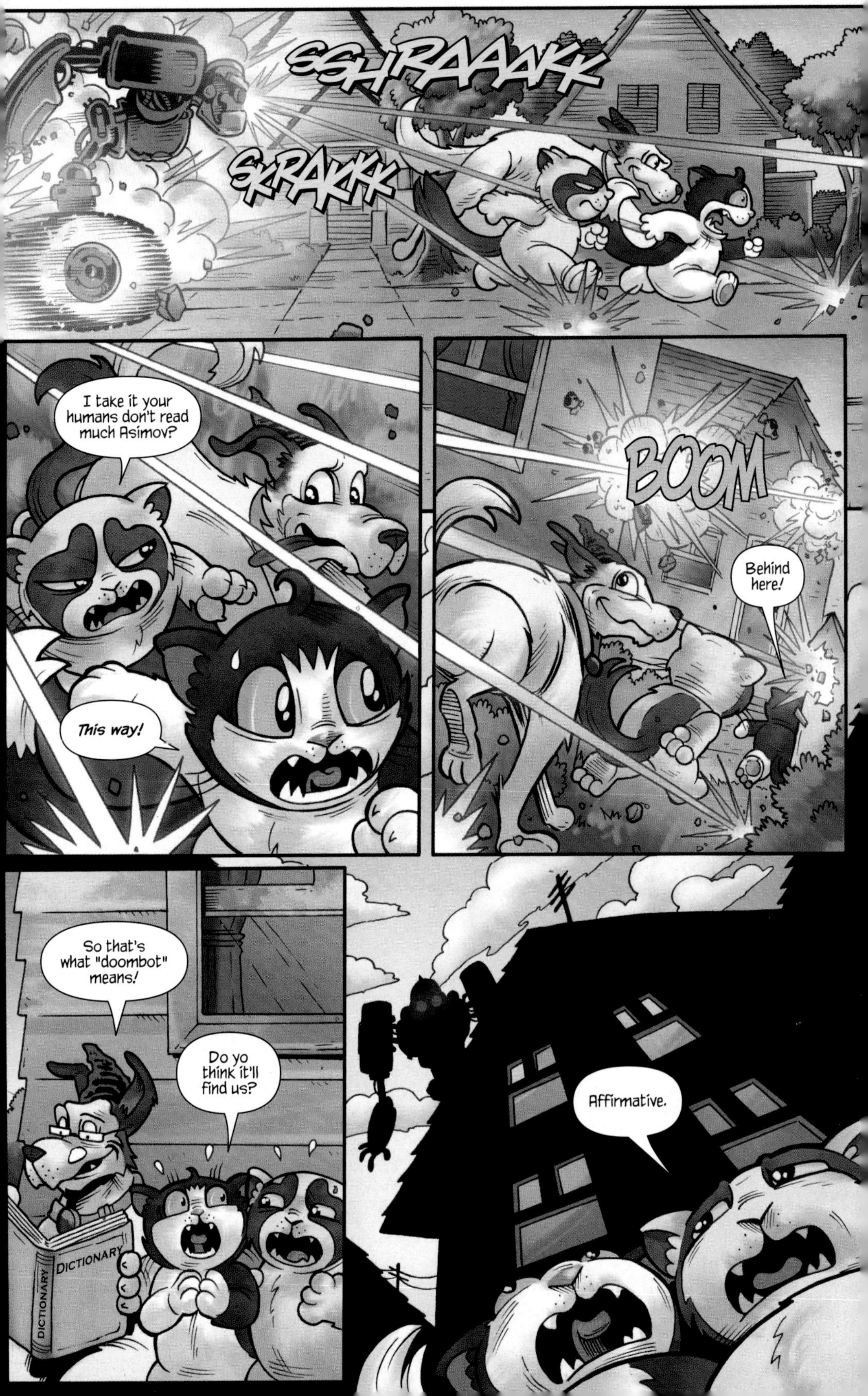

SSHRAAAKK
SKRAKKK
I take it your humans don't read much Asimov?
This way!
BOOM
Behind here!
So that's what "doombot" means!
DICTIONARY
Do yo think it'll find us?
Affirmative.

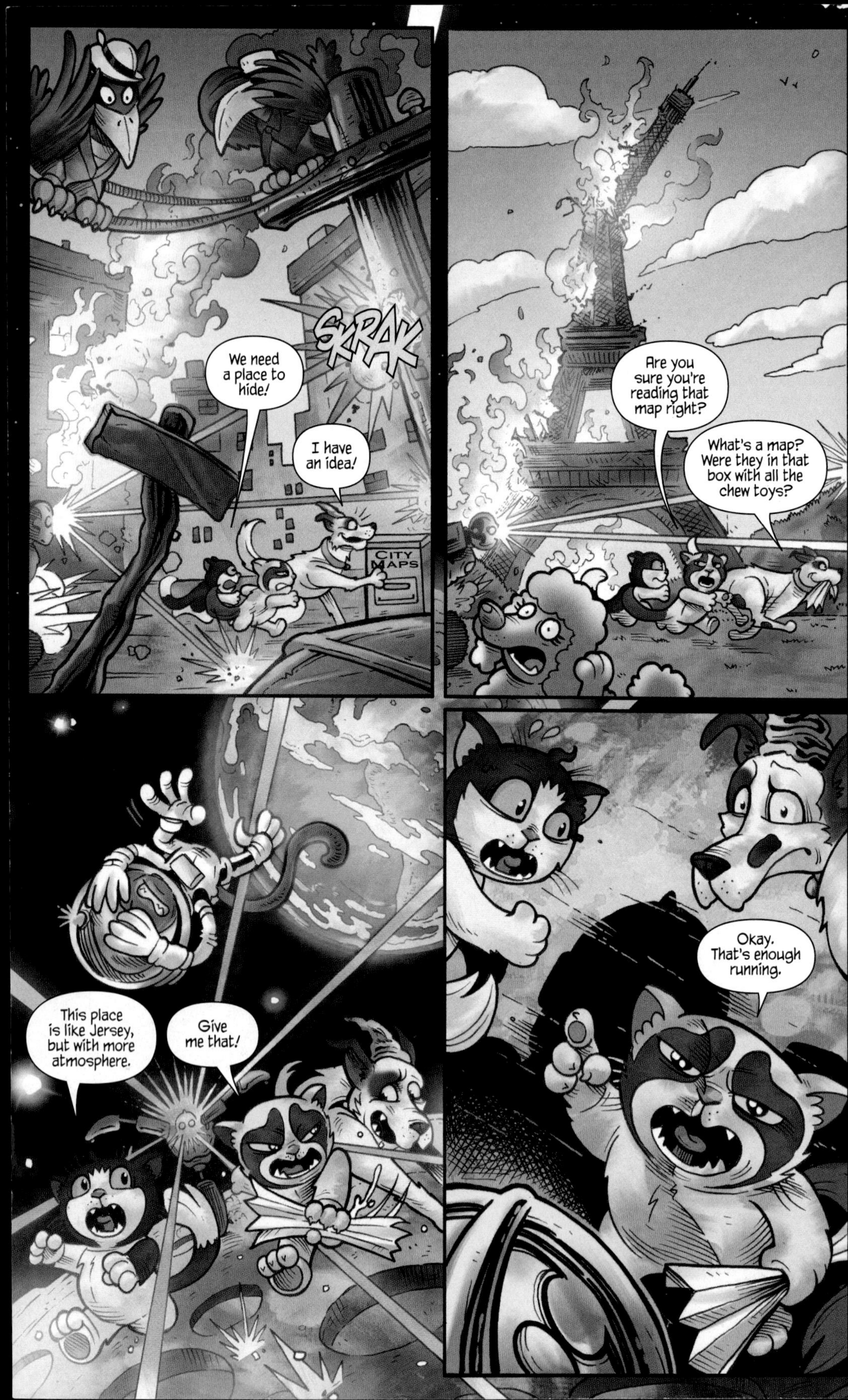
SKRAK
We need a place to hide!
I have an idea!
CITY MAPS
Are you sure you're reading that map right?
What's a map? Were they in that box with all the chew toys?
This place is like Jersey, but with more atmosphere.
Give me that!
Okay. That's enough running.

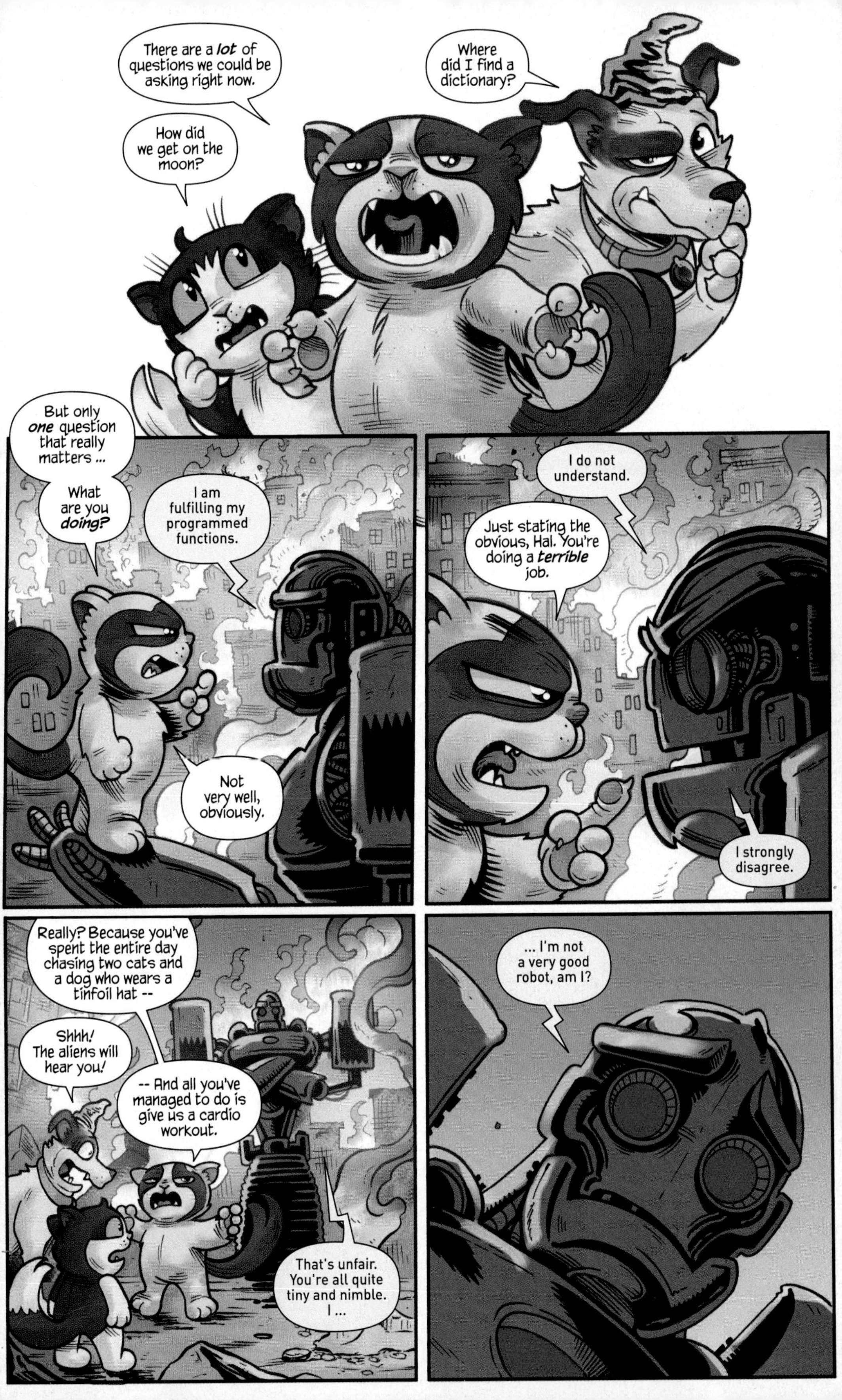
There are a *lot* of questions we could be asking right now.
Where did I find a dictionary?
How did we get on the moon?
But only *one* question that really matters ...
What are you *doing?*
I am fulfilling my programmed functions.
Not very well, obviously.
I do not understand.
Just stating the obvious, Hal. You're doing a *terrible* job.
I strongly disagree.
Really? Because you've spent the entire day chasing two cats and a dog who wears a tinfoil hat --
Shhh! The aliens will hear you!
-- And all you've managed to do is give us a cardio workout.
That's unfair. You're all quite tiny and nimble. I ...
... I'm not a very good robot, am I?

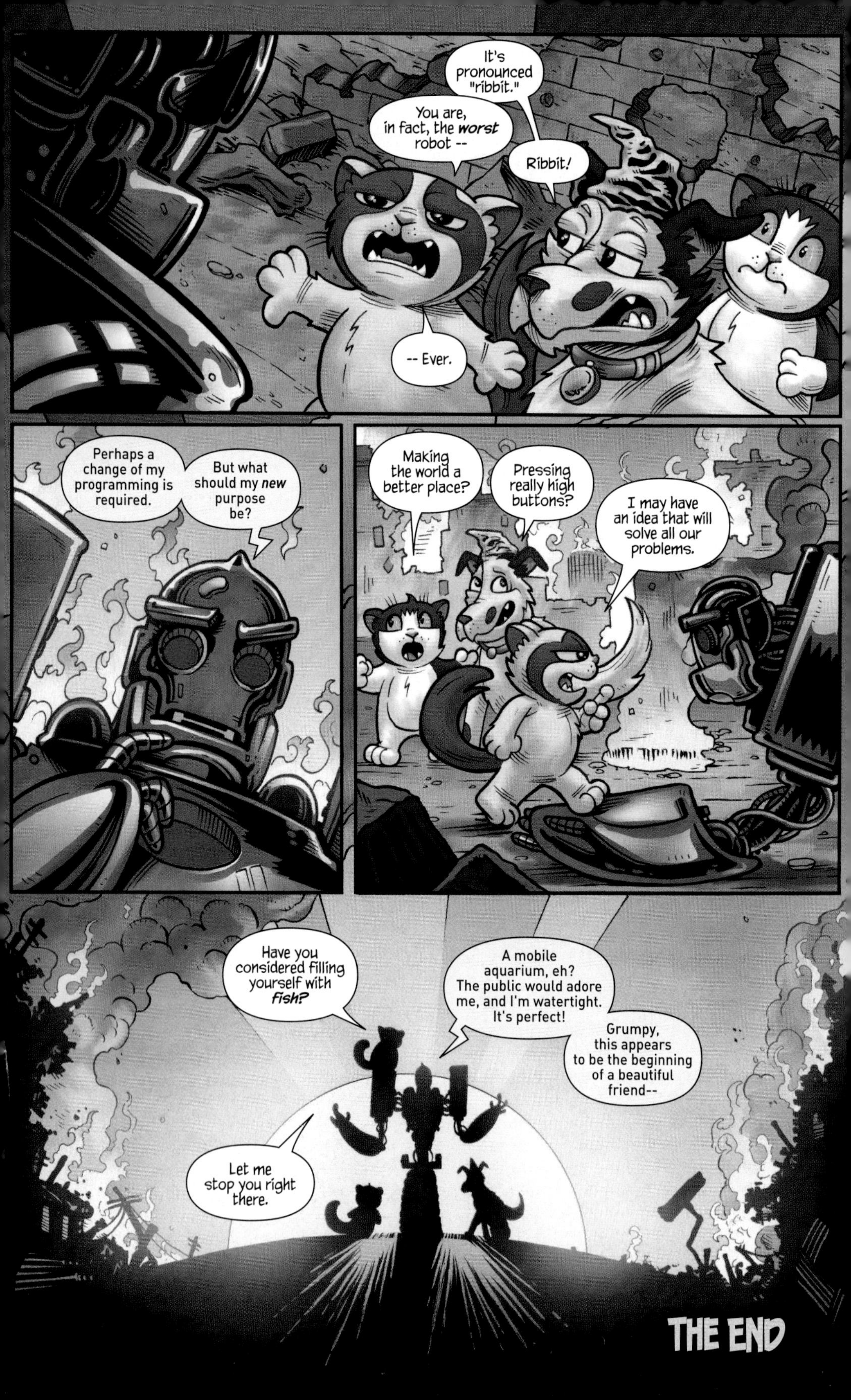
You are, in fact, the worst robot --
It's pronounced "ribbit."
Ribbit!
-- Ever.
Perhaps a change of my programming is required.
But what should my new purpose be?
Making the world a better place?
Pressing really high buttons?
I may have an idea that will solve all our problems.
Have you considered filling yourself with fish?
A mobile aquarium, eh? The public would adore me, and I'm watertight. It's perfect!
Grumpy, this appears to be the beginning of a beautiful friend--
Let me stop you right there.
THE END

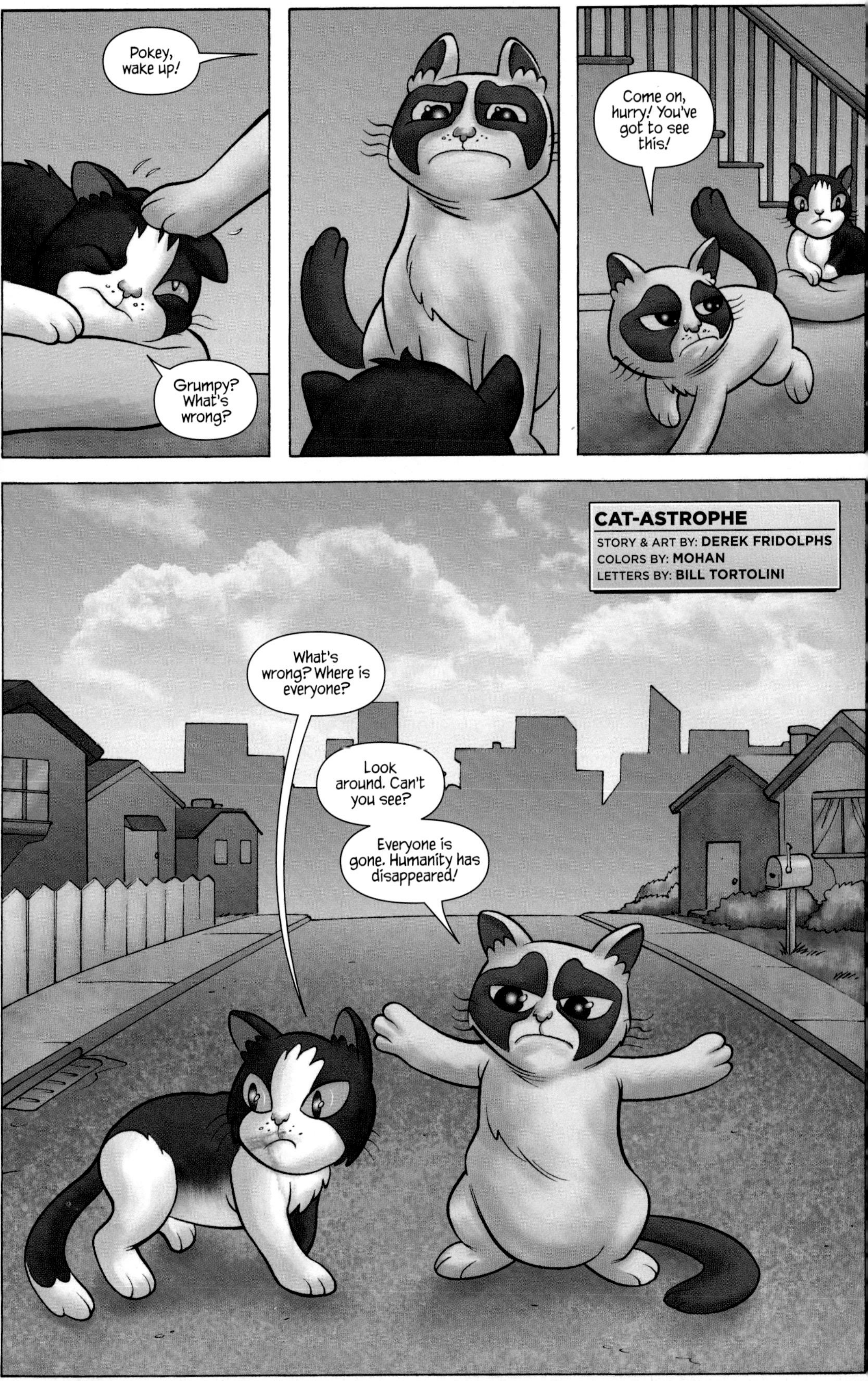
Pokey, wake up!
Grumpy? What's wrong?
Come on, hurry! You've got to see this!
CAT-ASTROPHE
STORY & ART BY: DEREK FRIDOLPHS
COLORS BY: MOHAN
LETTERS BY: BILL TORTOLINI
What's wrong? Where is everyone?
Look around. Can't you see?
Everyone is gone. Humanity has disappeared!

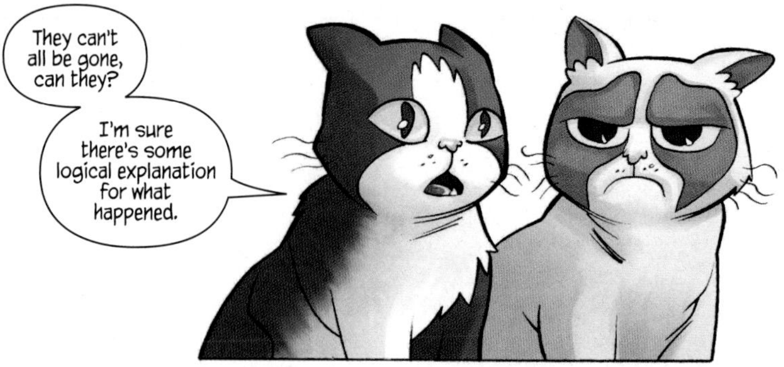
They can't all be gone, can they?
I'm sure there's some logical explanation for what happened.

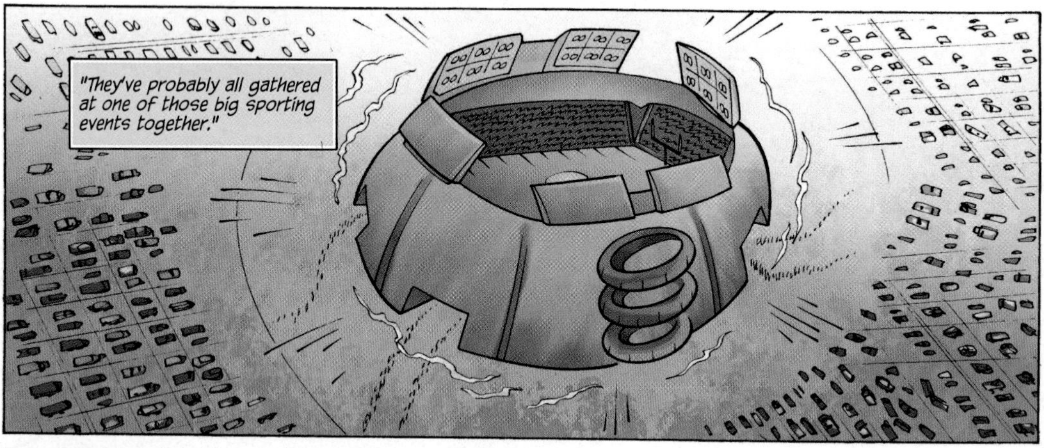
"They've probably all gathered at one of those big sporting events together."

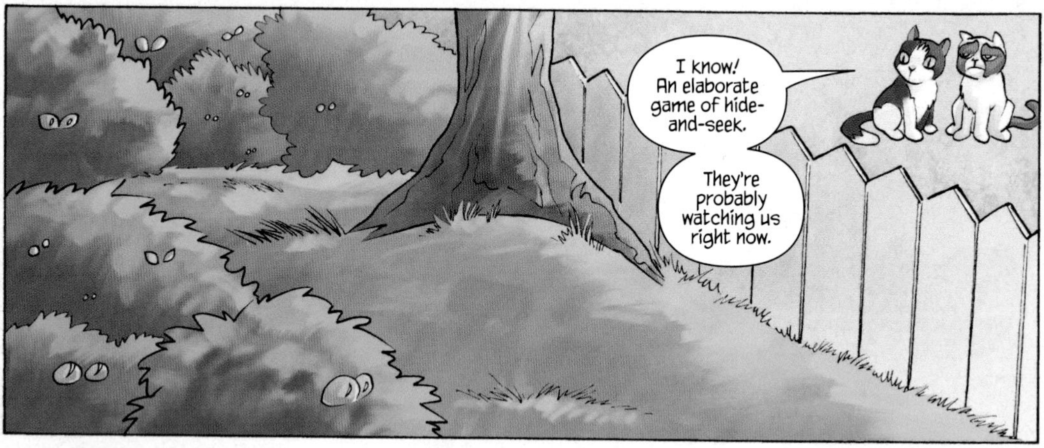
I know! An elaborate game of hide-and-seek.
They're probably watching us right now.

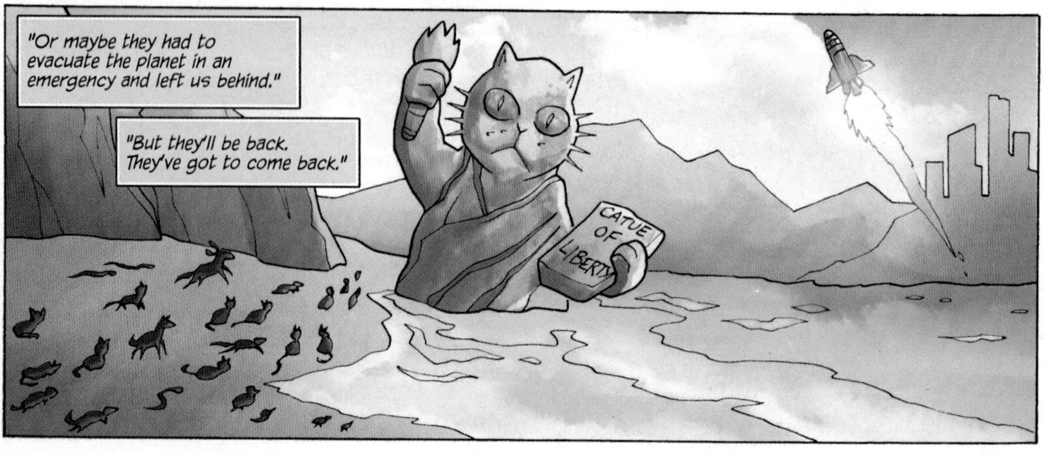
"Or maybe they had to evacuate the planet in an emergency and left us behind."
"But they'll be back. They've got to come back."
CATUE OF LIBERTY

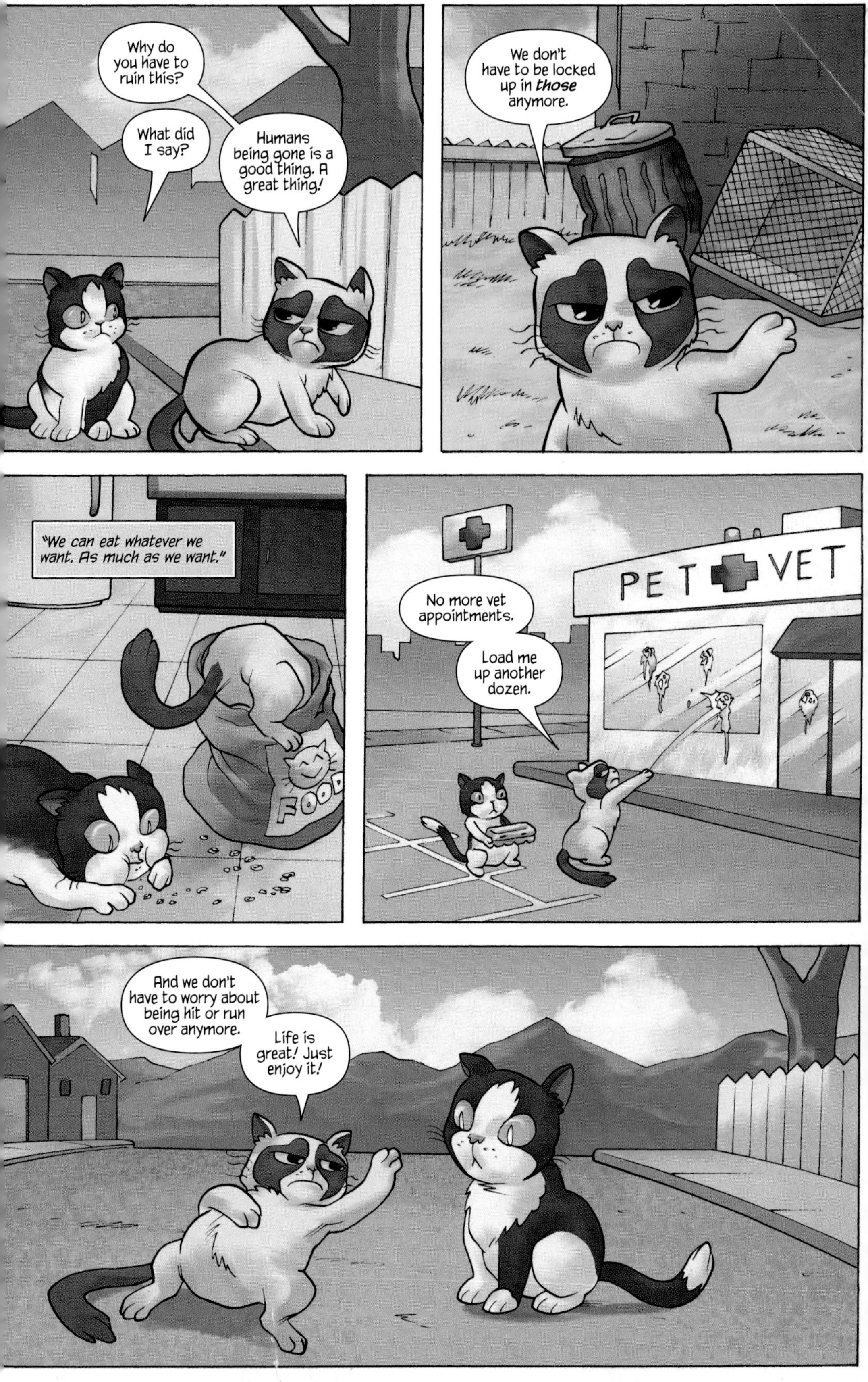

Why do you have to ruin this?
What did I say?
Humans being gone is a good thing. A great thing!
We don't have to be locked up in *those* anymore.
"We can eat whatever we want. As much as we want."
FOOD
PET VET
No more vet appointments.
Load me up another dozen.
And we don't have to worry about being hit or run over anymore.
Life is great! Just enjoy it!

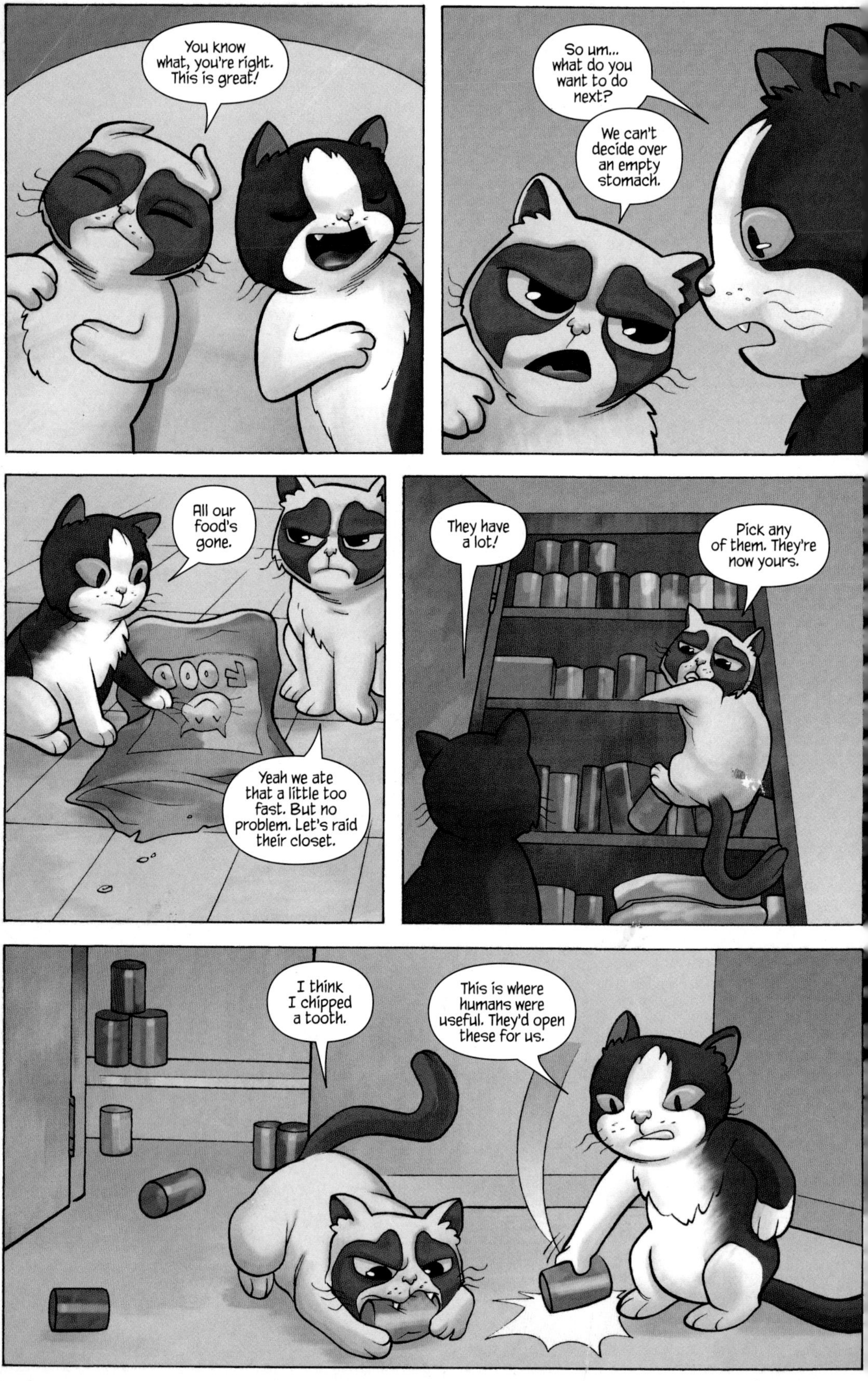
You know what, you're right. This is great!
So um... what do you want to do next?
We can't decide over an empty stomach.
All our food's gone.
FOOD
Yeah we ate that a little too fast. But no problem. Let's raid their closet.
They have a lot!
Pick any of them. They're now yours.
I think I chipped a tooth.
This is where humans were useful. They'd open these for us.

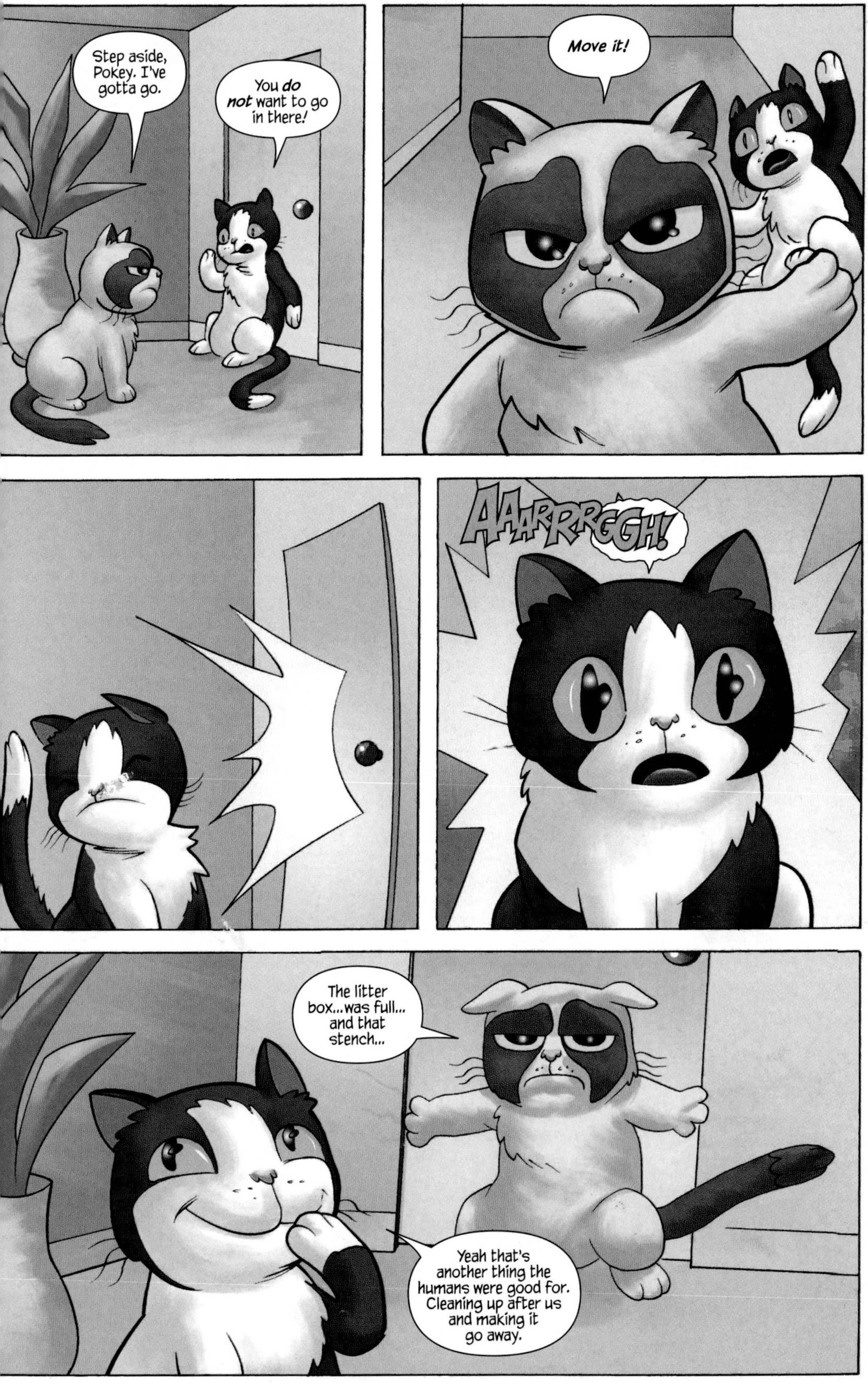

Step aside, Pokey. I've gotta go.
You *do* *not* want to go in there!
*Move it!*
AAARRRGGH!
The litter box...was full... and that stench...
Yeah that's another thing the humans were good for. Cleaning up after us and making it go away.

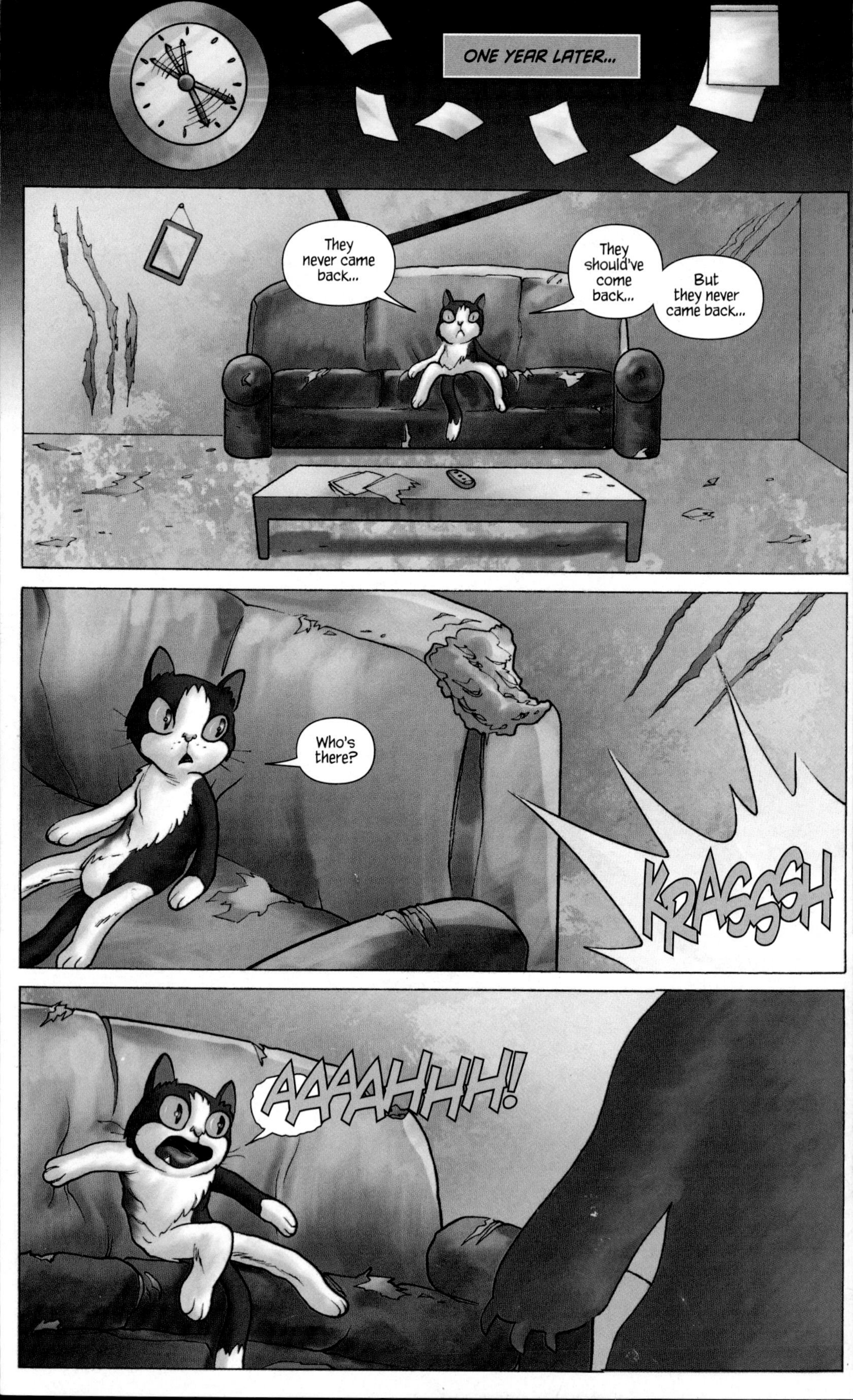
ONE YEAR LATER...
They never came back...
They should've come back...
But they never came back...
Who's there?
KRASSSH
AAAAHHH!

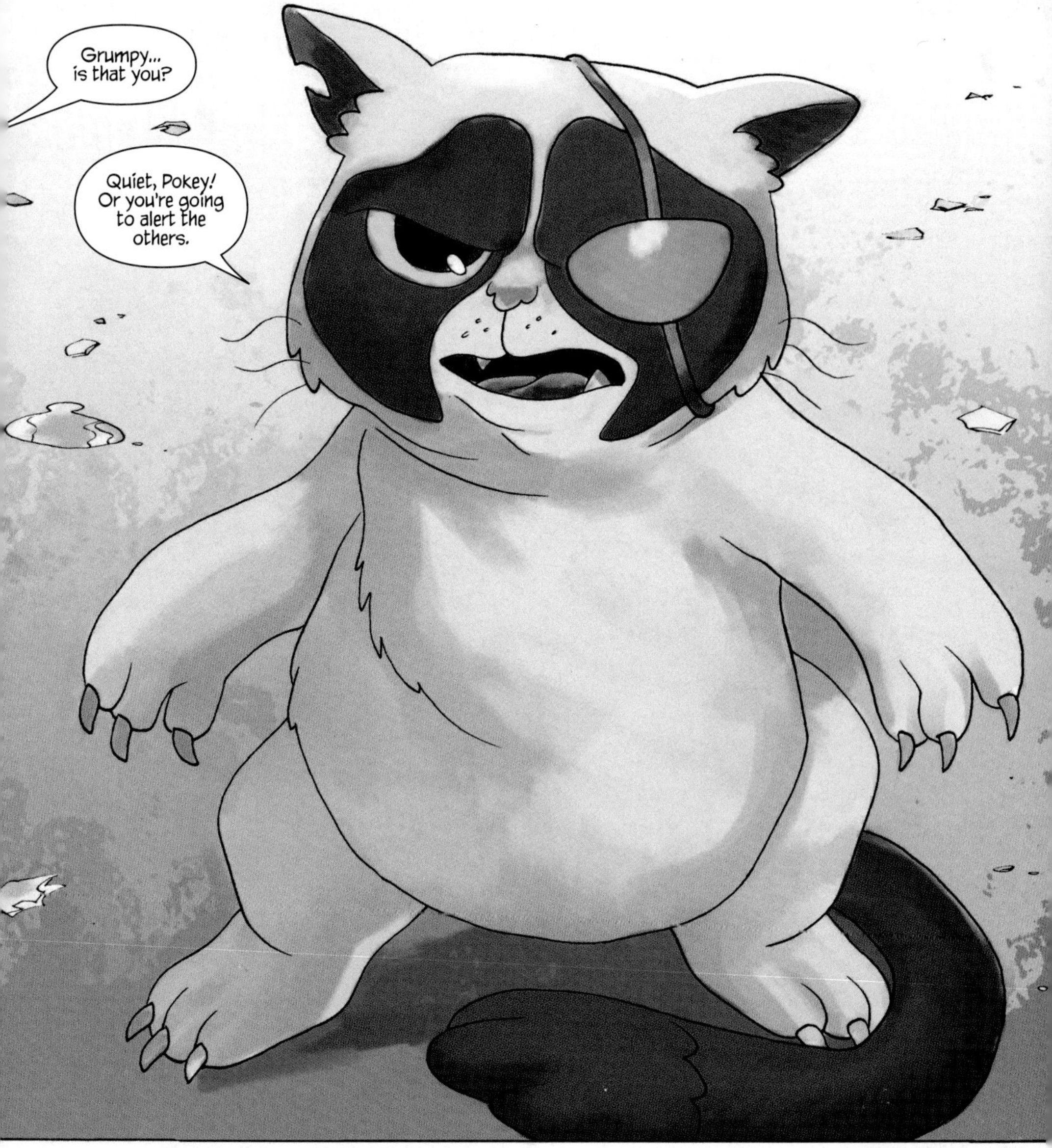
Grumpy... is that you?
Quiet, Pokey! Or you're going to alert the others.

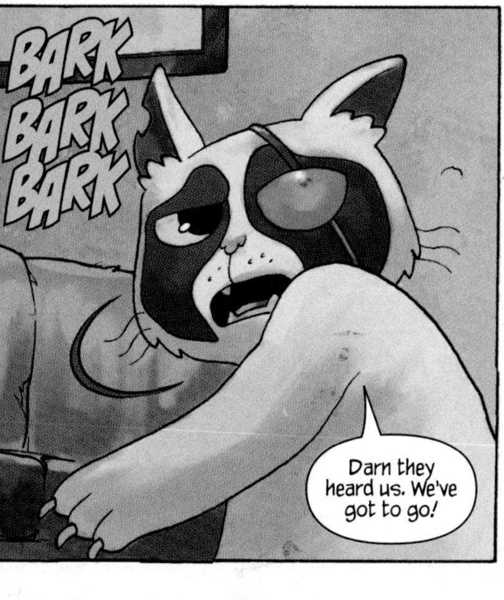
BARK BARK BARK
Darn they heard us. We've got to go!

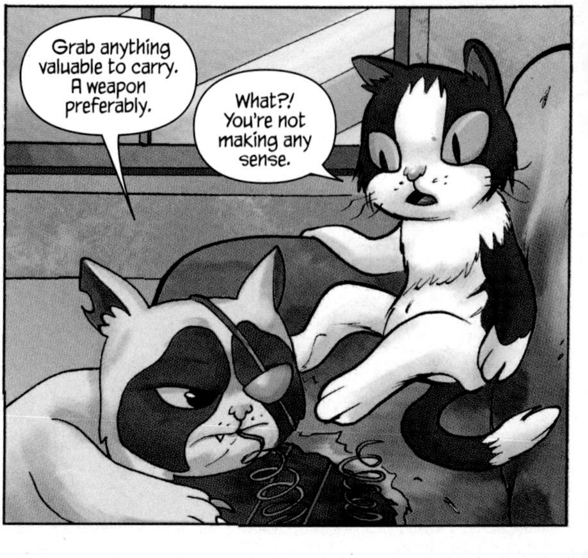
Grab anything valuable to carry. A weapon preferably.
What?! You're not making any sense.

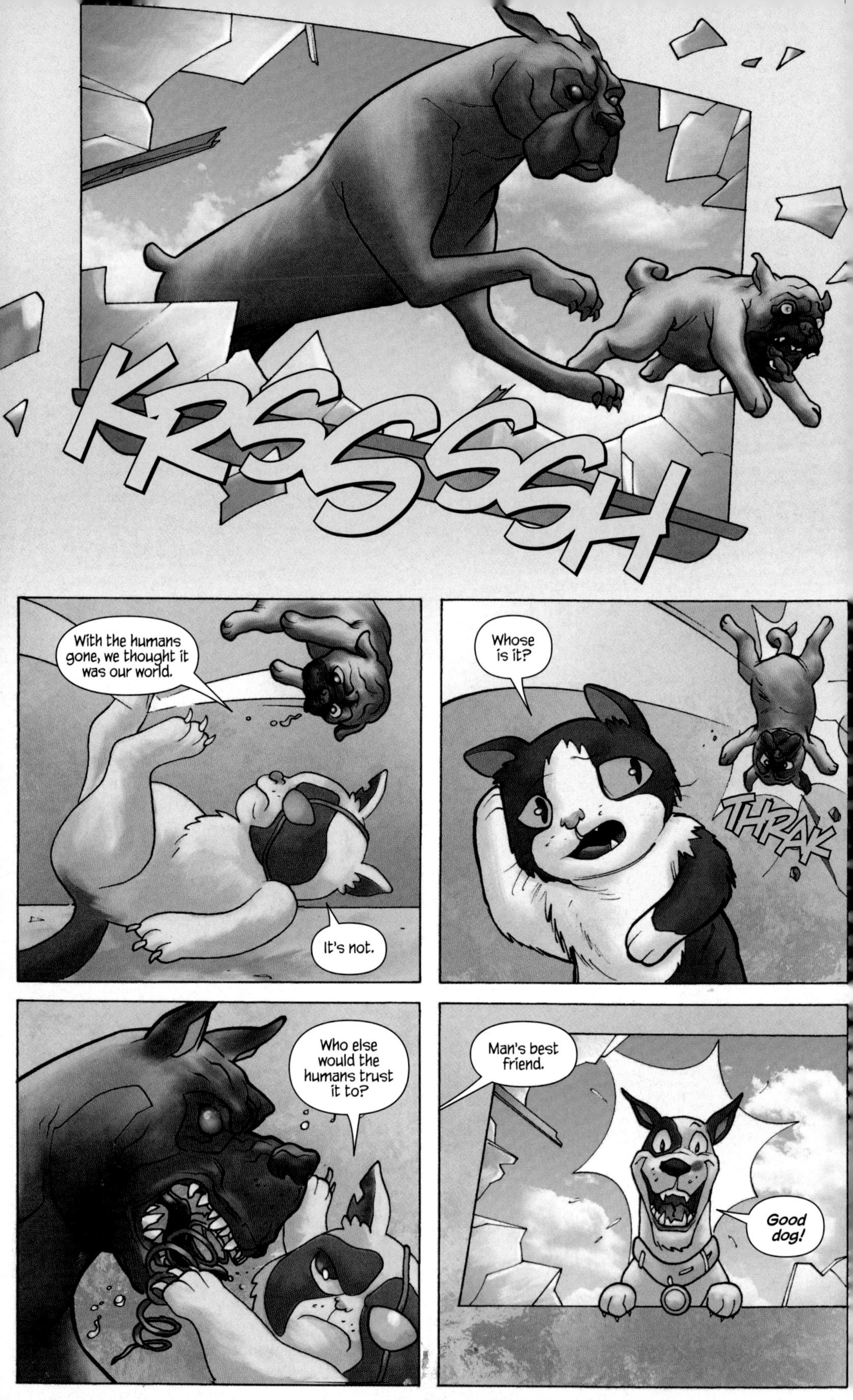
KRSSSSH
With the humans gone, we thought it was our world.
It's not.
Whose is it?
THRAK
Who else would the humans trust it to?
Man's best friend.
Good dog!

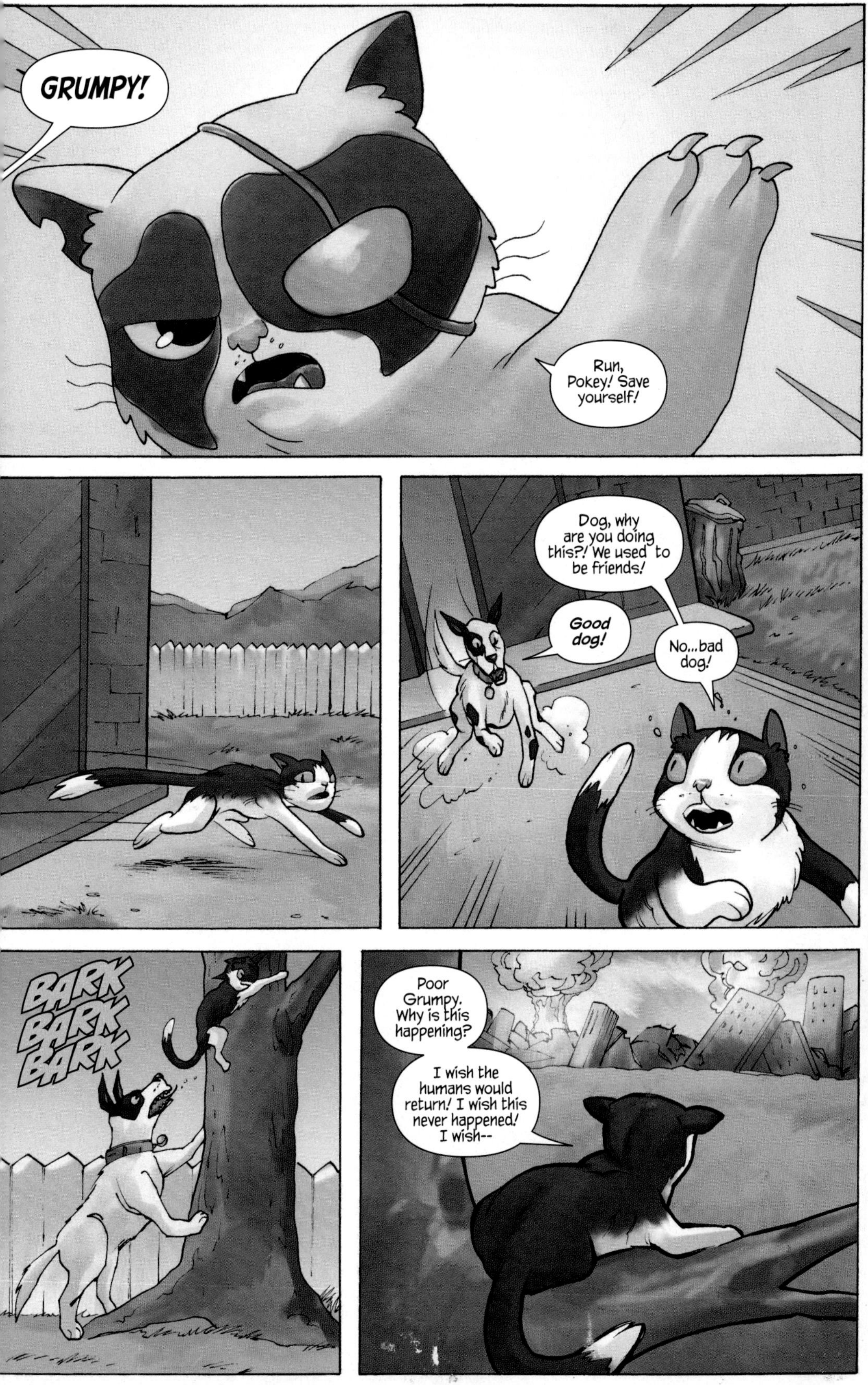
GRUMPY!
Run, Pokey! Save yourself!
Dog, why are you doing this?! We used to be friends!
Good dog!
No...bad dog!
BARK BARK BARK
Poor Grumpy. Why is this happening?
I wish the humans would return! I wish this never happened! I wish--

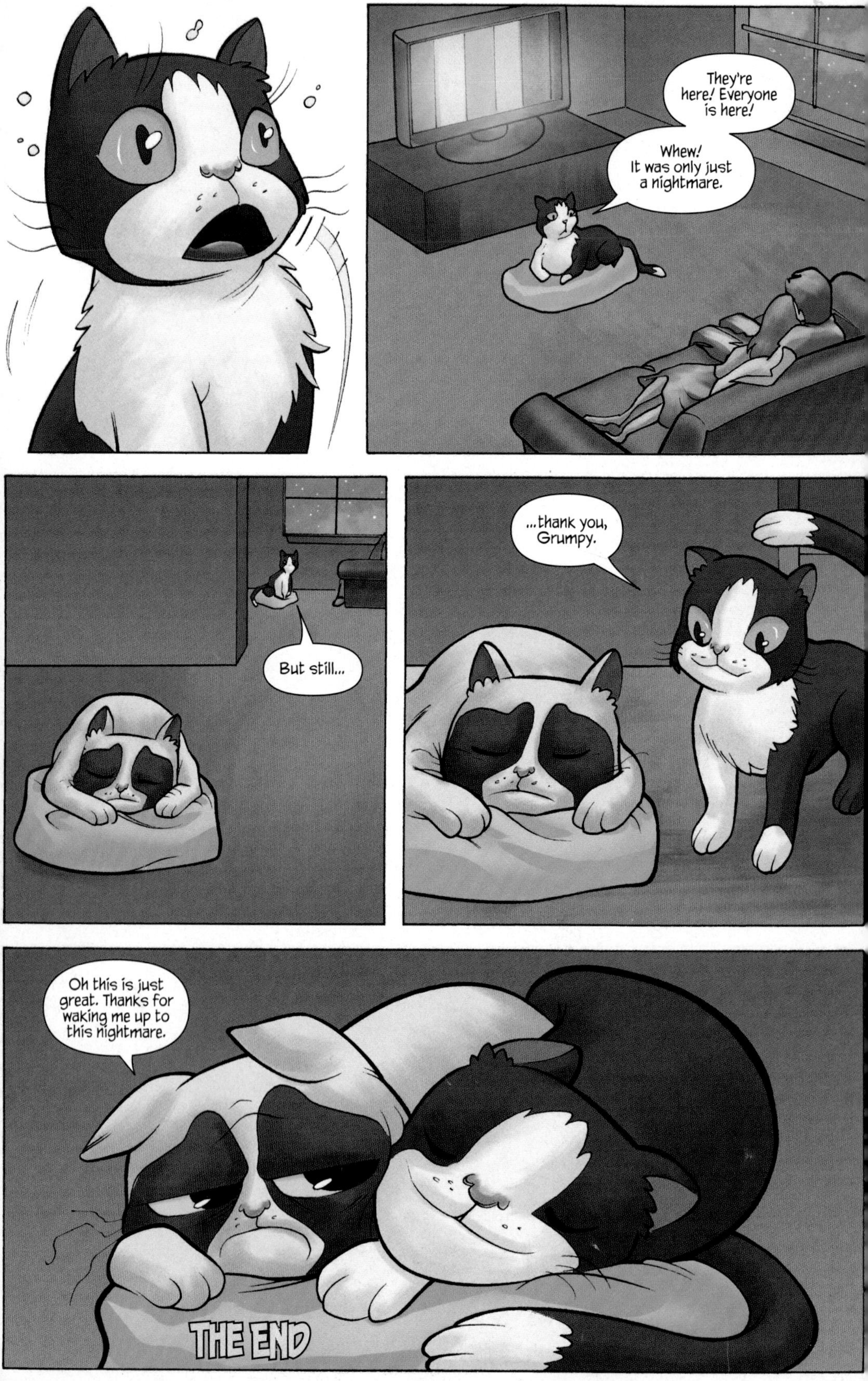
They're here! Everyone is here!
Whew! It was only just a nightmare.
But still...
...thank you, Grumpy.
Oh this is just great. Thanks for waking me up to this nightmare.
THE END

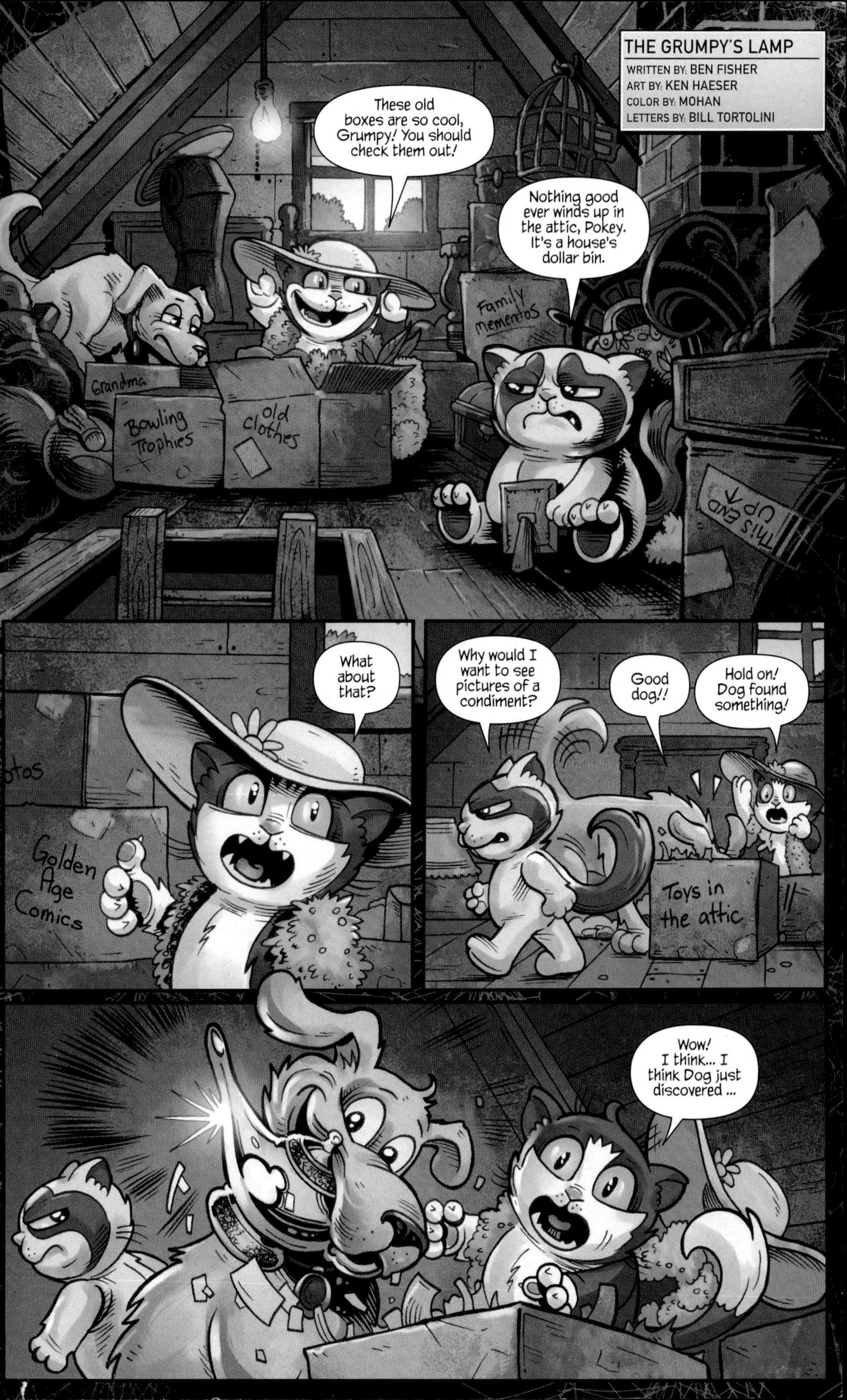
THE GRUMPY'S LAMP
WRITTEN BY: BEN FISHER
ART BY: KEN HAESER
COLOR BY: MOHAN
LETTERS BY: BILL TORTOLINI
These old boxes are so cool, Grumpy! You should check them out!
Nothing good ever winds up in the attic, Pokey. It's a house's dollar bin.
Grandma
Bowling Trophies
old Clothes
Family mementos
This End Up
What about that?
Golden Age Comics
Why would I want to see pictures of a condiment?
Good dog!!
Hold on! Dog found something!
Toys in the attic
Wow! I think... I think Dog just discovered ...

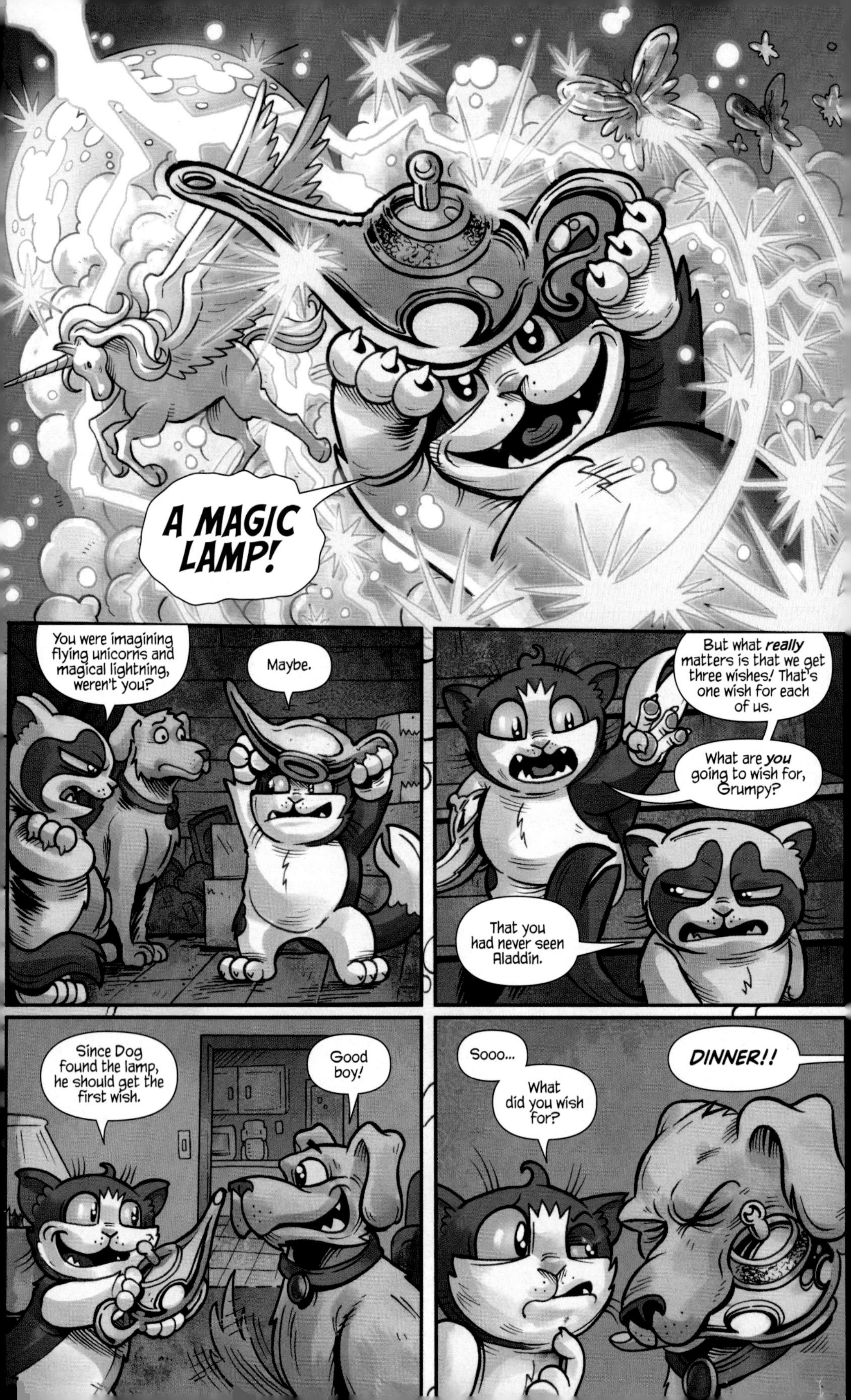
A MAGIC LAMP!
You were imagining flying unicorns and magical lightning, weren't you?
Maybe.
But what *really* matters is that we get three wishes! That's one wish for each of us.
What are *you* going to wish for, Grumpy?
That you had never seen Aladdin.
Since Dog found the lamp, he should get the first wish.
Good boy!
Sooo...
What did you wish for?
DINNER!!

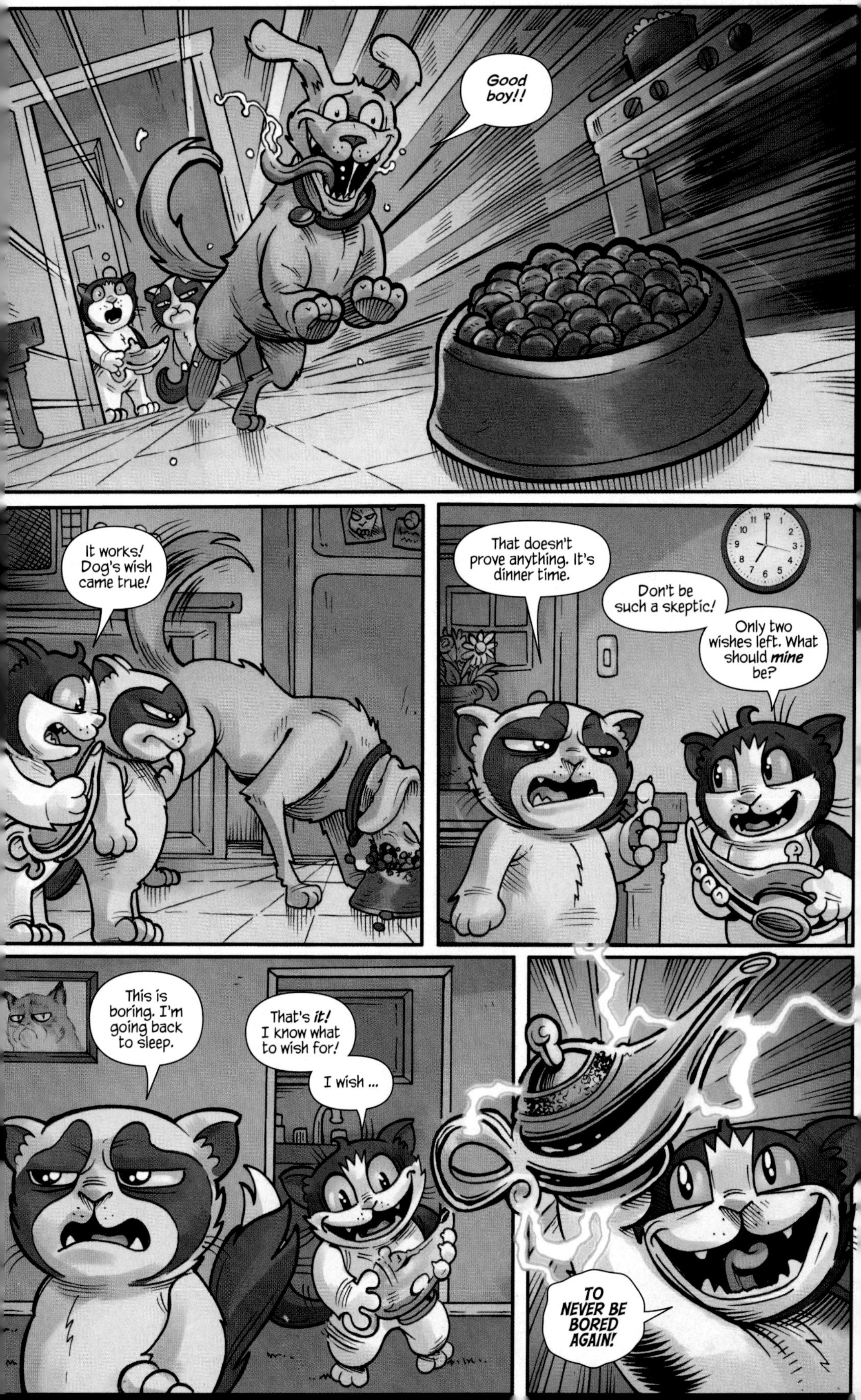
Good boy!!
It works! Dog's wish came true!
That doesn't prove anything. It's dinner time.
Don't be such a skeptic!
Only two wishes left. What should *mine* be?
This is boring. I'm going back to sleep.
That's *it!* I know what to wish for!
I wish ...
TO NEVER BE BORED AGAIN!

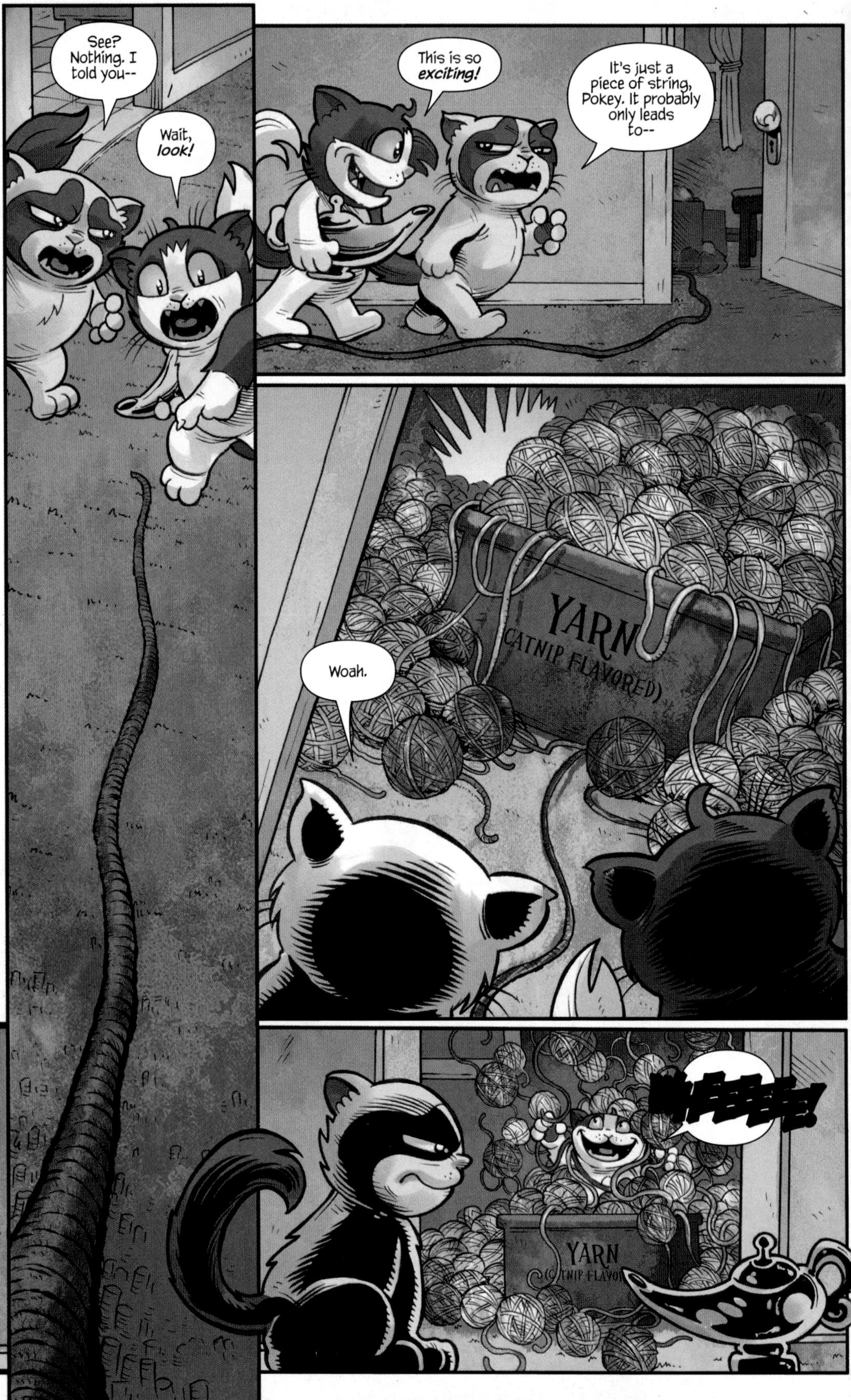
See? Nothing. I told you--
Wait, *look!*
This is so *exciting!*
It's just a piece of string, Pokey. It probably only leads to--
YARN
(CATNIP FLAVORED)
Woah.
WHEEEE!
YARN

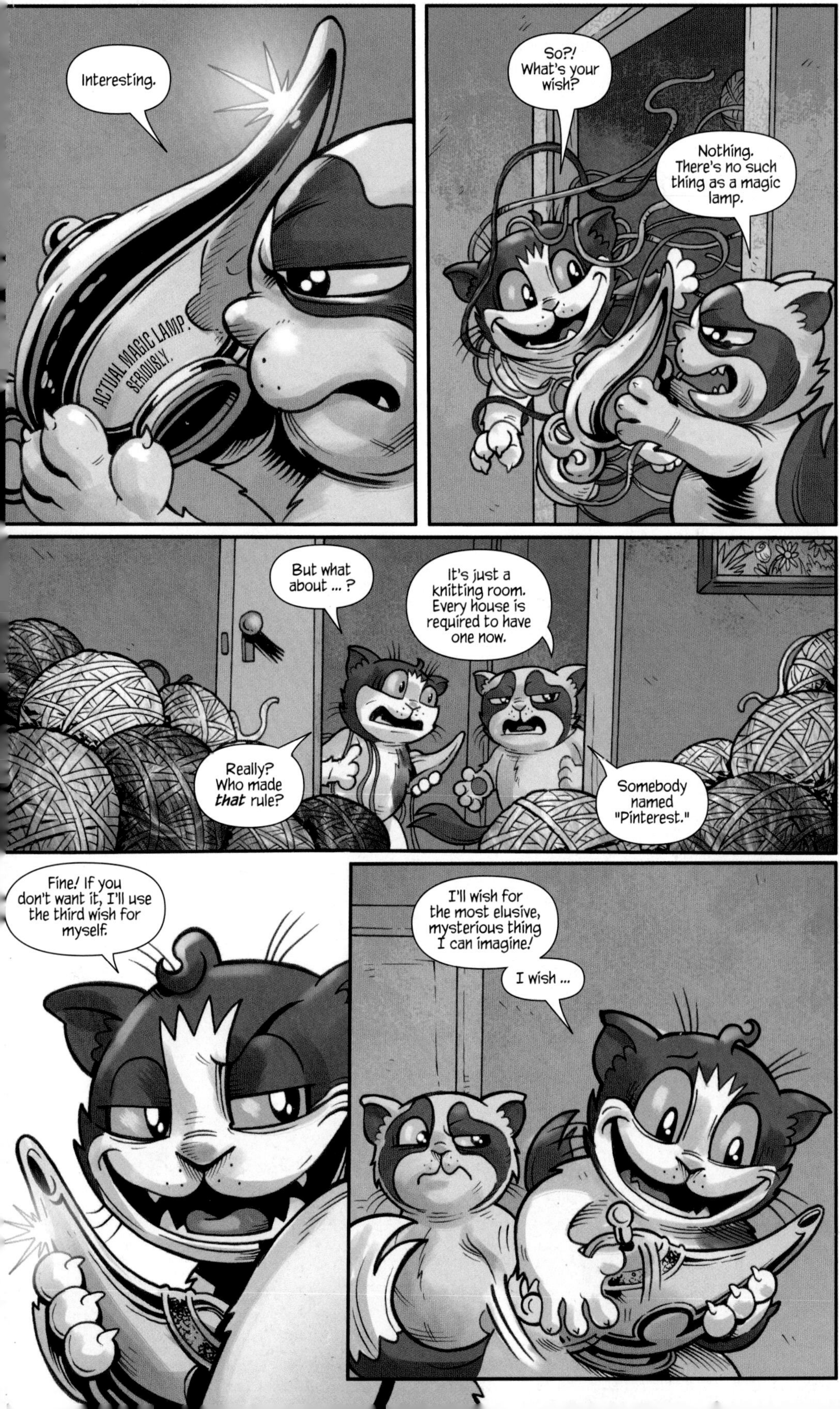
Interesting.
ACTUAL MAGIC LAMP. SERIOUSLY.
So?! What's your wish?
Nothing. There's no such thing as a magic lamp.
But what about ... ?
It's just a knitting room. Every house is required to have one now.
Really? Who made *that* rule?
Somebody named "Pinterest."
Fine! If you don't want it, I'll use the third wish for myself.
I'll wish for the most elusive, mysterious thing I can imagine!
I wish ...

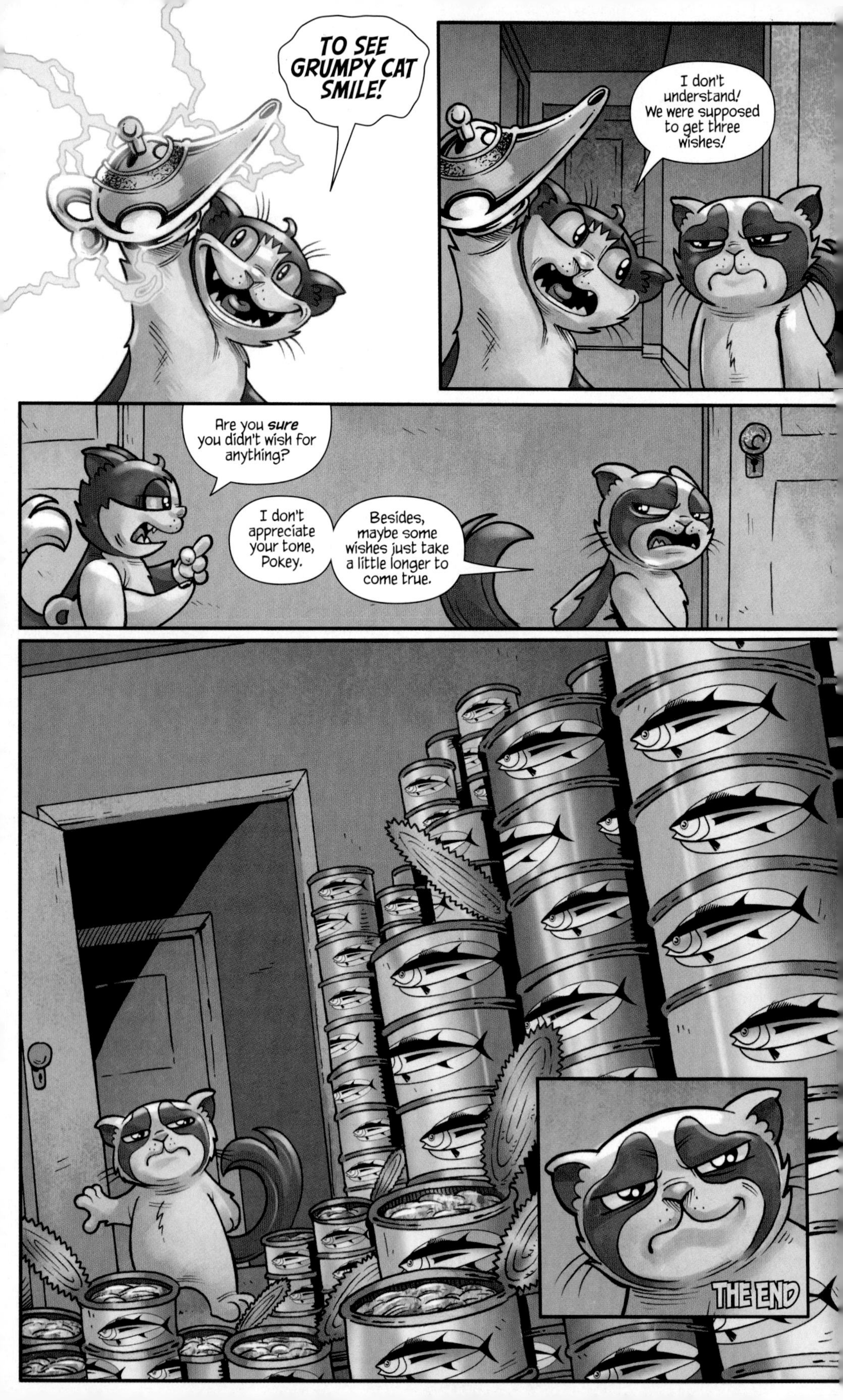
TO SEE GRUMPY CAT SMILE!
I don't understand! We were supposed to get three wishes!
Are you *sure* you didn't wish for anything?
I don't appreciate your tone, Pokey.
Besides, maybe some wishes just take a little longer to come true.
THE END

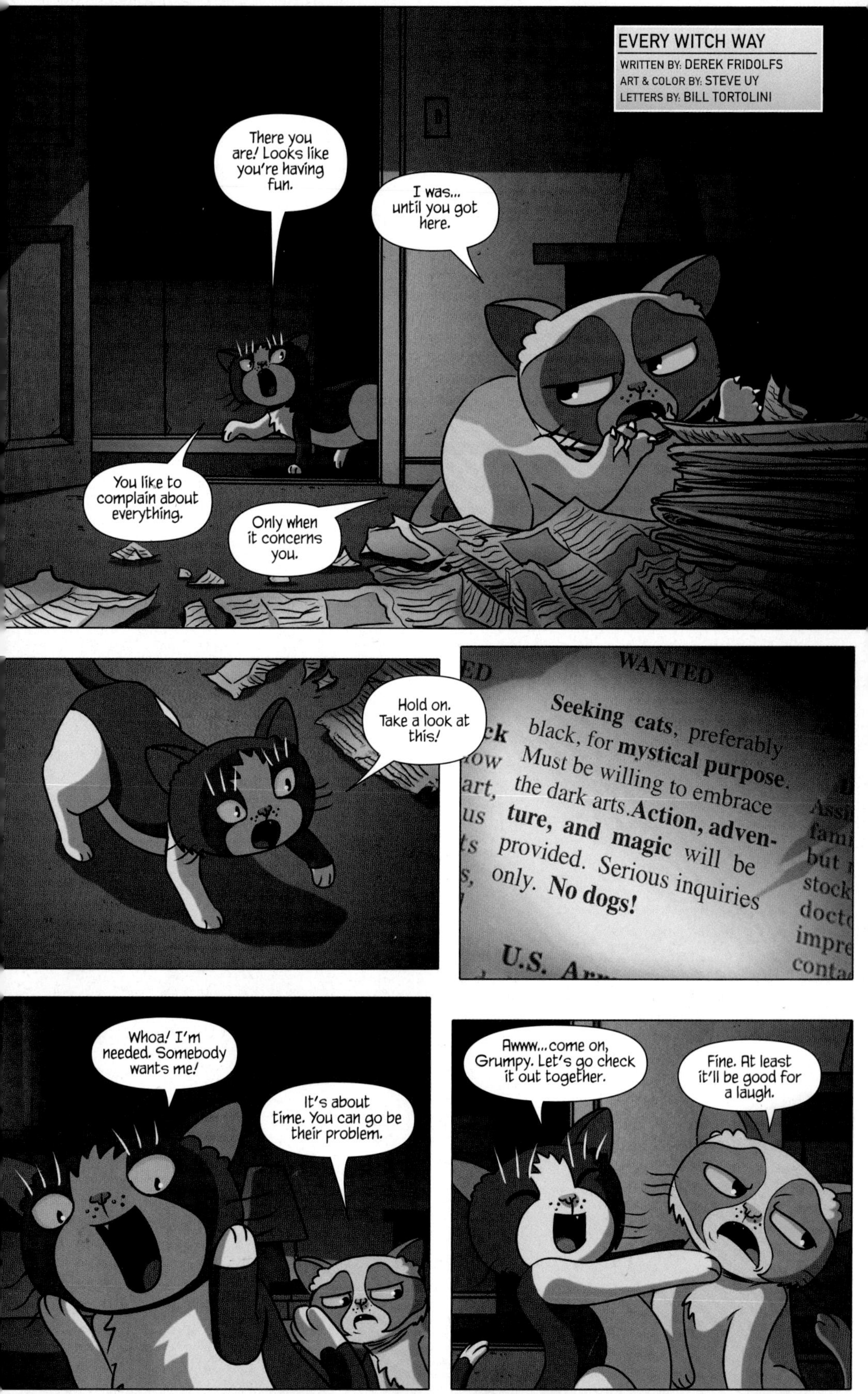
EVERY WITCH WAY
WRITTEN BY: DEREK FRIDOLFS
ART & COLOR BY: STEVE UY
LETTERS BY: BILL TORTOLINI
There you are! Looks like you're having fun.
I was... until you got here.
You like to complain about everything.
Only when it concerns you.
Hold on. Take a look at this!
WANTED
Seeking cats, preferably black, for mystical purpose. Must be willing to embrace the dark arts. Action, adventure, and magic will be provided. Serious inquiries only. No dogs!
Whoa! I'm needed. Somebody wants me!
It's about time. You can go be their problem.
Awww...come on, Grumpy. Let's go check it out together.
Fine. At least it'll be good for a laugh.

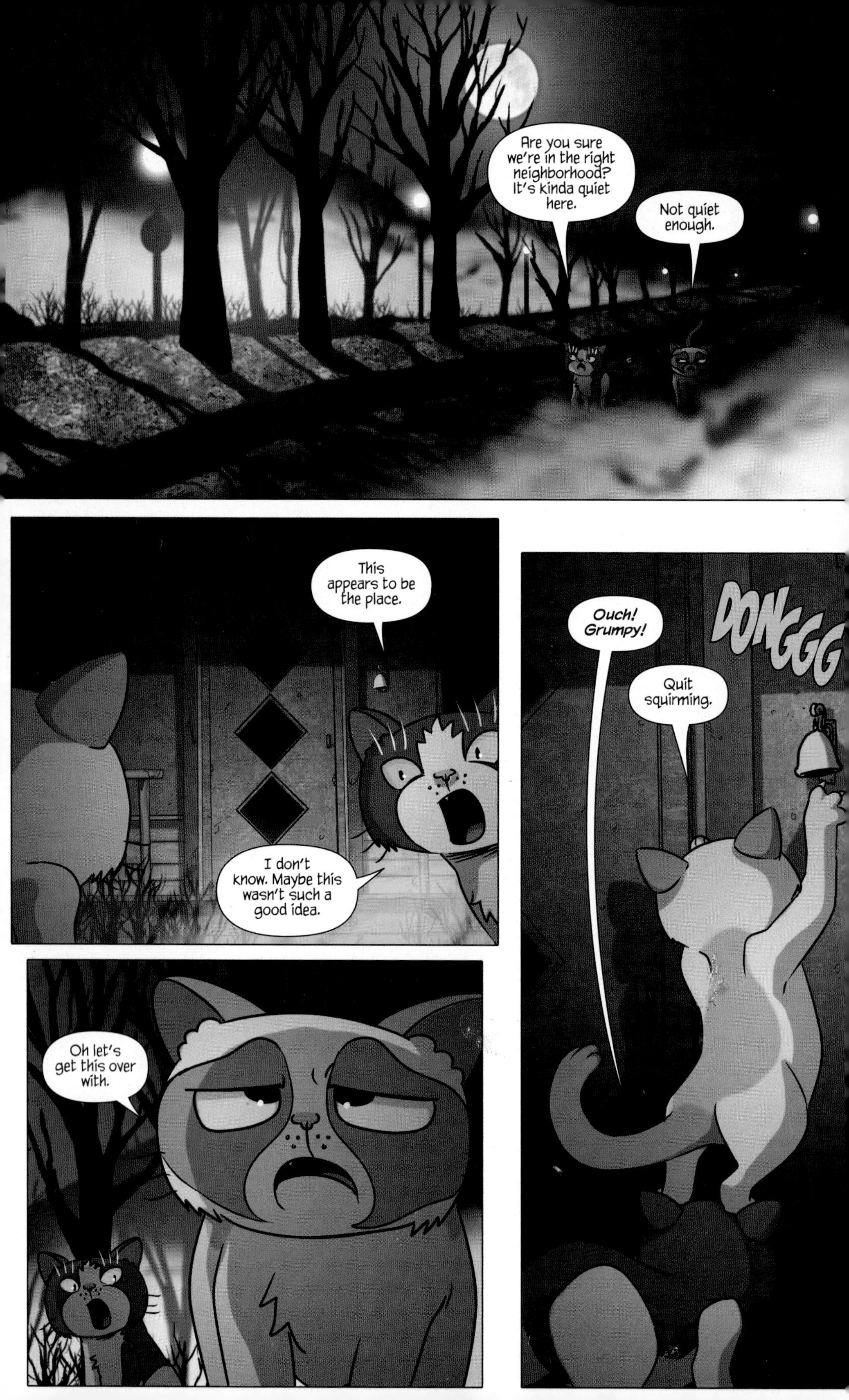
Are you sure we're in the right neighborhood? It's kinda quiet here.
Not quiet enough.
This appears to be the place.
I don't know. Maybe this wasn't such a good idea.
Oh let's get this over with.
DONGGG
Ouch! Grumpy!
Quit squirming.

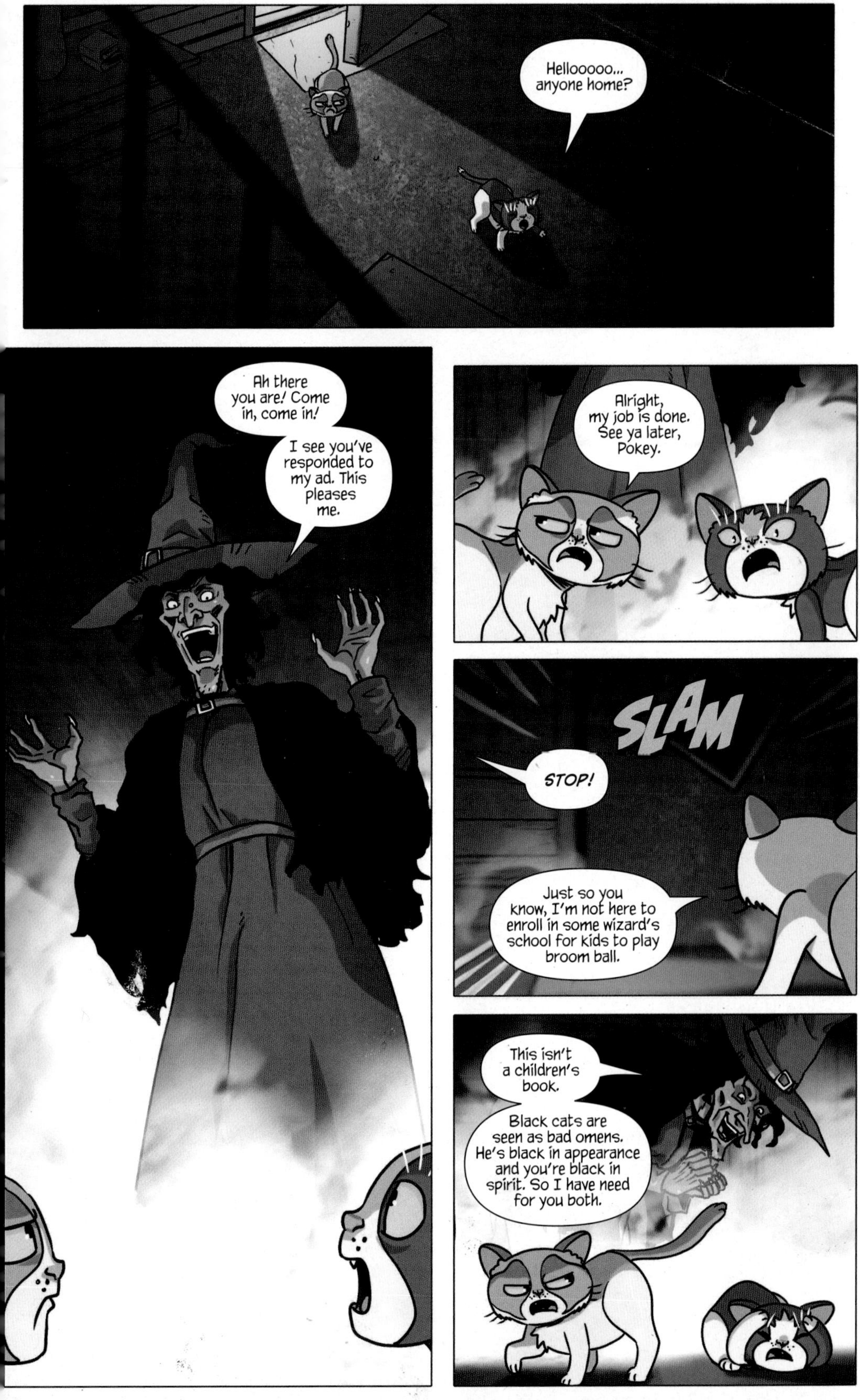
Hellooooo... anyone home?
Ah there you are! Come in, come in!
I see you've responded to my ad. This pleases me.
Alright, my job is done. See ya later, Pokey.
SLAM
STOP!
Just so you know, I'm not here to enroll in some wizard's school for kids to play broom ball.
This isn't a children's book.
Black cats are seen as bad omens. He's black in appearance and you're black in spirit. So I have need for you both.

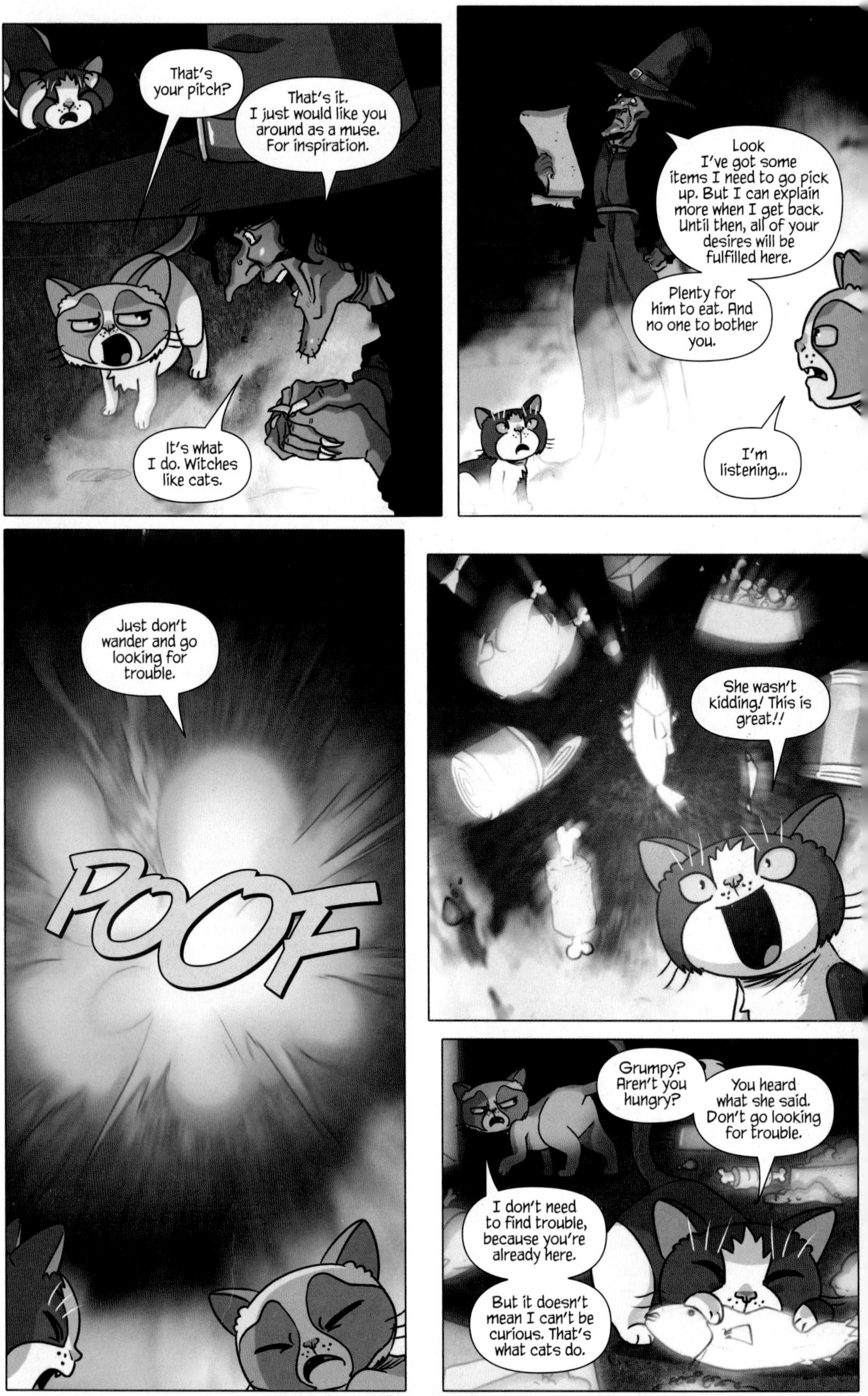
That's your pitch?
That's it. I just would like you around as a muse. For inspiration.
It's what I do. Witches like cats.
Look I've got some items I need to go pick up. But I can explain more when I get back. Until then, all of your desires will be fulfilled here.
Plenty for him to eat. And no one to bother you.
I'm listening...
Just don't wander and go looking for trouble.
POOF
She wasn't kidding! This is great!!
Grumpy? Aren't you hungry?
You heard what she said. Don't go looking for trouble.
I don't need to find trouble, because you're already here.
But it doesn't mean I can't be curious. That's what cats do.

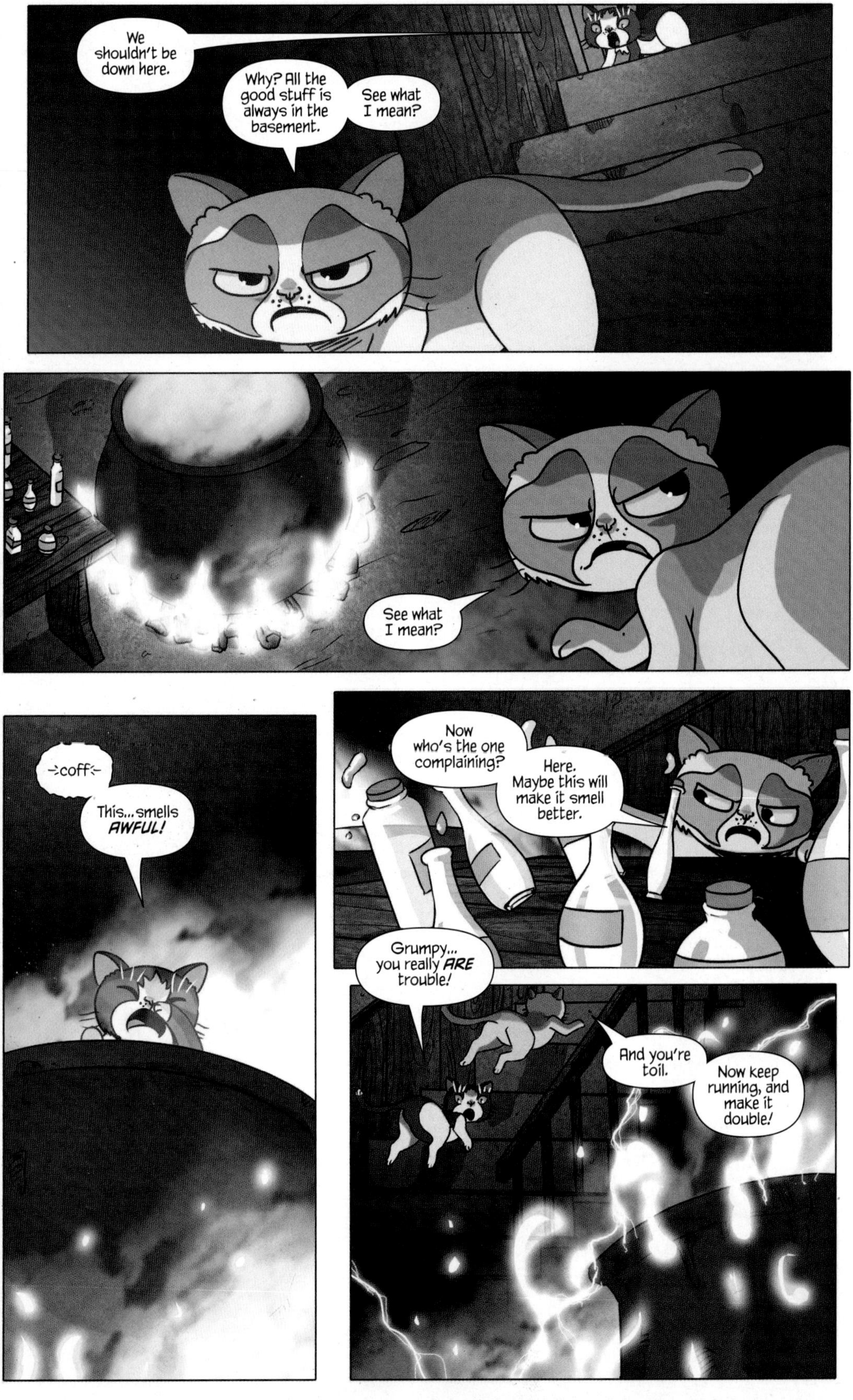

We shouldn't be down here.
Why? All the good stuff is always in the basement.
See what I mean?
See what I mean?
-coff-
This... smells AWFUL!
Now who's the one complaining?
Here. Maybe this will make it smell better.
Grumpy... you really ARE trouble!
And you're toil.
Now keep running, and make it double!

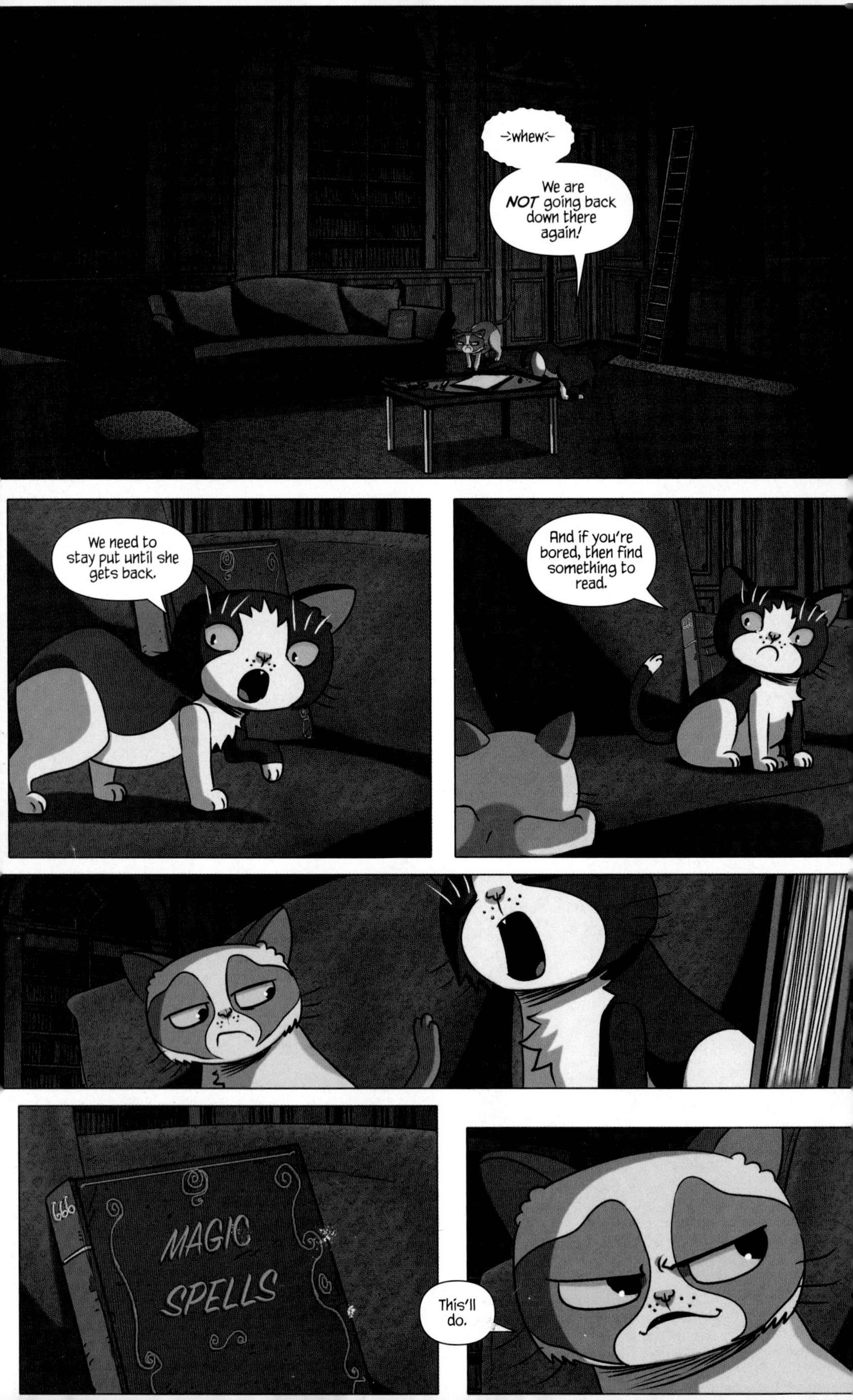
whew
We are NOT going back down there again!
We need to stay put until she gets back.
And if you're bored, then find something to read.
666
MAGIC SPELLS
This'll do.

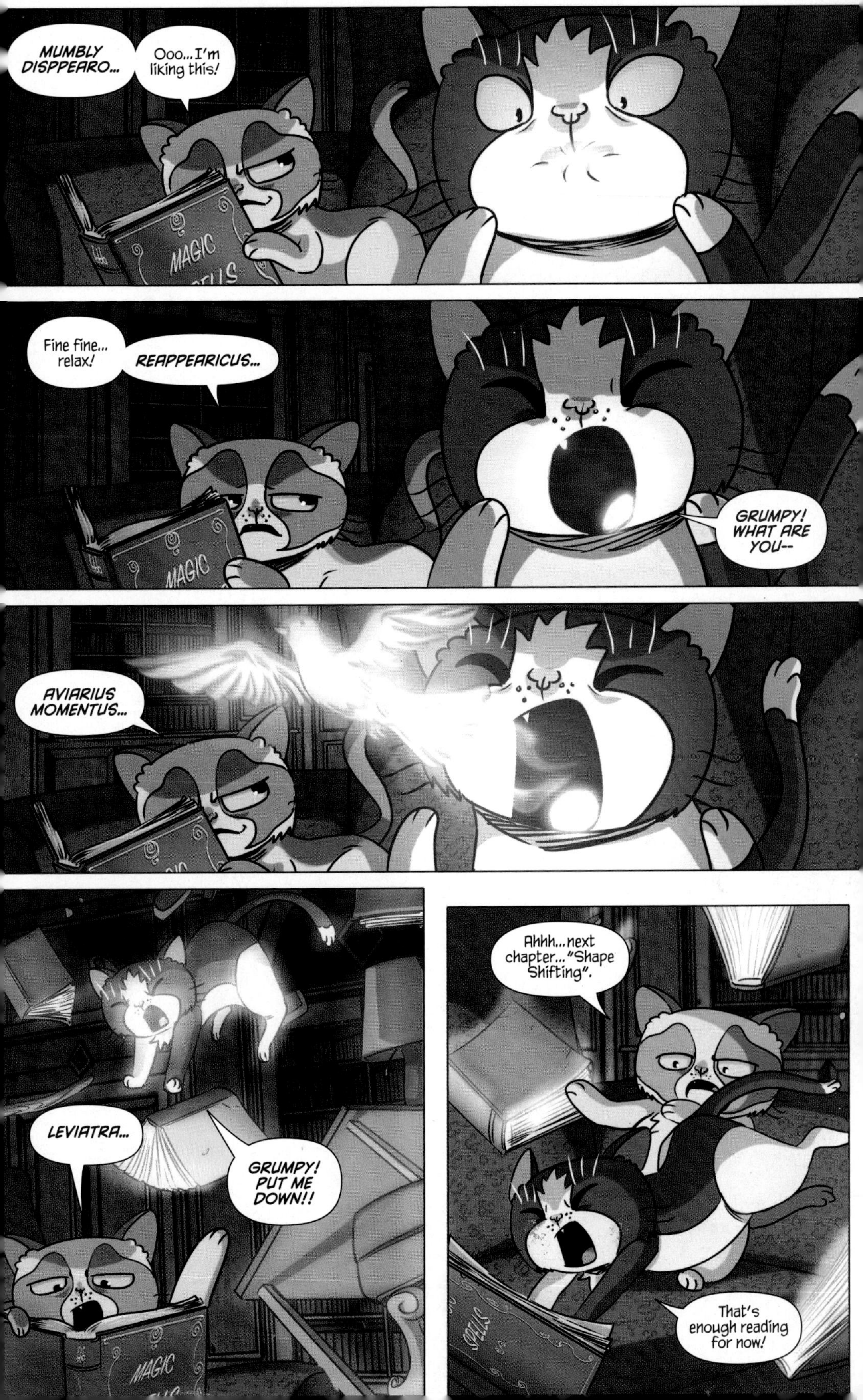
MUMBLY DISPPEARO...
Ooo...I'm liking this!
MAGIC SPELLS
Fine fine... relax!
REAPPEARICUS...
MAGIC
GRUMPY! WHAT ARE YOU--
AVIARIUS MOMENTUS...
LEVIATRA...
GRUMPY! PUT ME DOWN!!
MAGIC
Ahhh...next chapter..."Shape Shifting".
SPELLS
That's enough reading for now!

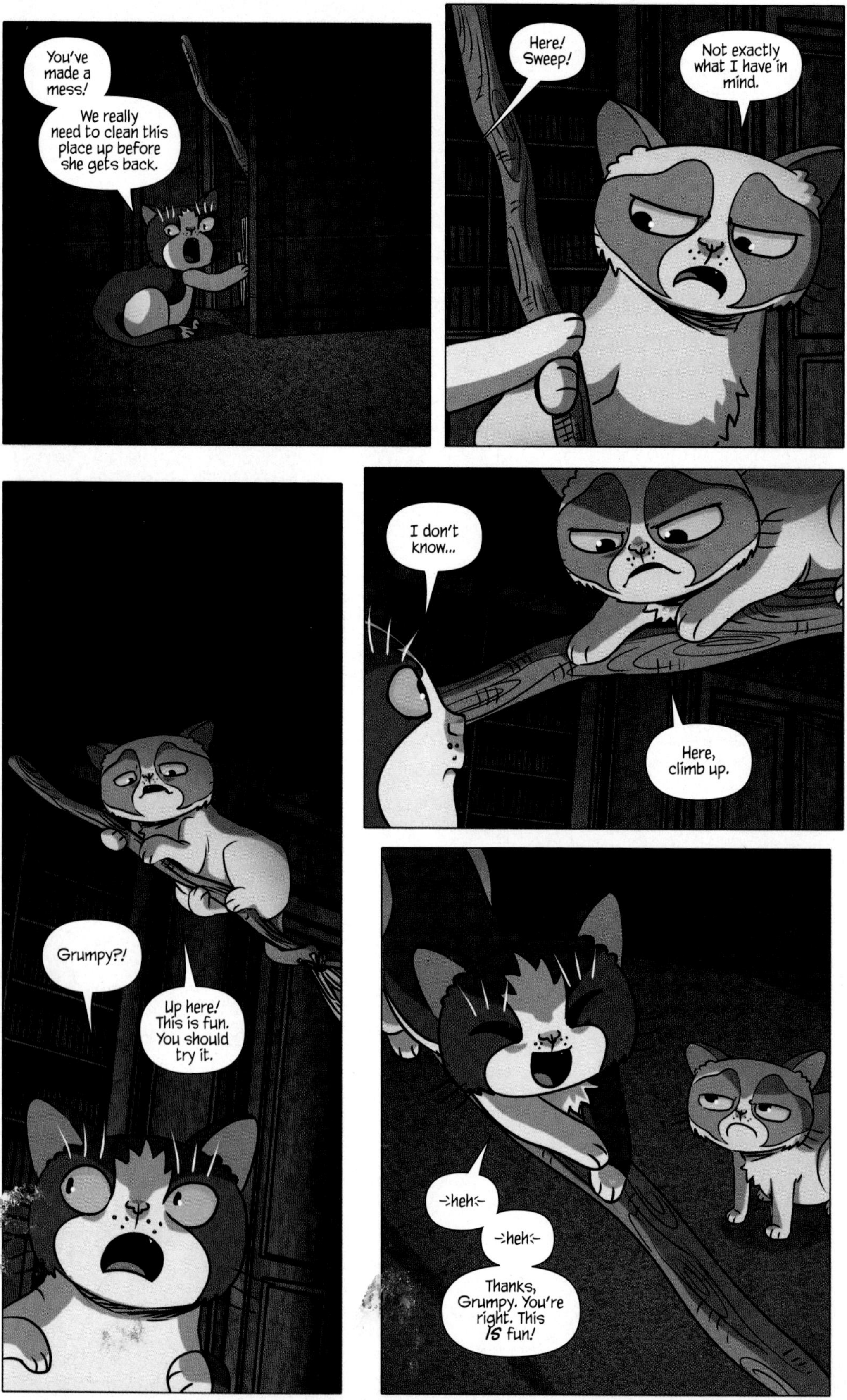
You've made a mess!
We really need to clean this place up before she gets back.
Here! Sweep!
Not exactly what I have in mind.
Grumpy?!
Up here! This is fun. You should try it.
I don't know...
Here, climb up.
heh
heh
Thanks, Grumpy. You're right. This IS fun!

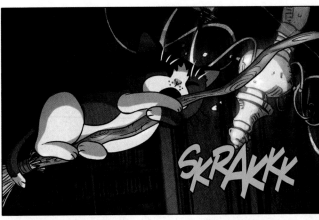

SKRAKK

Have a nice ride.

Wait! What?!

Help me, Grumpy!

KRSSSSH

MAKE IT STOP! *MAKE IT STOP!!*

I guess the ride's over.

KRRAACCK

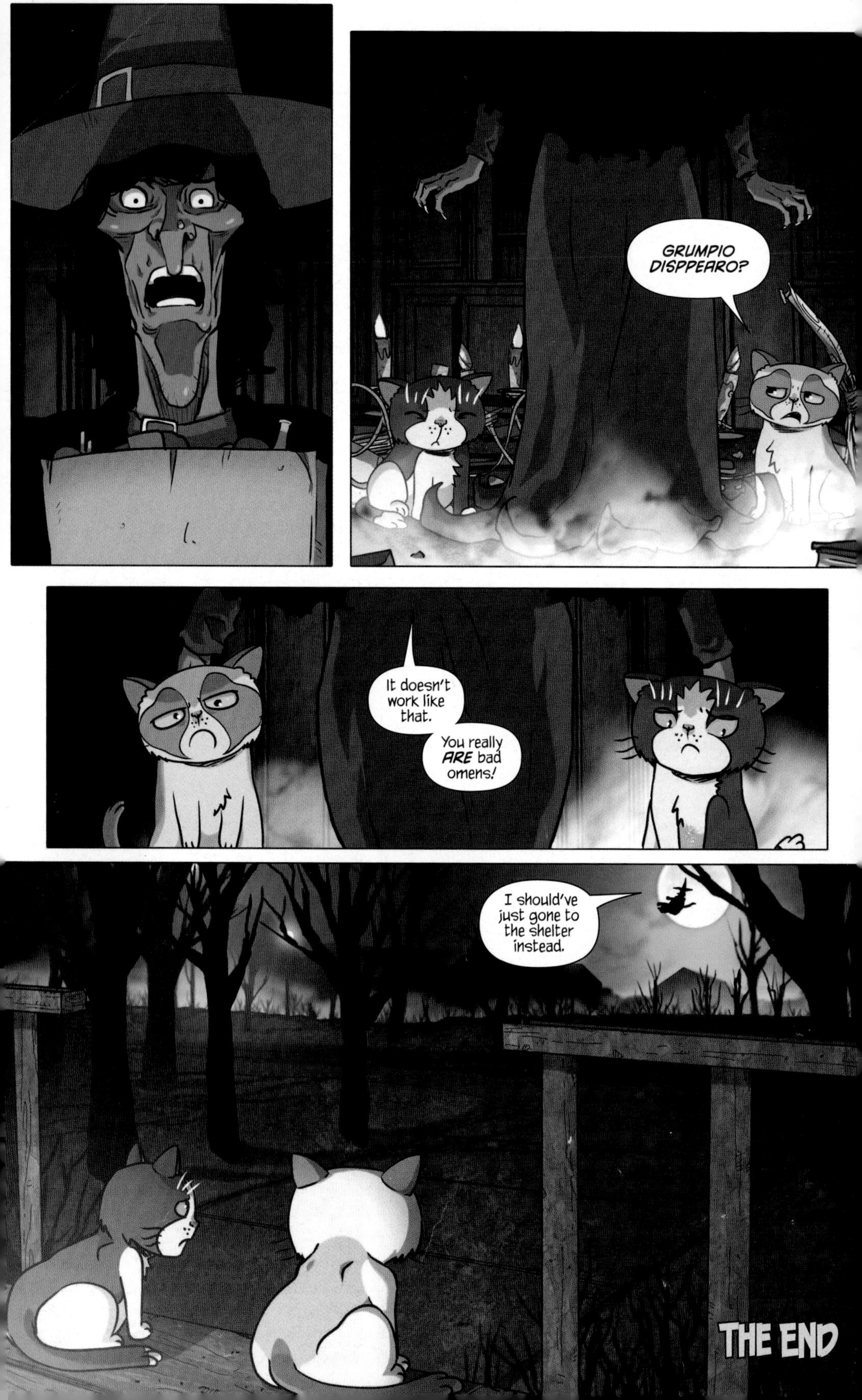
GRUMPIO DISPPEARO?
It doesn't work like that.
You really ARE bad omens!
I should've just gone to the shelter instead.
THE END

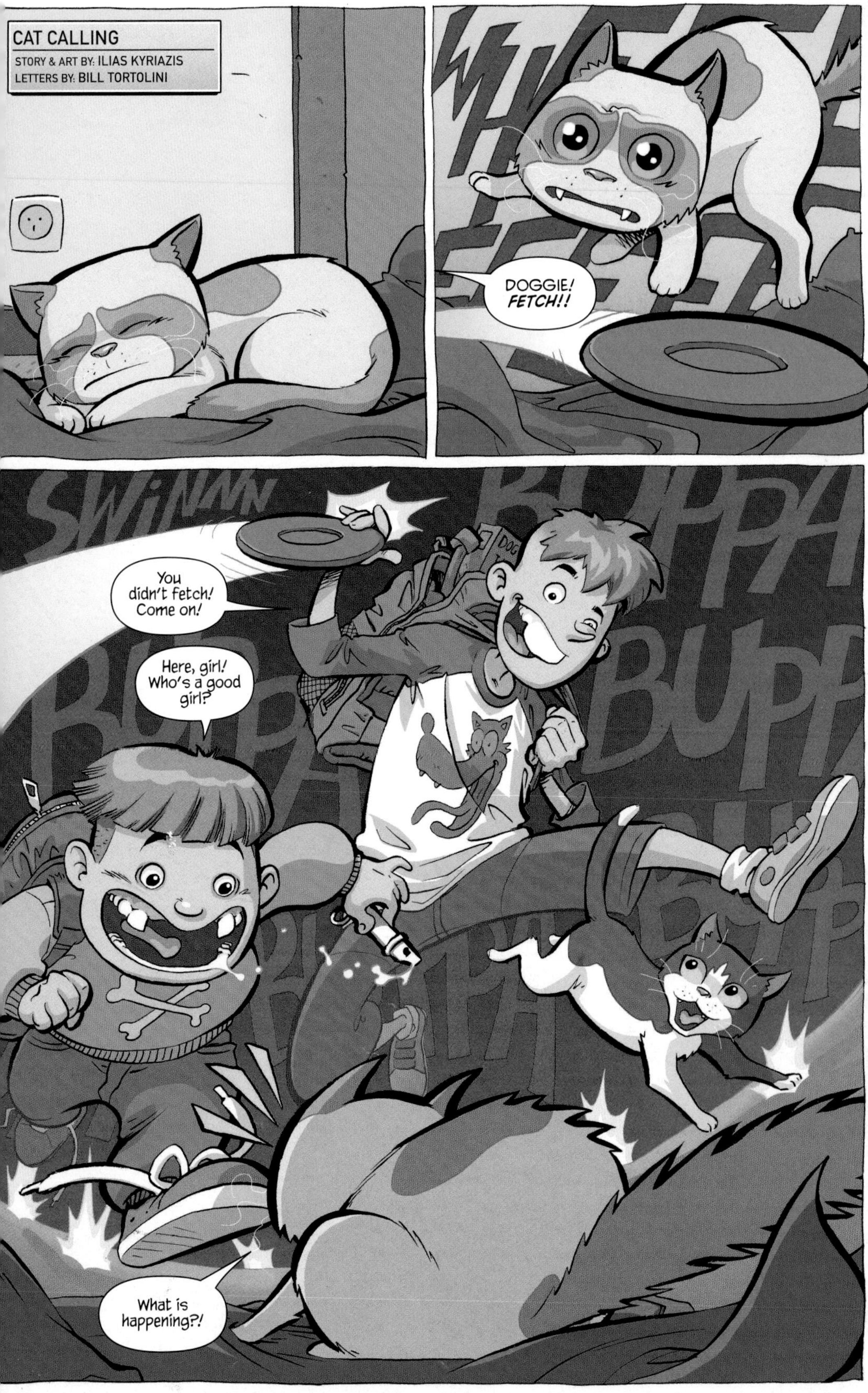
CAT CALLING
STORY & ART BY: ILIAS KYRIAZIS
LETTERS BY: BILL TORTOLINI
DOGGIE! FETCH!!
SWINNN
You didn't fetch! Come on!
Here, girl! Who's a good girl?
What is happening?!

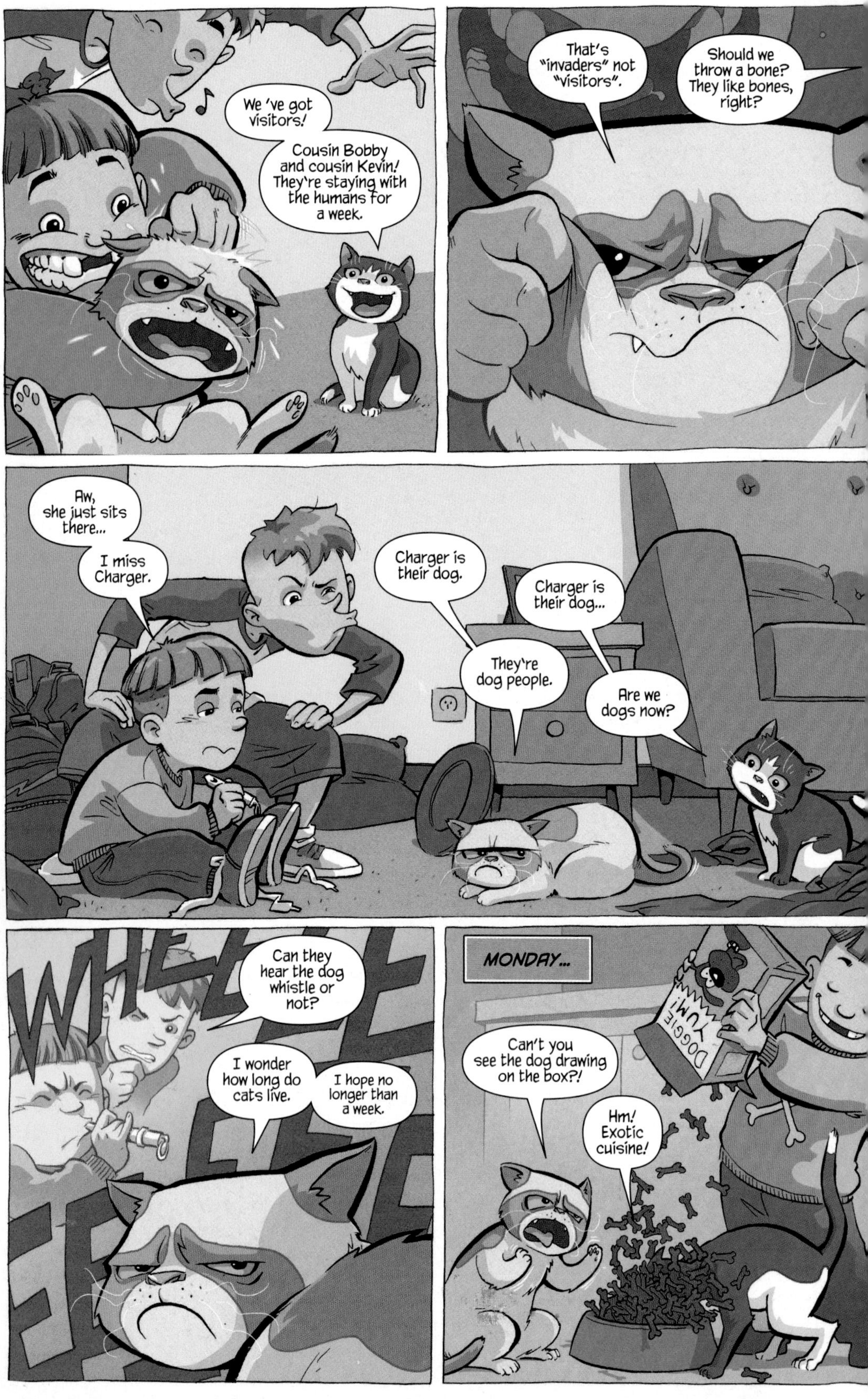
We 've got visitors!
Cousin Bobby and cousin Kevin! They're staying with the humans for a week.
That's "invaders" not "visitors".
Should we throw a bone? They like bones, right?
Aw, she just sits there...
I miss Charger.
Charger is their dog.
Charger is their dog...
They're dog people.
Are we dogs now?
Can they hear the dog whistle or not?
I wonder how long do cats live.
I hope no longer than a week.
MONDAY...
DOGGIE YUM!
Can't you see the dog drawing on the box?!
Hm! Exotic cuisine!

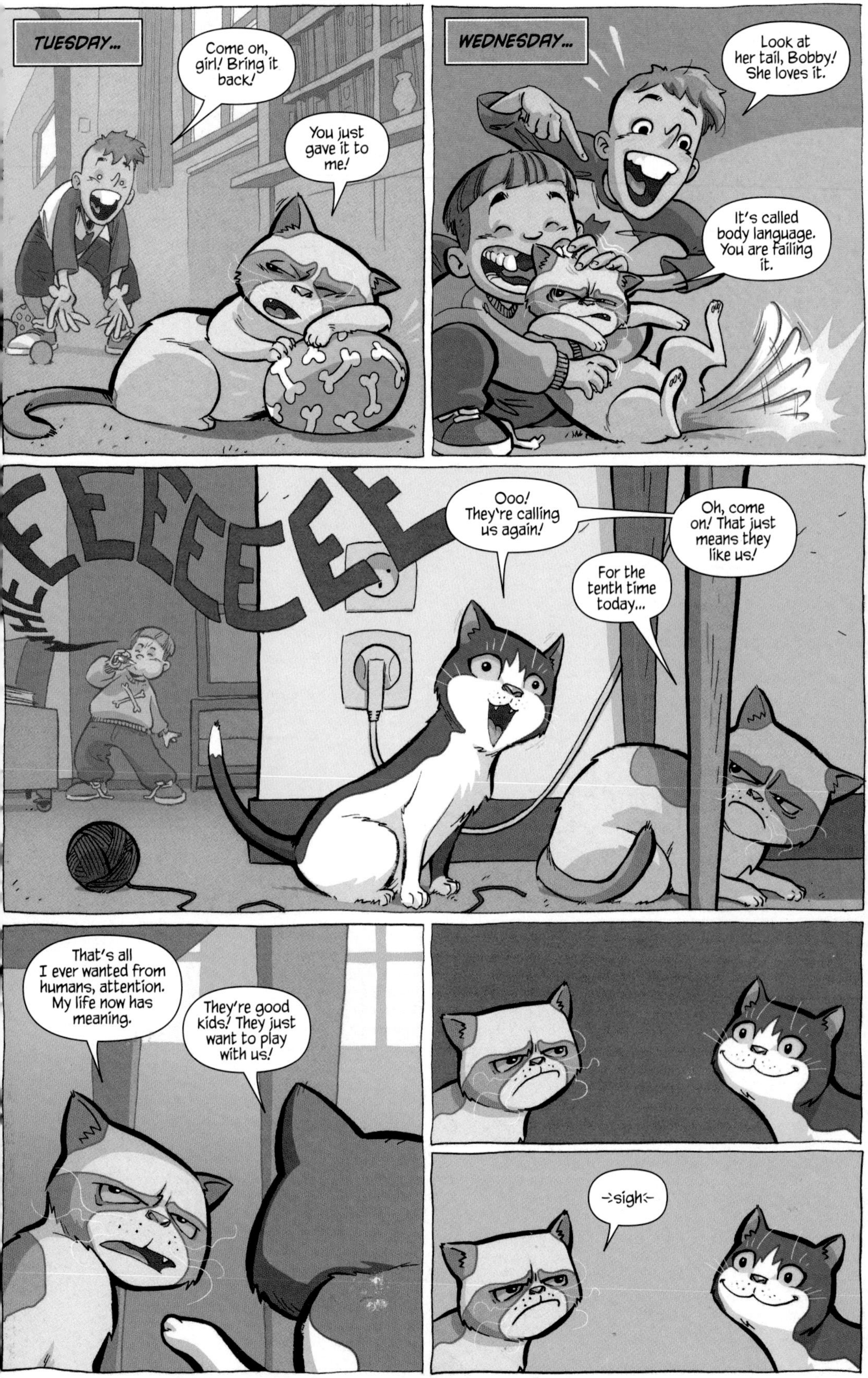
TUESDAY...
Come on, girl! Bring it back!
You just gave it to me!
WEDNESDAY...
Look at her tail, Bobby! She loves it.
It's called body language. You are failing it.
HEEEEEEE
Ooo! They're calling us again!
Oh, come on! That just means they like us!
For the tenth time today...
That's all I ever wanted from humans, attention. My life now has meaning.
They're good kids! They just want to play with us!
-sigh-

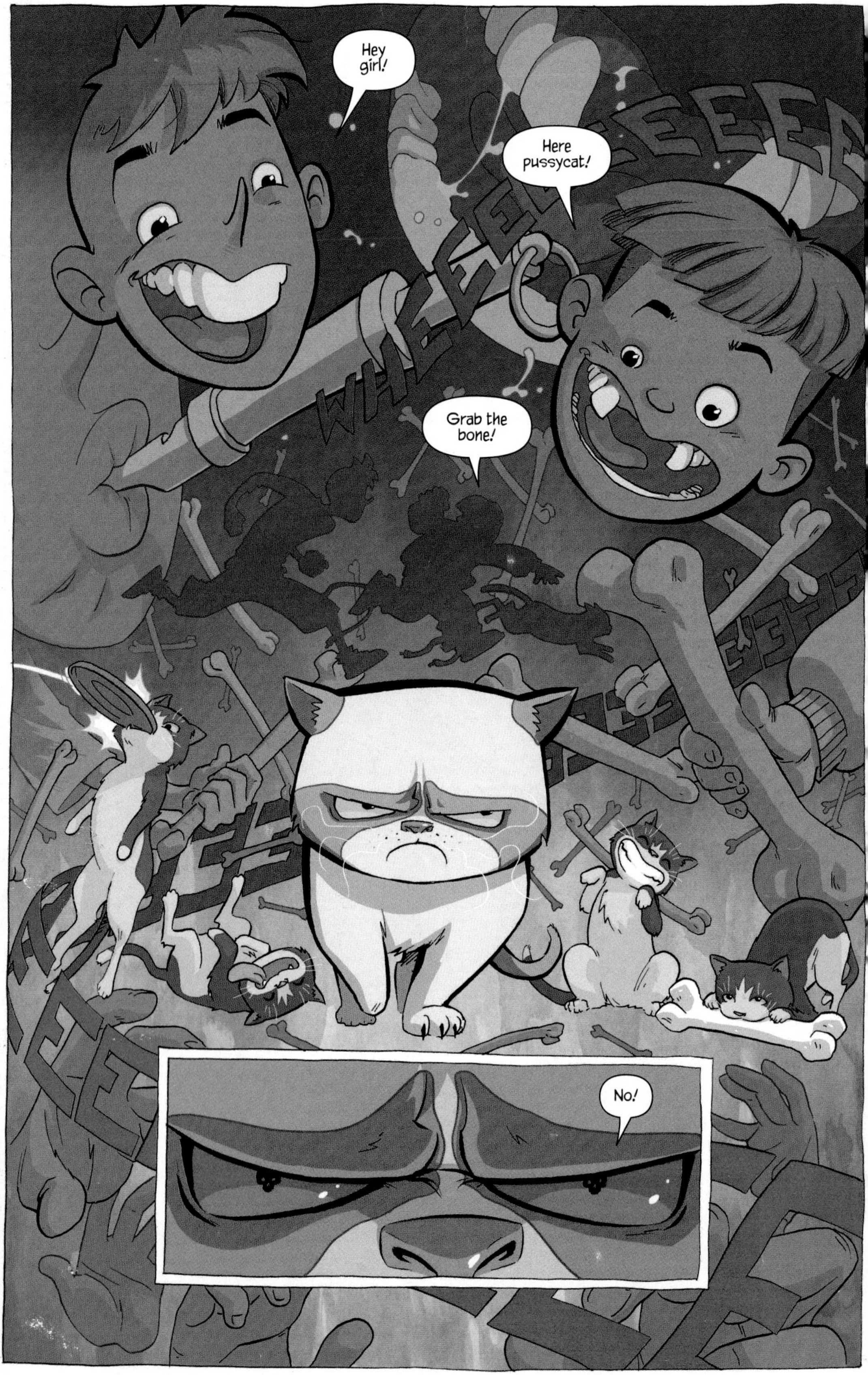
Hey girl!
Here pussycat!
Grab the bone!
No!

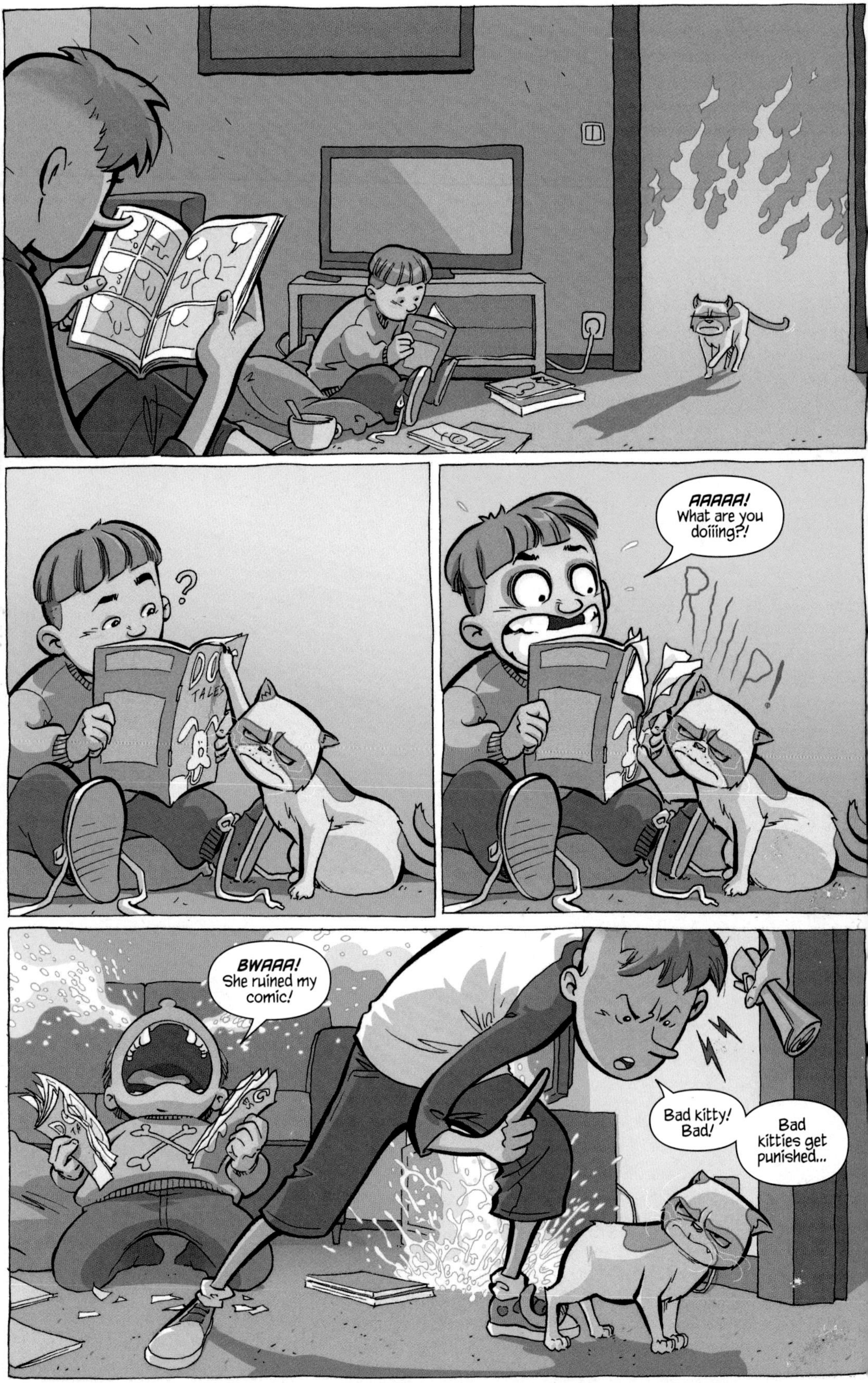
AAAAA! What are you doiiing?!
RIIIIP!
BWAAA! She ruined my comic!
Bad kitty! Bad!
Bad kitties get punished...

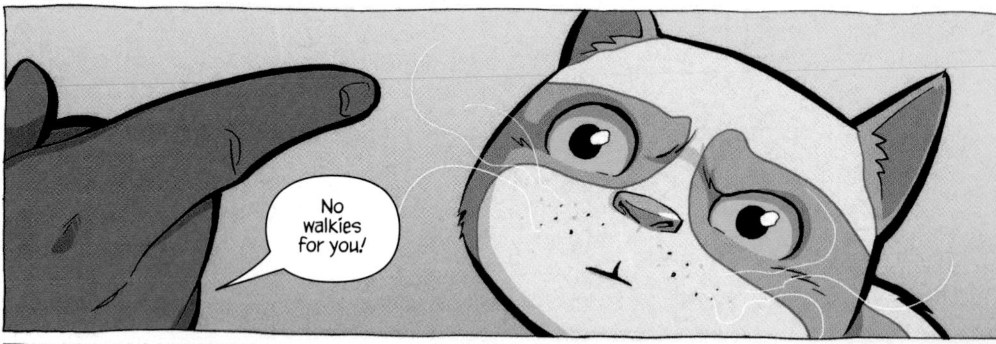
No walkies for you!

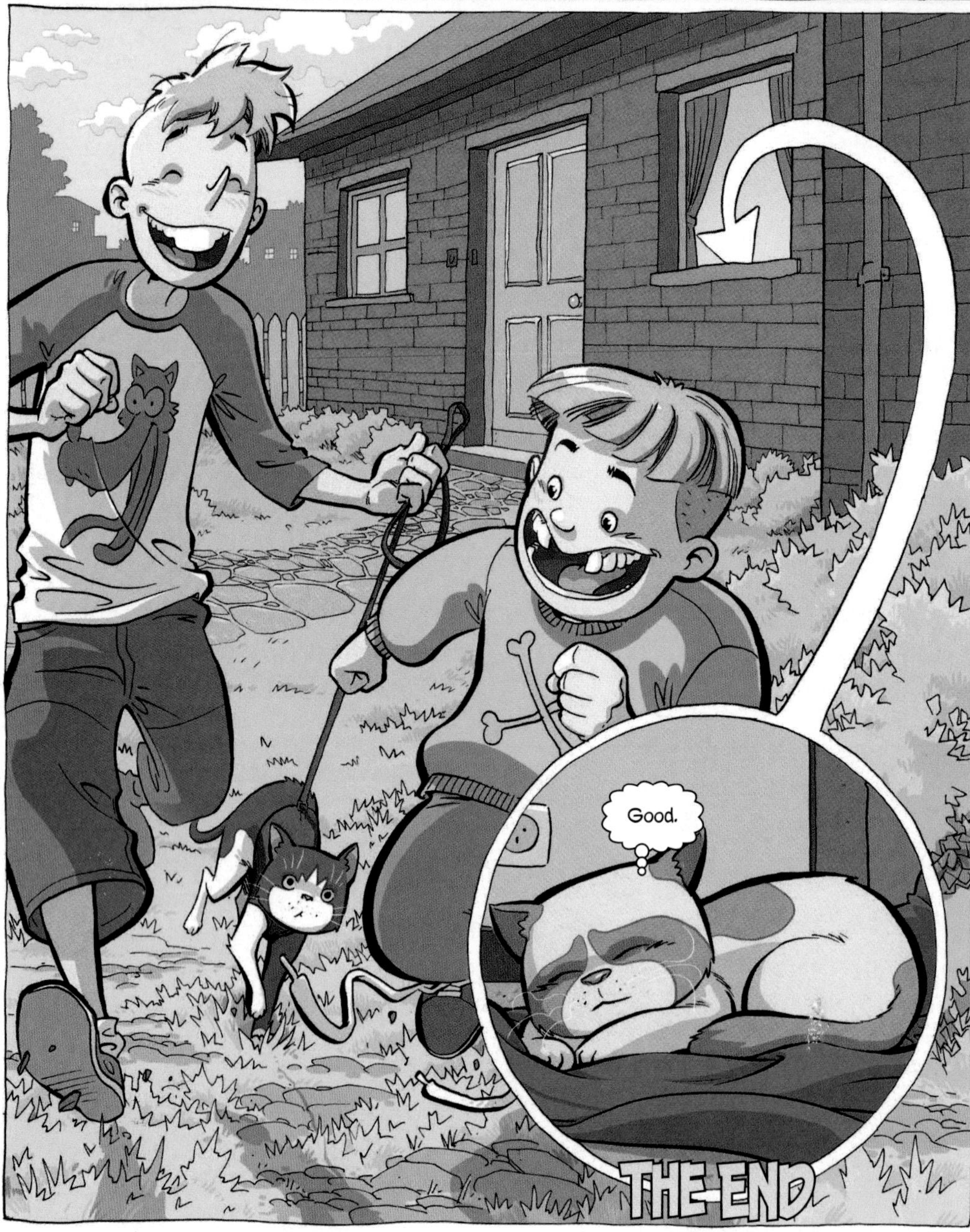
Good.
THE END

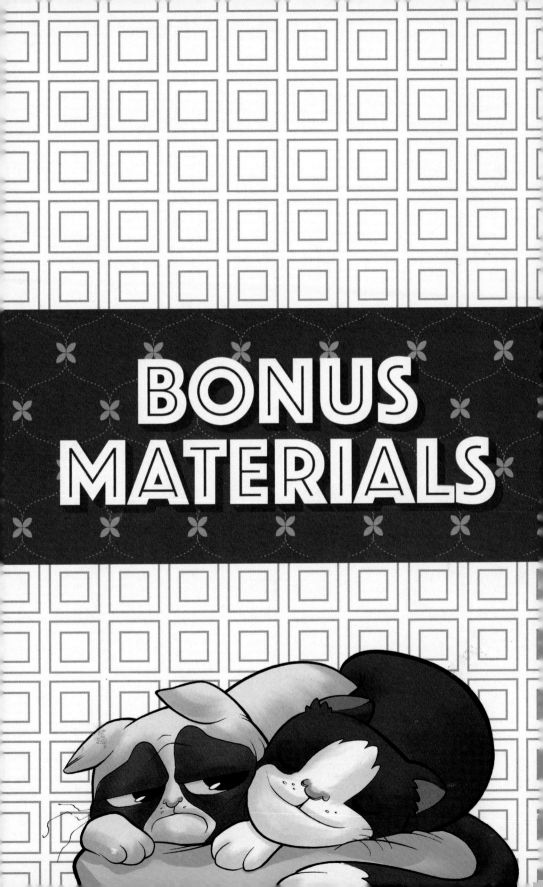

# BONUS MATERIALS

Issue 4, Cover A by: **Michelle Nguyen**

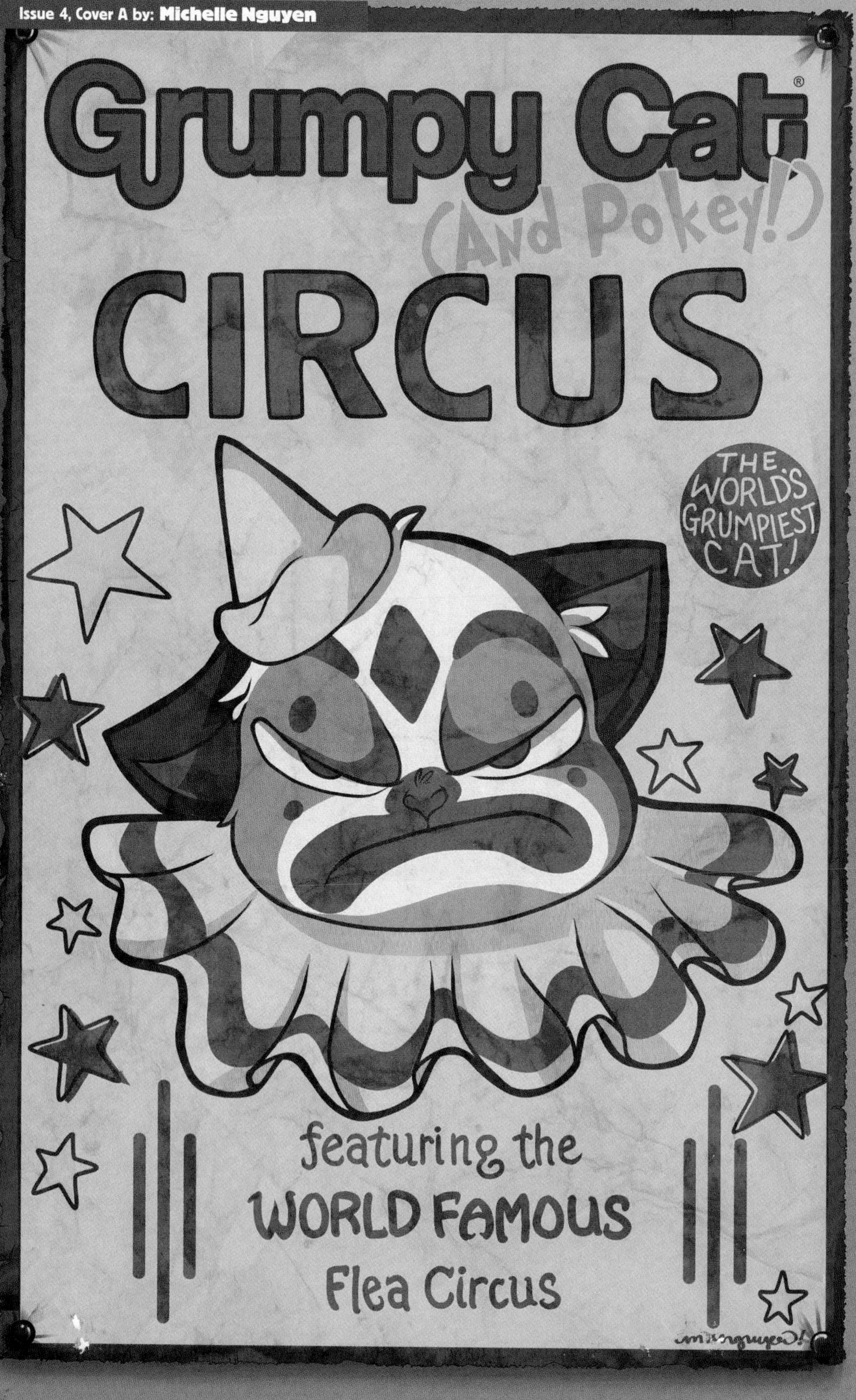

Grumpy Cat®
(And Pokey!)
CIRCUS
THE WORLD'S GRUMPIEST CAT!
featuring the
WORLD FAMOUS
Flea Circus

Issue 4, Cover B by: **Billy Martin**

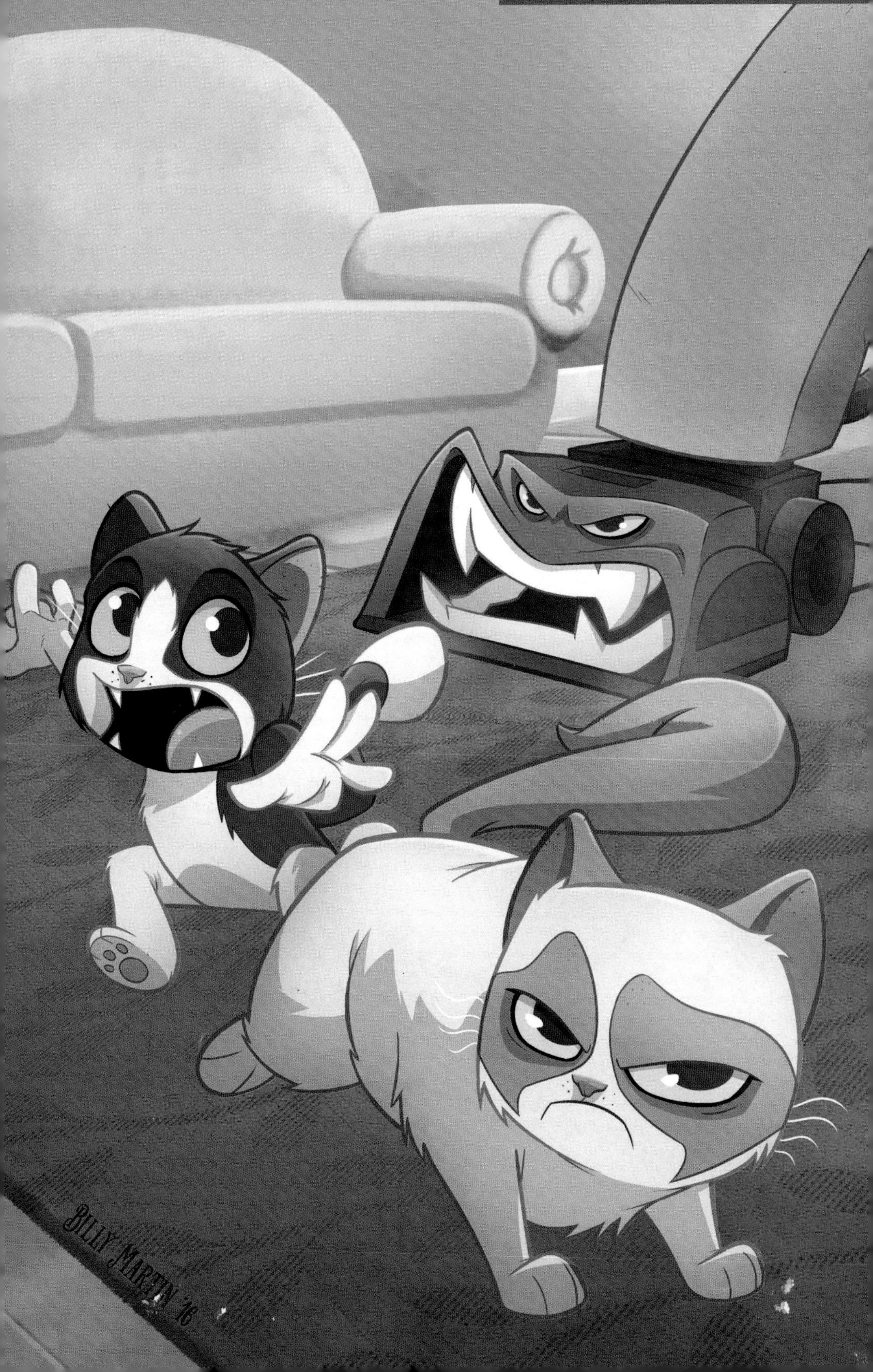
BILLY MARTIN '16

Issue 4, Cover C by: **Ken Haeser**

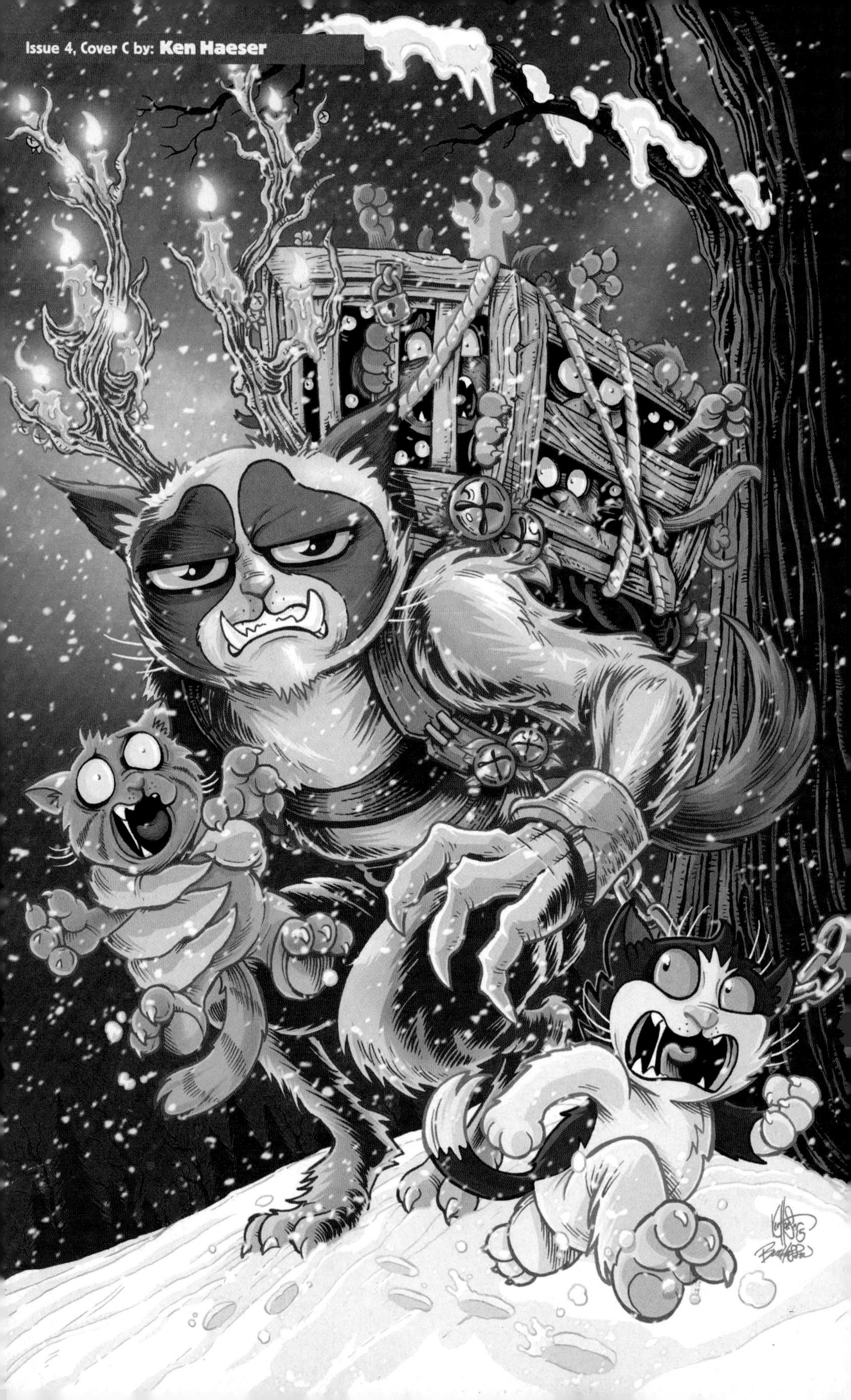

Issue 5, Cover A by: **Agnes Garbowska**

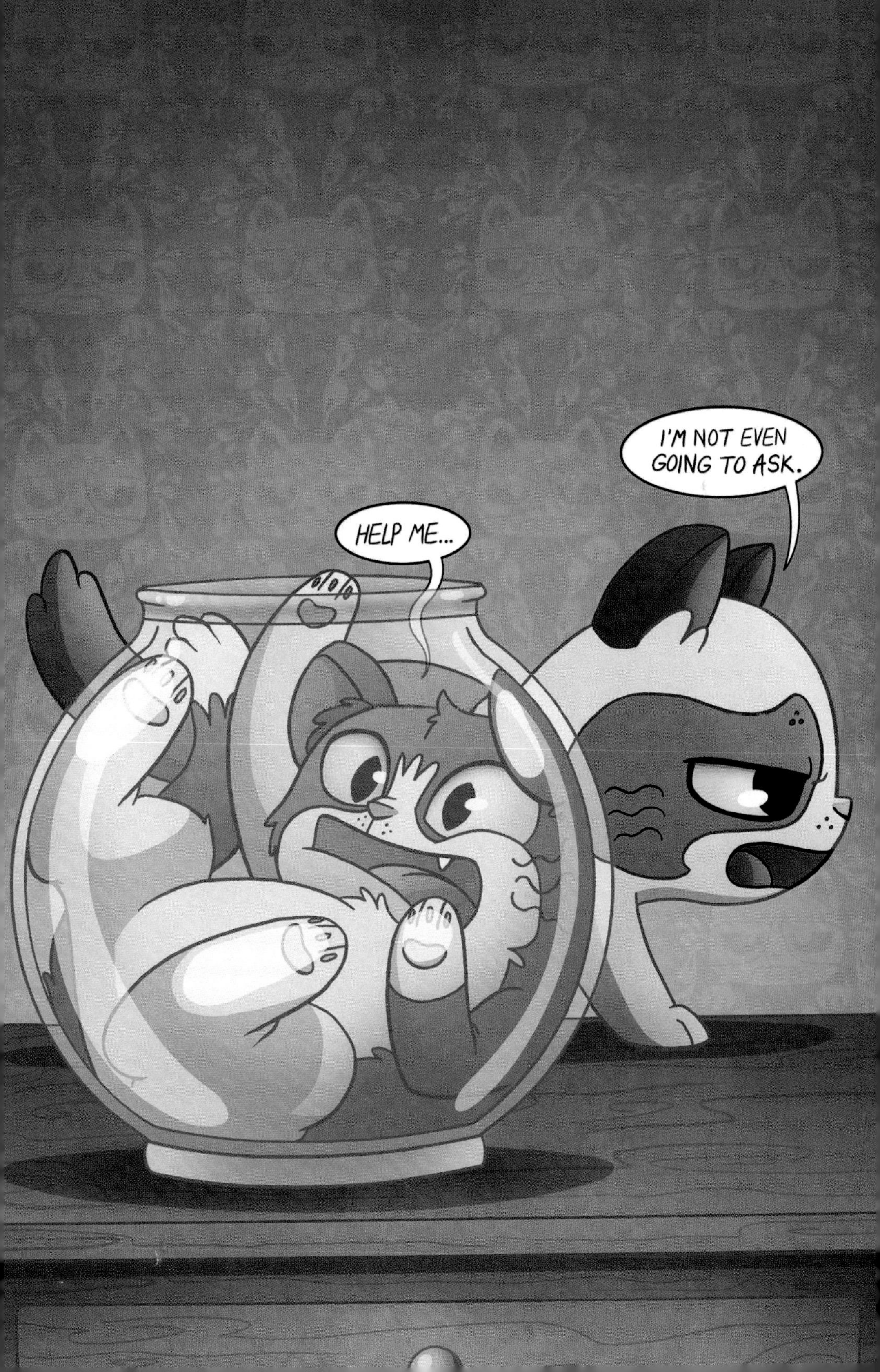
HELP ME...
I'M NOT EVEN GOING TO ASK.

Issue 5, Cover B by: **Ken Haeser**

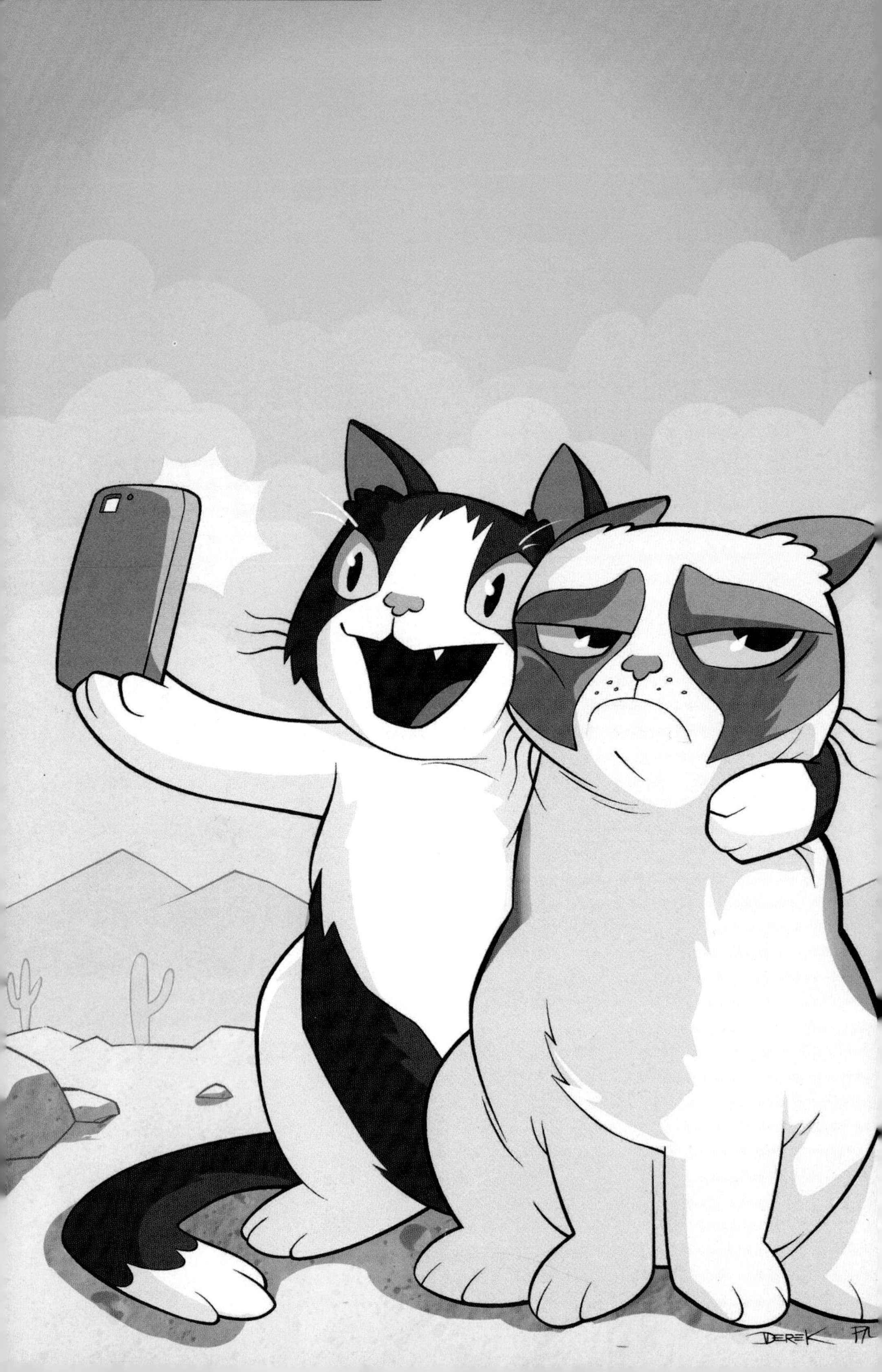

DEREK

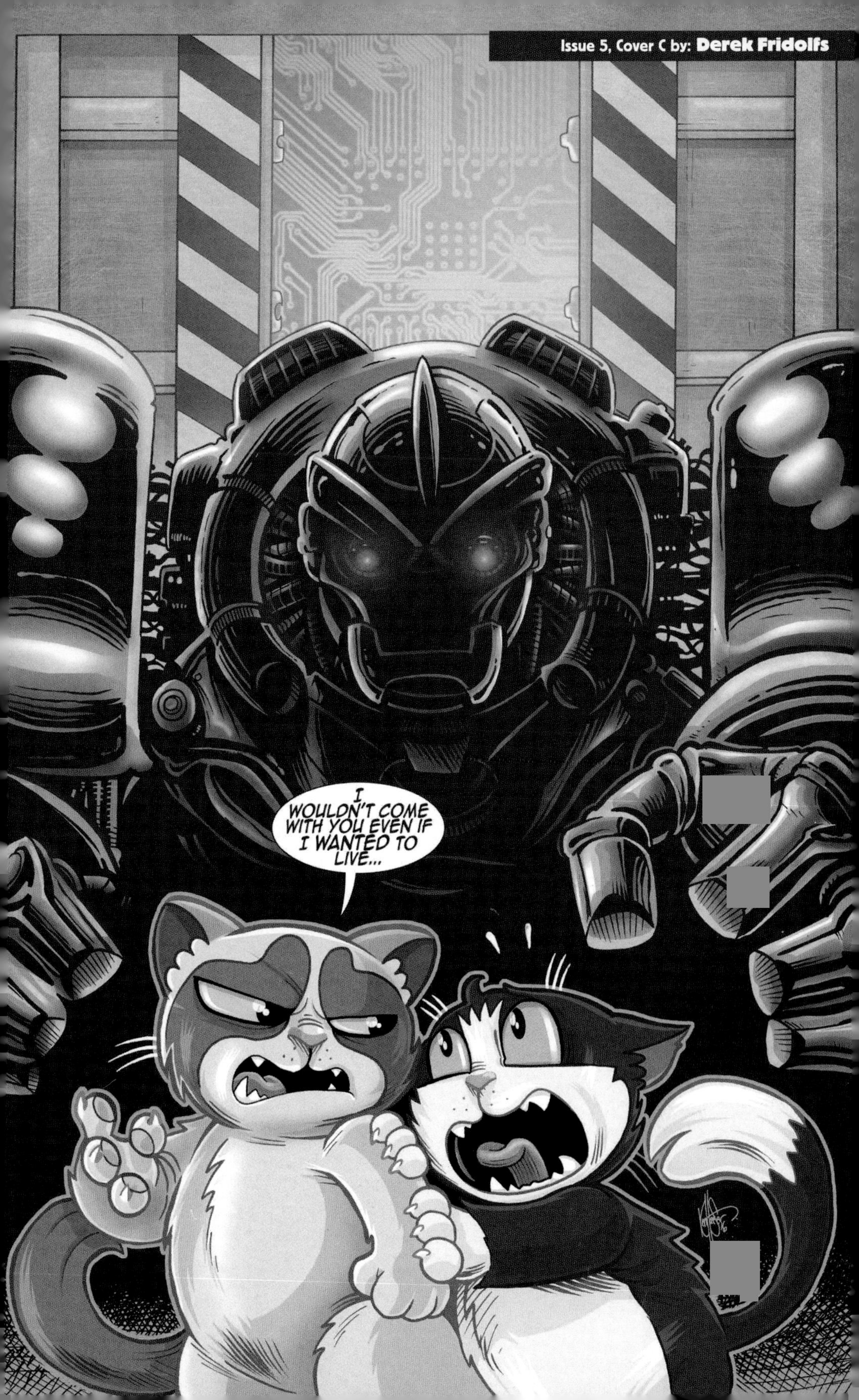
I WOULDN'T COME WITH YOU EVEN IF I WANTED TO LIVE...

Issue 5, Cover C by: **Derek Fridolfs**

Issue 6, Cover A by: **Agnes Garbowska**

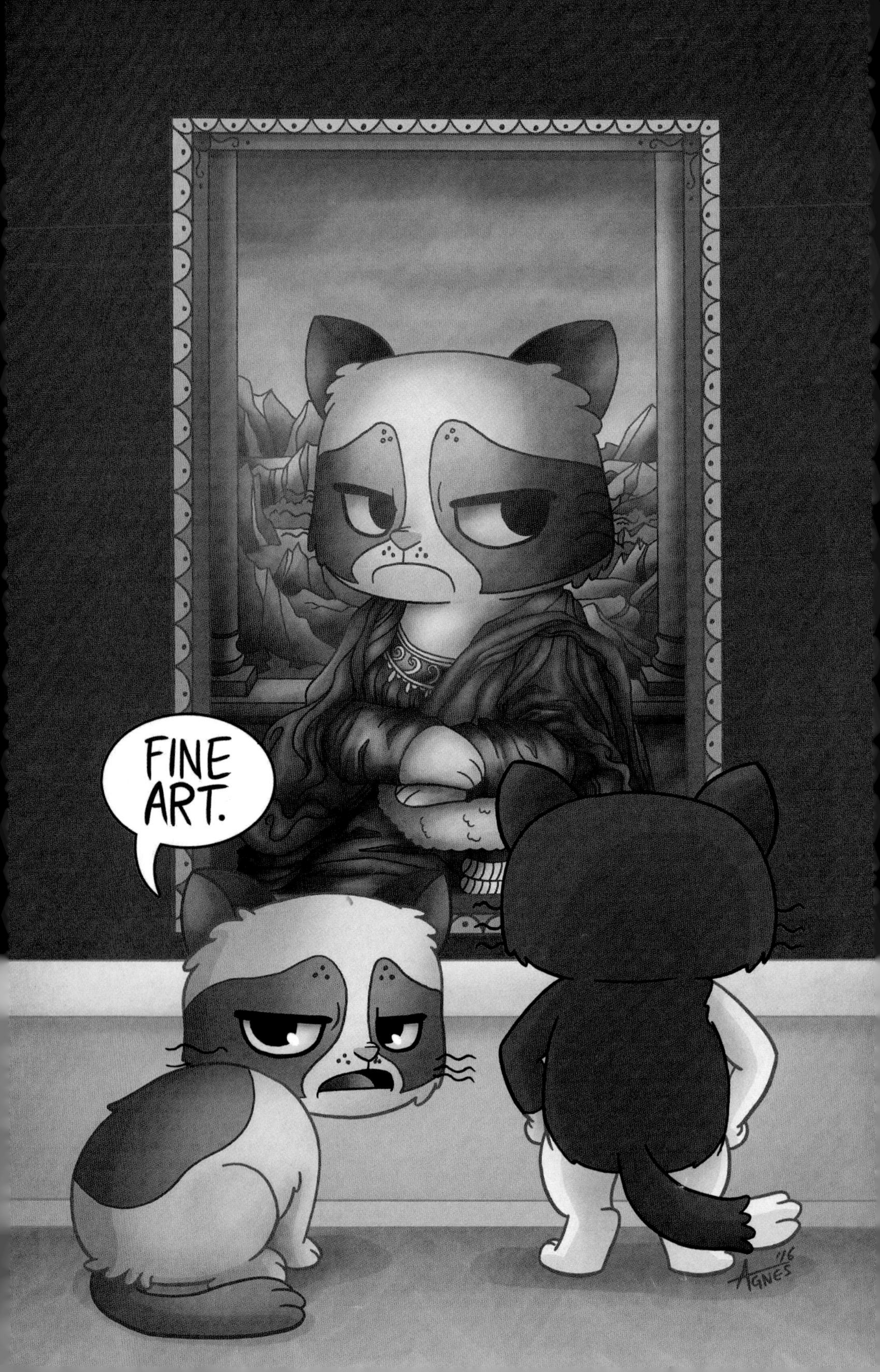
FINE ART.
AGNES '16

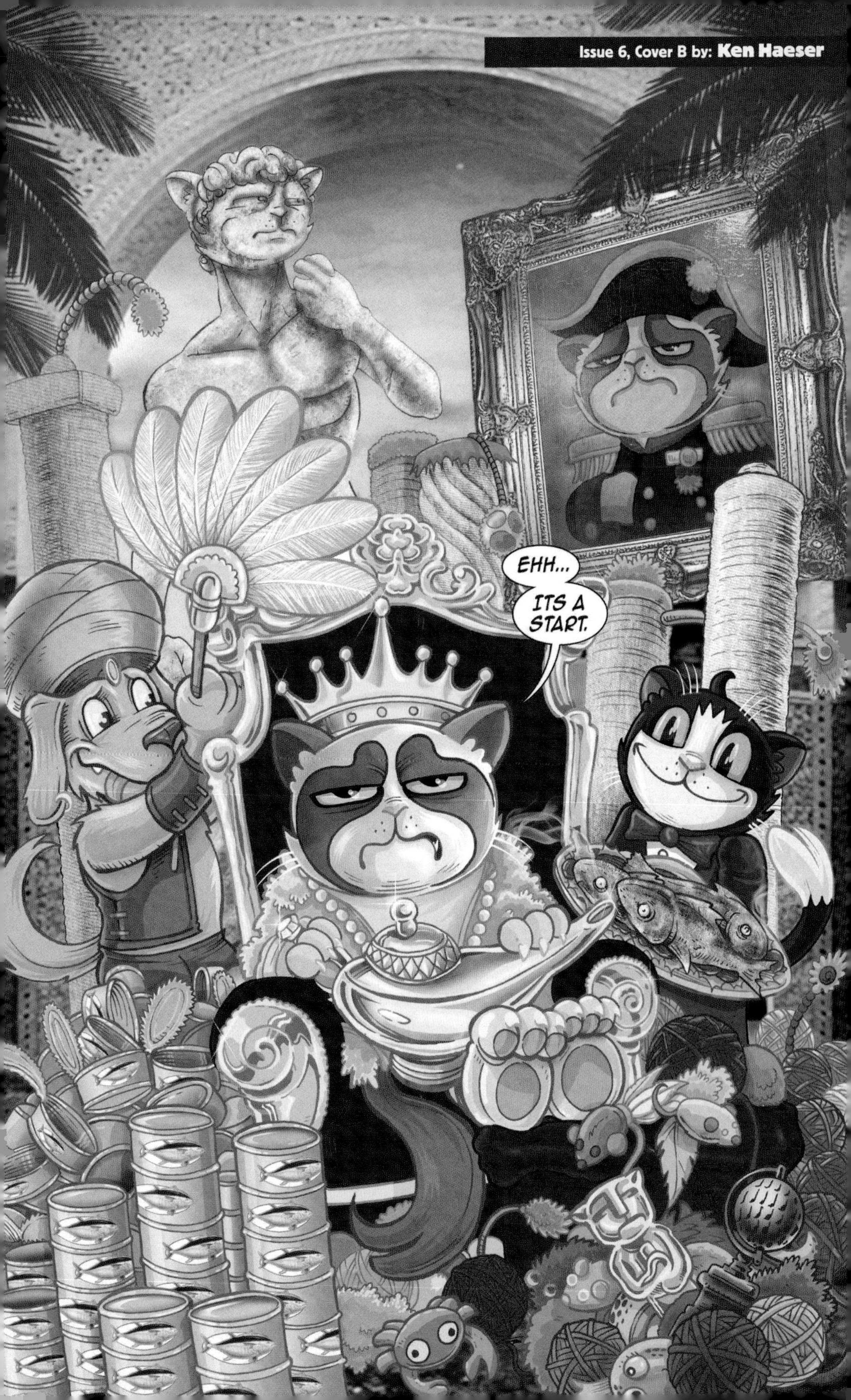
EHH...
ITS A START.

Issue 6, Cover B by: **Ken Haeser**

Issue 6, Cover C by: **RY-Spirit**

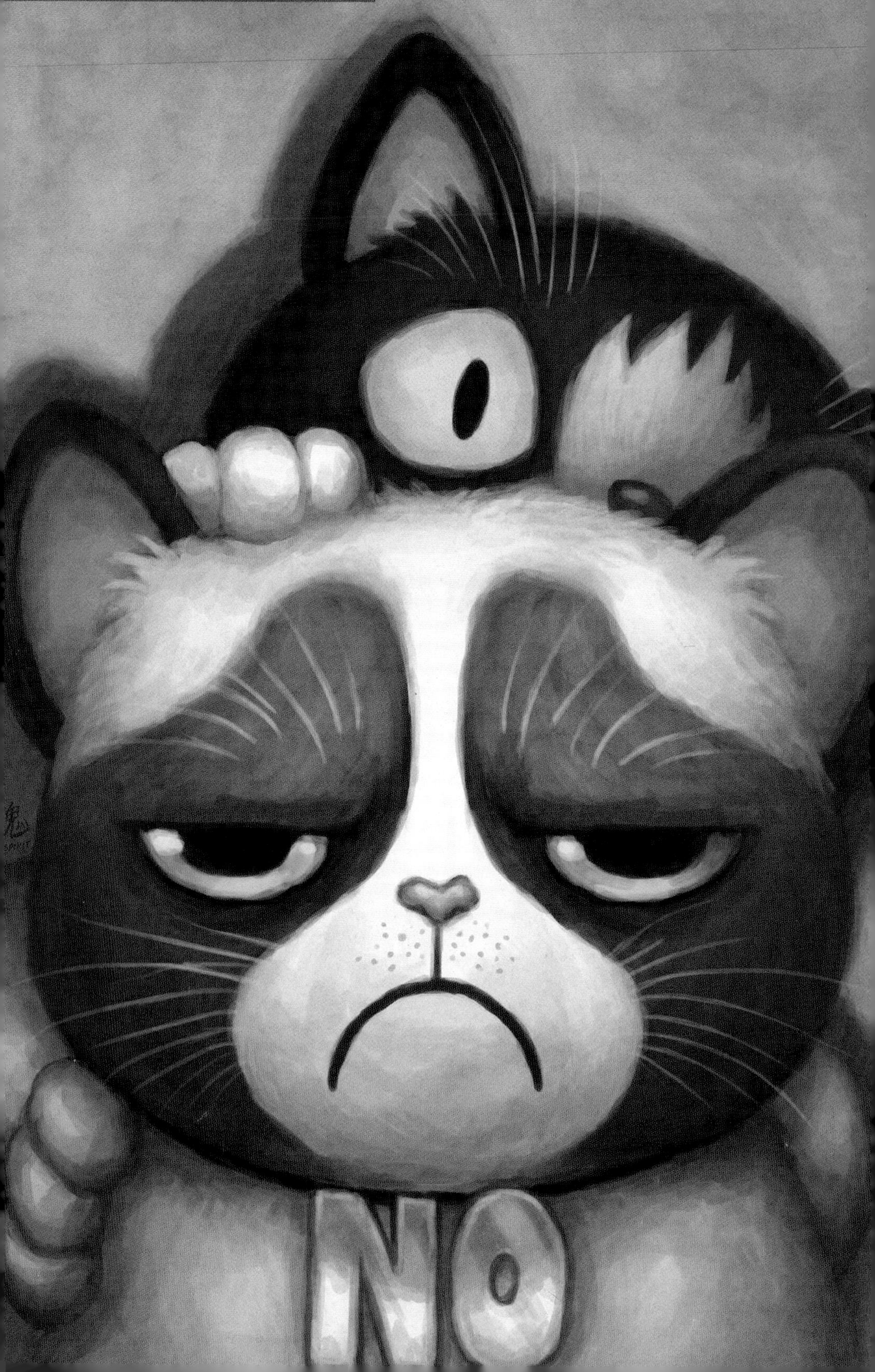

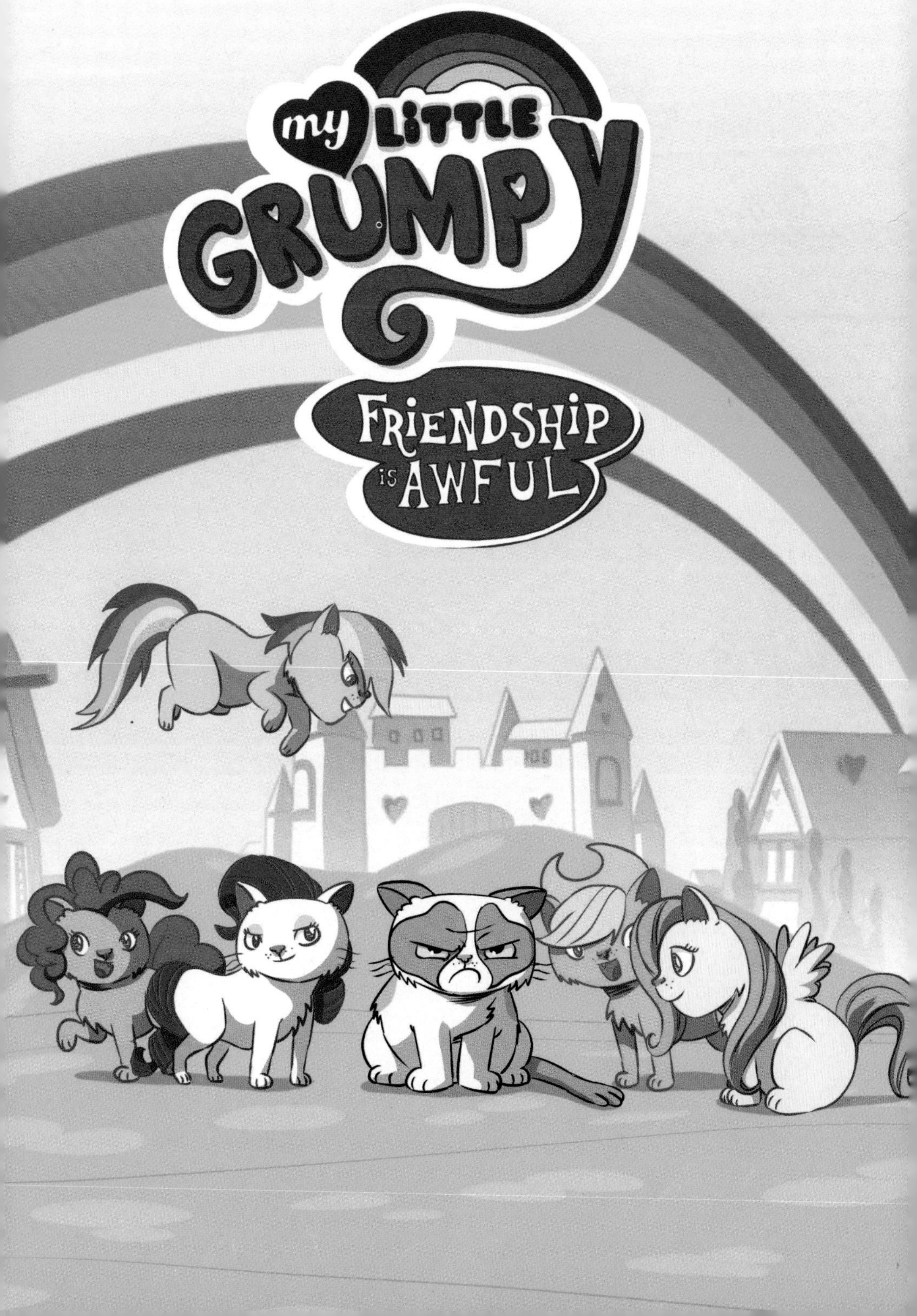
my LITTLE GRUMPY
FRIENDSHIP is AWFUL

## Collector's Series Grumpy Cat De-Motivational Posters.

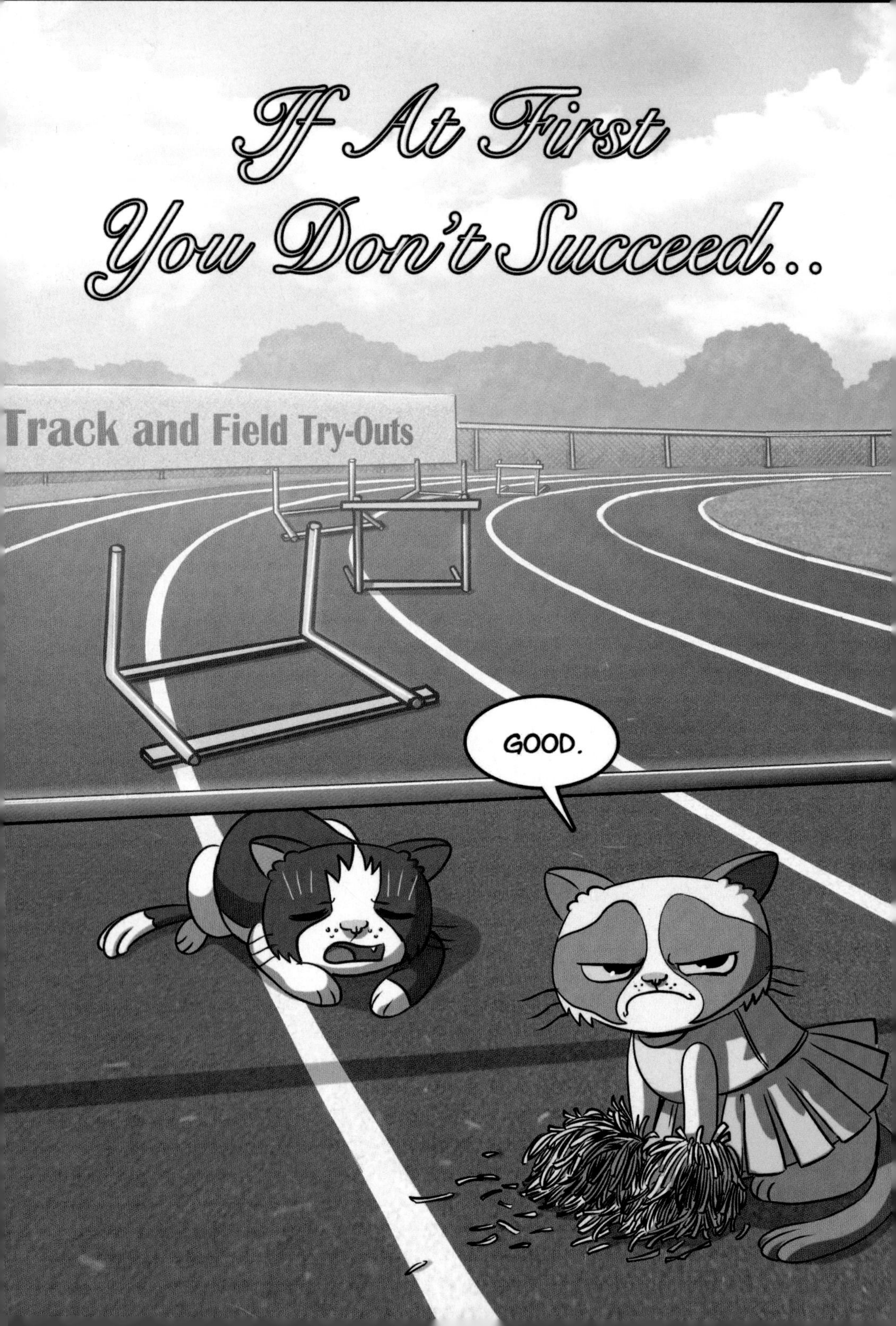
If At First
You Don't Succeed...
Track and Field Try-Outs
GOOD.

THE COLLECTED COMIC ADVENTURES OF THE INTERNET SENSATION!

# BOO
## THE WORLD'S CUTEST DOG™

JOIN BOO AND HIS FRIENDS AS THEY CREATE KITCHEN CHAOS, BECOME MOVIE STARS, CELEBRATE BIRTHDAYS AND MORE IN THIS WHIMSICAL, FUN-FILLED HARDBOUND BOOK PERFECT FOR READERS OF ALL AGES!

Sticker Sheet Inside!

COLLECTS ISSUES 1-3 & INCLUDES A STICKER PAGE!

COMING TO YOU FROM DYNAMITE IN JANUARY 2017